A Rob Wyllie paperb
First published in Great Britain in 2021
Derbyshire, United Kingd

Copyright @ Rob Wyllie 2021
The right of Rob Wyllie to be identified as the author of this work has been asserted by him in accordance with the Copyright, Design and Patents Act 1988
All rights reserved. No part of this publication may be reproduced, stored in a retrieval system, or transmitted. in any form or by any means, electronic, mechanical, photocopying, recording or otherwise, without the prior permission of the copyright owner.
All the characters in this book are fictitious and any resemblance to actual persons, living or dead, is purely coincidental.

RobWyllie.com

Past Sins

Rob Wyllie

PROLOGUE

A red letter day. Until yesterday, he'd not given a moment's thought to the origin of the phrase, but a quick two minutes on Wikipedia had provided chapter and verse. *A red letter day is any day of special significance or opportunity.* Well big deal, everyone knew that. *Its roots are in classical antiquity, where dating back to the Roman Republic, important days were identified on the calendar in red ink, a practice continued after the invention of the printing press.* Of course on reflection it was blindingly obvious and he began to muse that he may have once known it but that it had gradually slipped from his mind. What he definitely hadn't known however was that the UK still designated twenty-five of the things, and if they happened to fall on a weekday, judges sitting in the English Courts of Law would wear their traditional scarlet robes. He'd never been in front of a judge in the High Court and since he was far too smart for any of the stuff he'd done to be discovered, then there was scant chance of it ever happening. *Thank god for that.*

But getting back to today. Yes, it was to be a red letter day, the biggest in a career that had, let's face it, already been pretty illustrious by any standards. Which is why he'd remained seriously pissed off that those bastards of the Establishment, if that's what you called them, had been strangely reluctant to put him forward for the big one. *Knight Commissioner, Order of the British Empire.* Was that the right definition or was it now out of date with the Empire long gone? That didn't really matter, but what did matter was there was a long list of his so-called esteemed colleagues who'd already had it bestowed upon them, and they surely were nothing short of pygmies of the profession compared to himself. He knew what it was of course, all the speculation in the press all those years ago about Petra's death, caused by that meddling Scottish journalist who had tried to dig up dirt. But that was now long in the past, the story now faded old news. After today, they would have no choice. The public clamour would be so *immense* that they would simply *have* to give him one. *Sir James Parrish*. It had a nice ring to it, no doubt about it, and how much he looked forward to the day when he would insist his pathetic colleagues at the hospital addressed him properly. *Yes Sir James, no Sir James, of course Sir James.* That would be nice, no question about it, and no more than he deserved.

It had been his PA Ruby's idea to hold the unveiling in front of the world's press and Ruby who had persuaded the hospital both to let them do it and to move Freja Portman to a ward large enough to host the TV crews and all their paraphernalia. Super-efficient Ruby, pretty, capable and bursting with a sexuality that drove men crazy, himself included. Which stood in stark contrast to the sanctimonious little shit Portman, with her stupid eco-stunts and constant whining about climate change and how the world was being simply *ruined* for her generation. As if at seventeen years of age she knew shit-all about anything. But the thing was, the sweet little English rose had taken the world by storm, becoming simultaneously the most recognised and the most revered teenager on the planet. A living saint without having to go through the bother of canonisation, or whatever the hell it was the bishops did. He didn't like her at all, but that didn't matter, because little prim-arse Freja Portman was going to make him the most famous reconstructive surgeon in the world.

He had of course already test-driven the proper removal of her bandages ten days ago or more, and could tell back then, even through the bruises and inflammation, that his work had been successful. *Hugely successful.* She'd been a plain little cow before that guy had done the world a favour by spraying sulphuric acid all over her smug face, but now the cheeks were sculpted, the mouth wider, the lips fuller, her skin taut and flawless. He just hoped she bloody appreciated what he had done for her. Twenty minutes earlier he had re-applied her bandages, she happy to go along with another stunt in order to generate more publicity for her pathetic cause. *Stupid little cow.*

Now the world's media were beginning to file into the ward, the room set out theatre-style with accommodation for over one hundred hacks. A low platform had been erected at one end and on it sat a tall four-legged stool. In a few minutes the two of them would make their slow entrance, he guiding her by the hand, pausing for a few moments to milk the applause then helping her up on to the stool. He would make a short speech, emphasising how delicate and complex the surgery had been, and how a successful outcome had been in doubt right until the end. And then, dramatically, the bandages would be peeled away and the world would gasp at his amazing handiwork and soon would be *demanding* that the brilliant surgeon be showered with the wealth and honours he surely was now entitled to.

There were naturally some loose ends to be tidied up, but that wouldn't be too much of a problem. After all, he had always been rather good at tidying up loose ends, and getting away with it too. He'd heard the old saying of course, something about your past sins always catching up with you. Well maybe that was true for common people, but not for superior specimens like himself. Because for the supremely talented surgeon, it was so ridiculously easy to get away with almost anything.

Even murder.

Chapter 1

It was unusual in the extreme for Maggie and Jimmy to be meeting with Asvina Rani anywhere but in the glittering glass palace that housed Addison Redburn, the prestigious City law firm where Ms Rani was a Senior Partner. And she wasn't just any old senior partner either, she being considered by her peers in the profession to be the most accomplished family-law solicitor in the entire country and therefore the first choice whenever a billionaire, senior politician or A-list celebrity was experiencing a spot of marital difficulty. Generally if you wanted to make use of Asvina's services you came to her, no matter how famous or celebrated you were, her time being too precious and expensive to be wasted on unproductive and non-billable travel. But today, remarkably, she was coming to visit them in the unprepossessing shared office facility off Fleet Street which was the headquarters of Maggie Bainbridge Associates. That Asvina had been willing to undertake the short journey from her Canary Wharf office was all the more surprising in the light of the fact that she was approaching the thirty-fourth week of her pregnancy.

'You look amazing,' Maggie said, as she took her friend's coat and laid it over a spare seat in the meeting room, 'but huge too. Are you sure it's not twins?'

'Aye, or triplets even,' Jimmy said. 'Three wee guys would easily fit in there, if I'm any judge.'

Asvina grinned. 'No, just one, according to my gynaecologist at least. And it's a little girl, but I think you knew that already.'

'So what does Dav think about having his sleep disrupted for another six months?' Jimmy said.

'Not completely delighted if I'm being honest,' Asvina laughed, 'but my darling husband loves being a dad and knows it's the price you have to pay. And our boys are thrilled to be getting a little sister as you can imagine.'

'It will be lovely,' Maggie said, giving a mock grimace, 'except for the sleepless nights of course. But as everyone will tell you, the time soon whizzes by and before you know it they'll be off to school. But I'm sure you didn't come here just to bring us up to date with all of that.' She was sensitive to the fact that her best friend, polite though she would always be, liked to get down to business as soon as possible.

Asvina nodded. 'Yes, well as I hinted on the phone, it's rather a delicate and sensitive matter. Let me show you this.' After a brief rummage in her handbag, she withdrew a clutch of large photographs and placed them in a pile on the table facing them.

'Looks just like an ordinary office desk,' Jimmy said, wearing a puzzled expression as he looked at the uppermost picture.

'Correct,' she said. 'You might not recognise the location because all office desks look much the same but this is the workspace of my colleague Miss Jolene Cavendish.'

'Jolene?' Maggie said, smiling. 'You mean like in the song?'

'The same,' Asvina said. 'It's quite an unusual name isn't it? Anyway, Jolene heads up our Corporate Mergers & Acquisitions Support Services team.'

'That's quite a mouthful,' Jimmy grinned. 'So she's at your level Asvina, is she? Another big cheese?'

She laughed. 'Yes that's right Jimmy, she's a big cheese. We both report to Rupert Pattison, our Managing Partner.'

Which meant, Maggie reflected without a trace of envy, that Miss Cavendish was in the same million-plus earnings bracket as Asvina herself. Well, maybe a *little* envy although she herself didn't have any money worries to speak of. Her deceased husband Phillip had been a pig, but at least he had been a moderately well-off pig.

'Although to be fair she has to work much harder than me,' Asvina continued. 'She's dealing with huge multi-million pound mergers and takeovers that can keep a team of fifty or more busy for a year, sometimes longer. It's very complicated work.'

Being a lapsed lawyer herself, or more accurately, a disgraced lawyer, Maggie knew what that meant.

'So I'm guessing our Miss Cavendish generates a meaty fee income for the firm?'

'That's right,' Asvina said. 'It was over thirty million last year I think. Which is why this matter is so critically important to us.' She leant over the table and slid the topmost photograph to one side, revealing another picture of the desk. This time, it had an object placed on it.

'Good grief,' Maggie exclaimed. 'Is that a *witch's* hat?'

'Exactly. She's acquired a nick-name around our office. The witch-bitch, that's what they call her apparently, although no-one has ever said it in my presence.'

'Charming,' Jimmy said.

Asvina nodded, 'Yes, and that's far from the worst of it.' She pushed the picture aside, revealing another. This time, the object was all together darker and more sinister. A life-sized baby doll, eyes blackened with mascara, the face splashed with blood. Next to it, a chilling message, computer-printed on a sheet of A4 paper. *Death to the witch-bitch baby. Still-born in our prayers.*

'That's *sick*,' he said, shocked. 'Really sick.'

'Yes it is,' Asvina said. 'I should have said that Jolene Cavendish is pregnant too, and like me, not far off the birth date. Which makes it doubly sick.'

'It's awful,' Maggie said. 'And how long has this been going on for?'

'About three or four months we think. But it's escalated in the last week or two, cumulating in the baby episode.'

'Do you have any idea who might be responsible for this?'

Asvina raised an eyebrow. 'Now it's funny you should ask that question. Because that's why I'm here.'

'So that's going to be our mission is it?' Jimmy said, catching on. 'To find out?'

'Yes Captain Stewart,' she replied. 'That's going to be your mission, should you choose to accept it. Or at least that's part of it.'

'What do you mean?' Maggie asked.

'Well as you can imagine, Jolene has gone ballistic about all this. First of all, she's threatening to sue the firm for failing in its duty of care by allowing these incidents to continue. Then she says she will resign and take us to an industrial tribunal, citing constructive dismissal, again because we haven't done enough to stop it. You can imagine how all *that* will look if it gets into the papers, with her being nearly eight months pregnant and all that. Not good, I can tell you that.'

Maggie gave a wry smile. None of that would look good for the firm, but the shiny Canary Wharf tower hosted some of the most talented employment-law briefs in the land, well capable of defending its reputation against a disgruntled employee, no matter how senior. No, there was something else and she thought she knew what it was.

'I guess if she does leave, a lot of the business would go with her. If she's that good I mean.'

Asvina nodded. 'Got it in one Maggie. Rupert's absolutely beside himself that she'll walk out the door and take some of our biggest clients with her.'

'And so he's asked you to sort it out,' Maggie said.

Jimmy smiled. 'Sounds like one big hospital pass to me.'

'You could say that,' Asvina said, looking rueful, 'and I could have done without it to be honest, given my condition. But then I thought of you guys and my whole day suddenly brightened up.'

'We're touched,' Maggie laughed. 'So, to the mission.'

'Yes, the mission. It's in two parts I guess. First of all, we really do want to find out who is behind this vile harassment. Rupert has given that undertaking to Jolene and we are serious about following it through.'

'And the second thing?' Maggie asked, although she was sure she already knew what Asvina was going to say.

'We really don't want her to leave. Although she can be a bloody difficult woman, it would still be a disaster for the firm in all sorts of ways. Not just the loss of business but the damage to our reputation too. She wouldn't be shy in spreading around how she had been treated and that would badly affect our ability to attract new business and to recruit the best staff too. As I said, it would be nothing short of a disaster.'

'So you want us what, to try and persuade her to stay?' Jimmy said, furrowing his brow. 'God, I had some impossible missions dumped on me in my army days but this one looks right up there with the best of them. Or should I say the worst of them.'

'Yes, I know it will be tough but I have every faith in you two. I've told Rupert you've worked miracles in the past, which is why he's agreed to hire you. And you'll have a big compensation fund to work with, so money shouldn't be any problem.'

'What, to buy her off do you mean?' Jimmy asked.

'If you want to put it that way,' Asvina said. 'Rupert thinks everything can be fixed by money you see.'

'But I'm guessing you're not so sure,' Maggie said, picking up the nuance in her friend's response. She could see where Asvina was coming from. For Jolene Cavendish, the witch-bitch of Addison Redburn, this would be personal, and in her experience when things got personal, no amount of money could make it better. But then again, they said everyone had their price. They would just have to see how it all panned out.

Asvina nodded. 'Yes, if only it was just a question of money. She's a proud woman and rather in love with herself so I can see it being a difficult ask. But anyway, desks and passes are all arranged and you start at eight a.m. prompt, next Monday.'

'What?' Maggie shot her friend a surprised look.

'Didn't I tell you? I'm afraid you're going to have to work a little harder for your money on this assignment. So, we've told Jolene that you two will be joining her team, with the brief to find out who is behind this harassment campaign. The cover story as far as the rest of her team is concerned is that you are being brought in to help with the due diligence on the huge Hampton Defence deal they're working on. I'm sure you've heard of them?'

'Aye, I've heard of them all right,' Jimmy said. 'I used quite a bit of their kit in my army days. They make armoured personnel carriers and suchlike. But isn't there a big stink about it because they're being flogged to the Americans? With a lot of people saying the government should step in to block it?'

'That's absolutely right,' Asvina said, 'but the thing's even more complicated by the fact that there's a tranche of the stock going to some big-ticket private investors too. So it's big, horrible and complex and now it's getting to the critical point in the process and they're having to throw everything they've got at it. Believe me, it won't be any surprise to anyone to see additional resources being added to the team, more hands to the pump if you like. I doubt if anyone will even notice you.'

That caused Maggie to raise an eyebrow. Whilst it was true that the arrival of a dowdy-ish forty-two-year-old like herself was unlikely to be a cause for excitement, the same could not be said about her colleague. Six foot two and eyes of blue went the old song, and Jimmy Stewart could never enter a room without drawing admiring glances from every woman present. She often imagined him as a Hollywood heart-throb of old, a kind of intoxicating mixture of Cary

Grant and Clark Gable with a hint of his famous namesake thrown in for good measure. And the delightful thing was, he was blissfully unaware of the effect he had, an effect that she had exploited on a number of cases in the past. However, she had come to realise how much he hated being cast in the role of honey-trap, and had vowed to avoid such assignments in the future. Unless of course there was no option.

She saw he was frowning. 'But does that mean we're going to have to be there nine to five?' he said. 'Like in a proper job?'

Asvina laughed. 'Nine to five? I don't know what planet you come from Jimmy, but no-one works nine to five in our profession. Eight to ten more like, and I don't mean ten in the morning either. But don't worry, it will be made clear to everyone that you are being hired as investigators, to check out the background of some of those private investors I told you about.'

'Looking for dodgy ex-drug dealers and that sort of thing, do you mean?' Jimmy asked.

'I think they're more worried about Chinese involvement to be honest, but it amounts to the same thing. So anyway, no-one will be surprised if you're out and about most of the time.'

'Thank goodness for that,' Jimmy said, looking relieved.

'But the real job is to find out who is doing this to Cavendish?' Maggie said.

'From the firm's point of view, the real job is to get her to stay,' Asvina said. 'But yes, we do want to find out who is doing this too.'

'Any suspects at the moment?' Maggie asked.

'Well, Jolene has her suspicions, but it's a pretty long list I'm afraid,' Asvina said. 'She is rather paranoid I'm afraid, and I think she believes everyone hates her.'

Maggie nodded. 'And is that true? That everyone hates her?'

'Well as I said, she can be a difficult woman. Is she hated? I'm not sure I would put it that strongly, but I think the general view of her around the firm would be one of grudging respect rather than love. The witch-bitch sobriquet isn't new you see, she's carried it like a badge of honour for several years now. But the thing with the doll, that was different. That's a whole new level of bitterness, of a kind we haven't seen before.'

'Did the firm never think of calling in the police?' Jimmy asked. 'Because as you say Asvina, the thing with that doll is pretty sinister. That's properly threatening behaviour.'

'Well we did consider it of course, but the thing was, Jolene was totally against getting them involved, I'm not sure why. Rupert and I did discuss why she might feel that way, and all we could think of was she felt it might get in the way of any civil legal action she might take. But we haven't ruled it out of course and if there are any further incidents like it, we'll naturally consider that course of action.'

Maggie smiled to herself. She loved her friend dearly, but she knew that for Asvina, Addison Redburn ranked only behind her lovely family in things that were important to her. She could imagine how much it suited the firm to keep the police out of a matter that could turn out to be highly embarrassing for the firm. Much better to hire a biddable team of private investigators whose discretion could be relied upon, not that Maggie could really complain about that. This looked as if it was going to turn into a very juicy case, full of interest and intrigue, exactly as she and Jimmy liked it. Not to mention delivering a nice fat fee, which always came in decidedly useful.

She watched as Asvina gathered up the photographs and slipped them back in her handbag. As Maggie had expected, the meeting was to be short and sweet.

'So,' her friend said, getting up to leave, 'all clear?'

'Yup,' Maggie said, grinning, 'all clear.'

'Good. Oh, and there's just one thing I nearly forgot to mention,' Asvina said, shooting Jimmy a sympathetic smile. 'There's a dress code. So for you Jimmy that means suit, shirt and tie I'm afraid.'

She glided through the door without waiting for his reply. Which was just as well, given its decidedly uncomplimentary nature.

Chapter 2

Frank had decided it was worth digging out his best suit for today's assignment. It was the one he generally reserved for courtroom appearances, the smart navy job, slim-lapelled with a discreet pinstripe. Not as a sign of respect for the guy he was meeting, but so as not to let down his boss DCI Jill Smart, who was to accompany him to the House of Commons. Generally he had a disdain for politicians of all hues, considering them talentless leeches much in love with the sound of their own voices, and this guy, *Sir* Patrick Hopkins no less, he'd never even heard of. Looking him up on Google, it seemed he had some fancy title to do with the Duchy of Lancaster, which Frank had learned was bestowed by Prime Ministers on talented but troublesome members of their own side whom they couldn't quite trust to run one of the great departments of state. It appeared that the useful Sir Patrick had been endowed with a clutch of other responsibilities too, one of which apparently was pertinent to their meeting. *Chair of the All-party Honours Selection Committee.* Frank had no idea what the role of his little misfit Department 12B was to be in what Jill had described as a sensitive political matter, but he expected he would find out pretty soon.

The meeting was to be held in Portcullis House, the imposing modern edifice that sat on the Thames adjacent to Westminster Bridge and just a stone's throw from the Houses of Parliament itself. As he guessed, security was tight, notwithstanding the fact that his Metropolitan Police warrant card smoothed the path somewhat. He still had to go through the airport-style scanners but was thankful to be spared the full body-search by the hatchet-faced female guard who was on duty that day. He was met in reception by an unsmiling young woman attired in a grey business suit who gave no name, simply stating she was Sir Patrick's personal researcher. Of course, they all had researchers, these politician guys, steely-faced drones solely dedicated to clawing their way up the greasy pole, hoping against hope that several years' of blind servitude to the Party would result in the invitation to contest some no-hope seat in their opponents' heartland. And then a few years later if a sitting MP died, retired or committed some scandalous indiscretion, they might finally bag that safe seat that had probably been their dream since childhood. It wasn't a lifestyle he would have chosen for himself but he kind of understood why they did it. Show business for ugly people was how the political game had often been described, although it had to be said that Miss No-Name- Researcher was far from plain.

The young woman led him through to the elevators and swiped the control panel with her security pass. A distant whirr heralded the swift descent of the lift and soon the doors were sliding open, almost silently.

'We're on the top floor,' she said, still not giving him a glance. 'Come this way.'

He couldn't help reflecting how differently the scene would have played out if he had been his brother Jimmy, or at least looked a bit more like him. Not that they didn't share some similarities, and in fact people often did comment on the likeness if they saw them together. A shorter, fatter and older version of Jimmy was how he was invariably described, but that didn't bother him in the least. Well not much anyway.

A few seconds later the lift gave a discreet ping as it arrived on the sixth floor. The meeting room was immediately opposite, also requiring a sweep of the researcher's pass to gain entry. She pushed open the door and ushered Frank in.

A deep voice boomed out from the corner of the small room. 'Ah Rachel, so you've found our good Inspector running loose in the building. Welcome to Portcullis House Inspector Stewart. Grab a pew, anywhere you like. We don't stand on ceremony around here.'

Hopkins was a large grey-haired man of about sixty, attired in a crumpled white shirt with a striped tie which Frank guessed was one of these old-school regimental types. His ruddy features spoke of a lifetime enjoying the claret-fuelled lunches and dinners that reputedly oiled the machinery of government, but his demeanour was warm and welcoming and bereft of the pomposity that Frank was expecting. He knew that Sir Patrick had in his younger days been spoken of as a contender, and in recent years had come closer still, running a respectable second in two party leadership elections. But now his time had passed, and it seemed he was content simply to be useful to the Party in general and the PM in particular, his relationship with the latter endowing him with considerable power over his parliamentary colleagues.

Jill Smart had already arrived and as Frank had expected had decided to come in uniform.

'Morning ma'am,' he said, smiling as he pulled out a chair and sat down at the table. 'Looking good.'

'Cheers Frank,' she said, a sardonic smile crossing her lips. 'I wish I could say the same for you.'

'Best suit ma'am,' he replied with mock indignation, 'and I pressed the trousers too.'

'Run off and get us some drinks will you Rachel?' Hopkins said, giving her a dismissive wave. 'Tea, coffee, what will you have?'

A few seconds later the researcher returned, having evidently delegated the task of organising the refreshments to some other minion even lower down the food chain. And now it appeared it was she who was to open proceedings.

'So, Sir Patrick I think gave you some brief explanation on the phone Jill I believe?' So they were to be on first-name terms already were they? Fine by him, although he wasn't so sure how DCI Smart would feel about being addressed with such familiarity by this young kid.

'Only the briefest explanation,' Jill replied, 'a little difficulty with the birthday honours list, I think that's how you described it?'

'That's it in a nutshell,' Hopkins said, stepping in. 'Damned awkward the whole business is, damned awkward. Anyway, thank you so much for coming along today. I heard the Home

Secretary talking about your department's role in that damn Alzahrani business which is what gave me the idea to call you in.'

'We'll be happy to help in any way we can I'm sure,' Jill said. 'Isn't that right Frank?'

'Oh aye, any way we can. We're here to please.'

Rachel the researcher gave him a sharp look as if trying to work out if he was taking the piss or not. He returned a seraphic smile.

'So I'm sure you'll have heard about this Freja Portman business,' Hopkins said. 'A terrible thing all together, wasn't it?'

Frank gave Jill a searching look, wondering if either of them should say anything. The Portman business, as he described it, had not been the Met's finest moment, that was for sure. The force had known of course that right-wing activists would surely be targeting the climate conference in that London hotel where the teenager was giving a speech, but it had been their gaffer the Commissioner's decision that the policing should be low-key. Not in retrospect Dame Amanda's wisest move. So when that guy had stepped up with some sort of homemade water-pistol and sprayed sulphuric acid all over Portman's face, they had been caught unawares. With just two uniforms in the room, the hooded attacker had managed to flee via the fire doors and to the endless embarrassment of the force, hadn't been seen since. Neither Frank nor Jill had worked the case personally of course, but that didn't make the failure any easier to stomach. Collective institutional guilt, that was what they called it, and they both felt it acutely.

'Yes, it was a terrible thing,' Jill conceded, 'but I believe we are following up a number of promising lines of enquiry and hope to make an arrest soon.'

Frank smiled inwardly. *Promising lines of enquiry.* It was what they were taught to say when an investigation was going nowhere, and Jill was a master of making it sound convincing. But she needn't have worried, because evidently Sir Patrick's primary concern was not the scumbag who had disfigured the young climate activist but the surgeon who had so skilfully rebuilt her features afterwards.

'Jolly good,' he said. 'So this James Parrish, the surgeon chap. The fellow's become a bit of a national hero, and of course why shouldn't that be the case, because he did a terrific job on that young girl. Terrific job. Absolutely first class.'

'I'm sensing a *but*,' Jill said.

He gave a sigh. 'Well yes. It's that damn campaign in the *Chronicle*, lobbying for him to be given a knighthood. I'm hearing it's reached over a million signatures or likes or whatever it is.'

'Nearing two million now,' Rachel the researcher corrected, 'and they're tweets.'

'Yes, well that's good I'm sure,' Hopkins said, sounding uncertain, 'but the thing is, the *Chronicle* is one of our party's biggest supporters, which makes the whole thing somewhat problematic. If we were to defy the public clamour, if you know what I mean. It wouldn't look good for the PM or the party.'

Frank screwed up his face. 'I'm not sure I'm with you Sir Patrick.'

'This Parrish chap,' he repeated, making him sound as if he was an unsavoury member of his London club, 'you see, the PM has got some concerns that it might all blow up in his face sometime in the future. If we were to award the knighthood I mean. And of course we would wish to avoid that outcome, naturally.'

'Aye, I can see that,' Frank said, 'but I'm also guessing if your man Parrish isn't in the next honours list then it won't be popular with the public.'

'Yes indeed,' Hopkins said, nodding vigorously. 'The PM is very keen on winning a second term and as I'm sure you know, whether he does or doesn't has got sod-all to do with policy and everything to do with whether he remains popular in the country.'

'And knighting James Parrish wouldn't do that popularity any harm,' Jill said.

'No it wouldn't. So you can see why we are rather anxious to ensure that this matter is dealt with as swiftly and efficiently as possible.'

Frank found himself wondering when it was going to be revealed, the reason why they hadn't already booked James Parrish's kneeling appointment with Her Majesty the Queen. He didn't have long to wait.

'You see, Mr Parrish is presently on his *fourth* marriage,' Rachel said, more than a hint of disdain in her tone.

Frank gave her a puzzled look. By his calculation, the PM was on his third wife, so he doubted if the objection to Parrish's knighthood could be on moral grounds.

'Is that a problem?' he asked.

'Not in itself,' she replied primly, 'but you see, wives two and three died before their time, let's just put it that way.' The implication was unsaid but clear. *This was no coincidence.*

'Poor guy,' Frank said, deadpan. 'Must have been tough for him, suffering all that tragedy in his life. And what about his first wife? She still with us?'

'Yes, last time we checked,' the researcher said. 'That particular marriage didn't last long. Just two years.'

A short time indeed, Frank reflected, but if Parrish was on to his fourth already, the others couldn't have lasted much longer, given that from his photographs the guy looked no more than fifty years of age.

'So what, do you think there was something dodgy about these deaths then? Have you got any evidence?'

Hopkins shrugged. 'No, nothing like that. Nothing *concrete*. But there were some rumours about the third one. She drowned you see, somewhere up in Scotland. Loch More I think it was.'

Frank gave him an astonished look. 'Loch More? You're kidding me.'

'No,' Hopkins said, 'I'm pretty sure that's where it was. Why, do you know the place?'

'Aye, I suppose you could say that. My last case took me up there, so it just seems a weird coincidence that's all.'

'So it's your neck of the woods is it?' Hopkins asked.

'Not exactly. I'm from Glasgow.'

'I've never been,' Hopkins replied, half-apologetically. Frank wasn't surprised. He doubted if old Sir Patrick had ever been north of Watford.

'It's very picturesque, you'd like it.'

Hopkins gave an uncertain laugh. 'Yes, I'm sure I would. But coming back to the drowning, a reporter on one of the Scottish papers had her suspicions and did an investigation, but nothing came of it.'

Frank shrugged. 'Aye well, it's probably nothing then, but I'm guessing you're wanting us to take a look, is that it?' He turned to Jill and said, 'Well what's the verdict ma'am? Is this one for us?'

She laughed. 'I'm not sure if we have a choice. But yes, I'd say this is one for us.'

'Jolly good,' Hopkins said again, 'and I should have mentioned, we need this thing resolved pretty damn quickly. It's just six weeks before the final submission for the next honours list and the PM is anxious that he's not forced into a blind decision. Time is of the essence and all that.'

'Six weeks, are you joking?' Frank said, unable to hide his incredulity.

'We know it's quite a tall order,' the researcher said smoothly, 'but we have every faith in you and your team.' He noted, slightly peeved, that this was addressed to Jill and not him.

'Aye, well it takes six weeks just to get a case number set up on the computer,' he said, 'so I wouldn't raise your hopes too high.'

'I've already got us one,' Jill said, giving him a wry look. 'I thought it would be wise to come prepared just in case we were asked to move quickly. So yes Sir Patrick, we will take the case and yes, we can start right away.'

Frank recognised an ambush when he saw one and decided to say nothing. But really, what was he worrying about? The case seemed interesting enough and you could do a fair amount in six weeks with the right amount of cooperation from the local cops.

The only problem was, by some bizarre coincidence it seemed that one of Parrish's wives had drowned in Loch More. *Loch More, of all places.* Which meant that once again he would be dependent on help from the Police Scotland lads, no more than a month or two after he'd finished off the career of their Chief Constable. Sweet, as his best mate Eleanor Campbell might say.

But no matter, it was time to get started and as smooth Sir Patrick had made clear, time was of the essence. Head back to Atlee House, take a detour past the vending machine to grab a coffee and a Twix bar or two and then back to his desk in time for his wee appointment with Google. Search subject James Parrish FRCS.

Chapter 3

Thursday was their night, the once-a-week pub get-together that had been a ritual now for the two years she had known the Stewart brothers. The Old King's Head or was it just the King's Head, she could never remember which, had become as warm and comforting as an old pair of slippers, although Maggie couldn't really imagine Frank or Jimmy wearing that item of footwear. Too manly, too rugged by half, both of them. She was particularly looking forward to tonight, because when she worked it out, it had been four weeks or more since their last meeting. The truth was, it had all gone a bit flat since they'd wrapped up the Macallan case up in Lochmorehead, partially because of the awkwardness of her last encounter with Frank, but mainly because of the devastating news that had sent Jimmy into a spiral of despair.

Such was her thoughts as she made her way along Gresham Street, the pavement packed with early evening commuters heading home, causing her to have to weave in and out to maintain a reasonable pace. The situation with Frank was as puzzling as ever, but mainly because she had yet to fully resolve her own feelings in the matter. She liked him, in fact she liked him a lot, there was no getting away from it, and he, probably or was it possibly, felt the same way. And yet, when they had been alone at last, in the cosy lounge of that lovely little hotel on Loch Lomond, nothing had happened. They had talked of course, for an hour or more and it had been wonderful, and then they had gone upstairs together, and had stood at her bedroom door, neither it seemed daring to break the silence and say what they were really feeling. Then unexpectedly, he'd leaned forward and kissed her on the lips, gently, tenderly, considerately. But then he'd wished her goodnight and walked along the corridor to his own room without saying another word. Since then, she had replayed the scene over and over in her head and still struggled to make sense of it. Was she giving out the wrong signal, a signal that said we can be friends but nothing more? Because she knew Frank was a good man and she knew enough of him to understand that he was never going to cross that threshold of decency and propriety that was so central to his character. And there was something else, something in his life story that his brother had hinted at but had never explained. She could only imagine there had been some hurt in the past, a hurt that made him wary of giving his heart ever again. Bloody marvellous, that was all she could say about that.

As she expected, Jimmy and Frank were already at the bar when she arrived. That was par for the course as far as Frank was concerned, but far from normal in Jimmy's case. Usually she walked the mile or so from their Fleet Street office with her colleague, leaving around twenty-past five and arriving ten or fifteen minutes later to find his brother well into his second pint. But since Jimmy had got that call from his estranged wife Flora, the call that seemed to end his hopes of there ever being a reconciliation, he had started drinking, and not just on a Thursday too.

'Greetings Maggie,' Frank boomed. 'Usual is it? Large chardonnay?'

'And I'll have a double malt if you're buying,' Jimmy said. She detected the slightest of slurring in his speech and wondered how much he'd had already.

'Come on mate, go easy,' Frank said, as if answering her unspoken question. 'I'd just stick to the pints if I were you. It's not even six o'clock yet.'

'Since when did you become my flipping keeper?' his brother replied, with a sharpness that she had never heard from him before.

Frank shrugged. 'Well I did it for ten years when you were a kid but I never thought I'd still need to be doing it when you became all grown up, if in fact you've actually reached that state.' But then he seemed to realise how insensitive that sounded and changed his tone. 'Look bruv, I know you're hurting and I won't insult you by telling you to move on or any bollocks like that. But take it from me, the drink probably won't help, not in the long term at least. I tried it and it only made it worse.'

Then he gave a short laugh. 'But what the hell, one night's not going to kill you is it? Double malt it is pal, and yes, I'm buying.' He raised a finger to summon a barman. As he did so, she saw Jimmy reach out a hand and touch his brother lightly on the elbow, as if to thank him for his understanding. Of course, she knew from her own experience that Frank was right, one-hundred percent. When her own life was going pear-shaped, when her career and her marriage was tanking and she was in the public eye for all the wrong reasons, it seemed that only cheap chardonnay and lots of it could keep her half-sane. In the end, it was simply her all-consuming need to get her little son back into her life and the sharp talking-to she'd had from lovely Asvina that had brought her to her senses, forcing her to straighten herself out. Maybe that's what Jimmy needed too, the support of a friend who would offer sympathy but some straight talking too. But if she was to take on that role, what should she say? *It's over and you have to move on with your life*? *Don't give up hope, you can still win her back?* The former might bring him some peace, but she knew that deep in his heart he still had a burning love for Dr Flora Stewart and no amount of soothing words was going to make that go away.

'So have you looked out the suit then Jimmy?' she said, keen to change the subject. 'I'm looking forward to seeing you in it.'

He forced a grin. 'Aye well as it happens I'm buying a new one, but I can't say I'm happy about it. But needs must I suppose. Take one for the team and all that.'

'That's the spirit,' she grinned. 'Anyway, we'll only have to be in their office a couple of days a week at most. I'm sure you had to put up with a lot worse when you were in the army.'

'Aye, but I never had to wear a bloody suit then,' he said.

'What's all this about suits?' Frank said, picking up on the conversation as he sorted out the drinks.

'Maggie's trying to make me get a proper job,' Jimmy said, pulling a face. 'Monday morning with an eight o'clock start, over at Canary Wharf at Asvina's place.'

'Hardly that,' Maggie laughed. 'We've got a new case, that's all. A big one, and a very interesting one too.'

Frank gave a thumbs up. 'Aye, well I've got a new one as well, and *it's* a big one too. Bigger than yours I bet. In fact, *I'm* working on behalf of the Prime Minister no less, and it concerns someone really famous. In fact, *two* people who're really famous. Oh, and by the way Jimmy boy, I had to stick on *my* best suit when me and Jill Smart went up to Westminster to hear all about it, so I've no sympathy for you.'

'Listen to him,' Maggie said, chuckling. 'Best suits and visits to Westminster. Mr la-di-dah Stewart. What next, a knighthood for the famous detective inspector?'

'Funny you should say that, because that's what my case is all about. Knighthoods I mean.'

'Sounds intriguing,' Maggie said. 'Tell us more I pray.'

He smiled. 'Well I'd really love to but I can't. It's confidential and if I told you, I'd have to kill you, if you'll pardon the cliché. Maybe later, when I get more into it. But the thing is, this one's so hot it'll probably leak into the papers anyway. In fact, I guarantee it will.'

As she caught his glance, she saw him move his head imperceptibly in the direction of his brother, as if to ask, *how do you think he's doing?* In response, she gave the faintest of shrugs. And then, as Frank began to speak, she realised why he had been so keen to catch her attention.

'There is one other thing mate,' he said, speaking slowly. 'It looks like this investigation might take me back up to Lochmorehead. There was something that happened there a long time ago that needs looking into it. I just thought I'd better mention it, given the situation with your Flora and all that.'

Your Flora. It was a nice touch, and so typically Frank, the very essence of kindness and decency, and once again she felt the fuzzy warmth that always overcame her when she was in his presence, a feeling that she felt he shared. Making it all the more bloody annoying that so far neither of them had actually got off their backsides to do something about it.

'Aye, well thanks for telling us,' Jimmy said, breaking his silence. 'And will you be needing our help on this case like you did on the last one?' From his tone, Maggie couldn't tell whether this was something he would welcome or not.

Frank shook his head. 'I doubt it, but we'll see. Look, if there's anything I can do, you know, whilst I'm up there...' He stopped abruptly, she guessing that he was already regretting what he had just said.

'What could you do?' Jimmy spat the words out. 'It's over and I just have to get used to it. Move on with my life, that's what everyone's saying behind my back isn't it?'

'Woah, steady,' Frank said. 'We just want what's best for you, isn't that right Maggie?' It wasn't hard to see he was uncomfortable with the direction the evening was heading. Normally Thursday night meant having a few drinks and a few laughs and a bit of a catch up about their respective cases, sprinkled with idle chat about nothing in particular. Deep and meaningful conversations about relationships and feelings had decidedly not been on the agenda before.

'Yes, of course,' Maggie said, wondering what more she could say. Once, she had cast herself as Austen's Emma Woodhouse, quite certain that with her intervention she could somehow fix the broken marriage of Jimmy and Flora Stewart. But she soon realised, like the eponymous heroine, that things were not so straightforward in the real world, especially when she'd learnt of the appearance of one Hugo Blackman on the scene. Like Flora, Hugo was a doctor, the acquaintance going back to their student days at Glasgow University, and by all accounts he was as handsome as he was accomplished. From a distance it seemed that Jimmy's wife had moved on and in Maggie's opinion, it was only a matter of time before a letter requesting a divorce dropped through Jimmy's letter-box. She had thought about that often in recent days and worried how he might cope with it when it appeared. But it seemed that Jimmy had decided to snap himself out of his uncharacteristic gloom, because he broke into a smile and said,

'Aye well I appreciate that guys, I really do. But come on, we're here to have a bit of a jolly, not to mope over my stupid troubles. So I'm going to stick something on the jukebox, although I'm not sure it's exactly appropriate given my circumstances.'

'What do you mean?' Maggie said, looking puzzled.

'Have you not heard it?' he said. 'That bloody annoying tune Frank's been humming since he got here.'

'Have I?' Frank said, surprised. 'Aye, well I suppose I have, now I come to think of it. You see, in my new investigation...'

'Your *secret* investigation,' Maggie said.

'Aye, that one. So the guy who might or might not be up for a knighthood has been married four times, and his first wife, turns out it was her name. Since I found out, I've not been able to get the bloody tune out of my head.'

Maggie gave Frank a look of astonishment. 'Don't tell me. No way.'

'Aye, it's one of Dolly Parton's. Her most famous number.' Impervious to the disdainful looks of the surrounding drinkers, he broke into a tuneless warble.

'Jolene, Jolene, Jolene, Jolee-ee-ene, something-something just because you can.'

Chapter 4

'They call it the weekly stand-up. It's another one of these things that we've imported from corporate America I think. They get the whole team in a room and run through the programme for the week ahead. And everybody is standing up, that's where the name comes from, obviously.'

Maggie, slightly breathless, was trying to explain to Jimmy why Monday morning's eight o'clock start had unexpectedly turned into a seven-thirty. She found his peevishness amusing given that he wouldn't have been exactly unused to unsocial hours in his time as a Captain in the bomb-squad. But maybe that was one of the reasons he'd left the army, to get a lie-in every now and then.

'Sounds like a load of bollocks to me,' he said, as the jostled their way through the commuter throng making for the Addison Redburn office on Canary Wharf.

'Well, it's our first day. Probably not wise to complain too much, not until we've got our feet under the desk a bit.'

'Fair enough boss,' he said, smiling. 'Actually, I'm quite looking forward to it, especially meeting the witch-bitch in person. She sounds like a real piece of work.'

'Yeah she does,' Maggie agreed. 'But just make sure you don't let slip her nickname in front of her. That probably wouldn't go down too well.'

'She'll already know. In fact I bet she secretly revels in it. Jolene the Witch-Bitch. It's got a certain ring to it, don't you think?'

As they approached the building, Jimmy tapped Maggie on the shoulder and pointed ahead. 'Here, what's this all about?' A small group had gathered in front of the revolving door, carrying a selection of obviously home-produced placards. *Keep Hampton British. Say No to US Asset-Strippers. Stop the Sale.* An overweight dreadlocked woman of about forty wearing a stained parka came over to Jimmy and thrust a leaflet in his hand.

'Will you sign our petition please?' she said, giving him the sort of smile that Maggie had seen a hundred times before, in fact almost every time a woman was within fifty feet of Jimmy Stewart. A smile that telegraphed *I'm interested*.

'Aye, if you like,' he said. 'But it's my first day, so if you don't mind, I need to get on.'

'Of course,' she said, smiling at him again before standing aside.

Asvina Rani had arranged their security passes a day or two earlier and so their entrance to the building went smoothly, the revolving door responding spookily to their approach and delivering them into the impressively high-ceilinged atrium.

'Third floor I think,' Maggie said as they grabbed the nearest elevator. It felt just like the first day in senior school, the awkwardness and self-consciousness, wondering if you would fit in. The lift announced its arrival with a quiet ping, the doors sliding open to reveal a brightly-lit open-plan office with an array of desks packed tightly in a strict geometric pattern. Every few yards or so a tall potted plant made an unsuccessful attempt to soften the stark atmosphere. It reminded her of a factory farm, except here instead of chickens there were row upon row of worker-bee junior lawyers chained to their desks churning out deadly dull contracts and torts and non-disclosure agreements and such like. At least when she had been in the profession, even as a spectacularly unsuccessful barrister, she'd had the excitement of her courtroom appearances to look forward to. Now she couldn't imagine ever going back to her old life, and these few days she would spend in this corporate hell-hole would surely serve to remind her of that.

It was just twenty-past seven, but already the room was full, groups of staff standing alongside their desks clutching take-away coffees and chatting quietly. She guessed that Miss Cavendish was not one to tolerate lateness, so it was as well to be early just to be on the safe side. Or maybe they just wanted to get in before the protest mob turned up outside the front door.

'Good morning guys.' The voice was loud and shrill and to Maggie's ears bereft of any warmth. There was still a good six minutes before the scheduled start of the meeting but here was Jolene Cavendish already taking the stage, which explained why the team was already gathered. This must be the routine, she thought, arrive early in order to catch out any members of her team who had the temerity to actually turn up precisely on time. A muted *good morning Jolene*, distinctly perfunctory in nature, was the response. Looking around the room it wasn't hard to come up with a word that described the atmosphere. *Sullen*. Maggie estimated there was around forty or so staff in the room, and if they all hated their boss as the looks on their faces suggested, then finding out which of them had taken that hatred a stage further was going to be no easy task.

'Right,' Jolene said briskly, 'do we all know what's ahead of us this week? You Harry, do you know?'

She nodded her head in the direction of a man who was standing a few feet away from Maggie. She guessed he was maybe a couple of years younger than herself, slim to the point of skinniness and with cropped hair dyed a vivid blonde. If it wasn't for the suit he could have been taken for central-casting's archetypal football hooligan instead of a corporate lawyer with a big-time firm. He gave Jolene a sullen look then said,

'Draft contracts. We need to have the draft contracts completed and in front of Hampton's board by Friday. Everybody knows that Jolene.' There was no mistaking the tone of insolence.

'Clever boy Harry,' Jolene said. 'So if you're so clever, what in the name of god was it you presented us with on Friday?' She held aloft a thick document, a document that the man obviously recognised.

'Only a working draft Jolene,' he said sullenly. 'It still needed some work.'

'Actually Harry, this was *only* a pile of shit, and it needed more than *some* work. What it actually needed was to be thrown into the shredder and never to see the light of day again. Instead I wasted several hours of my precious weekend wading through this crap and that's time I'm never going to get back, is it?'

She gave a theatrical pause before repeating the question, this time directing it at the unfortunate victim.

'Is it Harry? *Is* it?'

'No Jolene,' he said, looking her straight in the eye. 'But I already told you it was just a working draft. You just weren't listening. As normal.'

Maggie caught Jimmy's eye and could see he was thinking the same thing. *Shouldn't have said that*.

'No Harry, let me correct you there. *You* think it's a working draft when in fact it is, as I think I made perfectly clear, a pile of shit. You know, maybe you need to consider if you've chosen the right profession. Barista perhaps, assuming you know the difference between a latte and an americano?'

A flicker of anger passed across his face and for a moment Maggie thought he was going to say something, but he evidently thought better of it, giving a morose shrug instead. She couldn't help but be fascinated by the dynamics of the little scene that was being played out in front of her. Jolene Cavendish was the gorilla in the room, the four-hundred-thousand-a-year partner, but what was he? Maybe mid-to-late thirties and yet still slaving away at the legal coal-face, still on the lowest rung of the career ladder, resigned to a life of endlessly drafting and re-drafting dull agreements that no-one would ever read properly if at all. It was a career going nowhere, but everybody had to pay the bills so he probably had no choice but to slog it out.

She knew what it was like, thinking back to her time at Drake Chambers when if she got given any cases at all, they were the crappiest briefs, no-hopers and badly-paying to boot. By the time she reached her fortieth birthday, any dreams of becoming Queen's Counsel were long in the past. That was until the Alzahrani case catapulted her into the public eye, placing the coveted silk tantalisingly in reach, only for it to explode in her hands, destroying her life and career at the same time. It was when she was at her absolute lowest point that Jimmy Stewart had come into her life, and it was no exaggeration to say that without him, she doubted if she would have been able to carry on. And of course, if she hadn't met Jimmy, she wouldn't have met Frank either. The old chestnut, every cloud has a silver lining, had turned out true for her. Now she wondered if Harry was facing a cloud just around the corner, and if there would be a silver lining for him too.

'Ok, I'll take another look at it,' he said, giving another sullen shrug. 'You'll have it by lunch-time.'

'By eleven o'clock if it's not *too* much trouble.'

'Whatever.'

The guy wasn't exactly respectful, Maggie thought, but that didn't excuse they way Jolene was treating him, and in public too. One thing was sure, Jimmy had been right in his assessment of this woman. *What a piece of work*.

'So, I think we are all clear on what the task is for the week ahead,' Jolene continued, seemingly unfazed. 'Draft contracts to be with Hampton by twelve noon on Friday. The transfer of assets documents, the financial terms and conditions documents, the guarantees and warranties documents, the default remedies documents bla-dee-bla-dee-bla. All of them, is that clear? And I don't give a shit if any of you have parents' evenings or a dying mother or if you've just been diagnosed with a terminal illness, we put in the hours and we complete these documents on time. No excuses. Is that clear?'

Nobody said anything.

'Is that *clear*?'

A smattering of nodding heads and a couple of reluctant-sounding mumbles confirmed that, at least for some of the team, it was clear.

'Right,' she said. 'So just a quick bit of housekeeping before we get started. We've got two new members joining us today, Maggie and Jimmy. They call themselves legal investigators but what they actually are are private *dicks*.' She gave a short laugh at her own joke. 'They'll be looking into the backgrounds of some of the dodgier private investors in our deal, to make sure there's nothing that's going to pop up and bite us on the arse later. So if they ask you for information in this regard, I'm sure I can rely on you to help them.'

Once again, nobody said anything. God, this was going to be a tough one, Maggie thought. Jolene clearly ruled the place through fear and as she had already seen demonstrated with the unfortunate Harry, didn't suffer fools gladly. So getting anyone to talk might prove to be a tall order, with everyone worried in case they said the wrong thing.

'Right, get to it and no pissing around,' Jolene barked, then gestured at Maggie as she turned away. 'I'll see you two in my office at ten sharp.'

Jimmy raised an eyebrow. 'Charming, don't you think? I can see why she's not too popular around here. Even my old Colonel didn't talk to us that way.'

'Yeah, but you all had guns,' Maggie said.

'True enough,' he said, 'but plenty of people around here were shooting daggers. I don't think we'll have any problem making a list of suspects, do you?'

She grinned. 'No, that's true enough but it's eliminating them that might prove a bit more of a challenge. And that's assuming we can get any of them to open up to us in the first place, given they're all shit-scared of her.'

Out of the corner of her eye, she saw they were being approached by a young woman. A beautiful young woman, whom Maggie guessed to be in her mid-thirties, slim and willowy with a shock of carrot-red hair held back by an elaborate French plait. And at that moment, she realised it might not be quite so hard to get the information they needed after all. Not when it looked as if around half the team was female and she had Jimmy Stewart on her team. Now this vision of loveliness was making a bee-line towards her colleague, which made Maggie wonder for a moment about the origin of that phrase, because anytime she had seen a bee, they seemed to fly in anything but a straight line.

'Hi', the young woman gushed, 'I'm Emily, Emily Smith. Welcome to the mad house.' The introduction was directed at Maggie but her gaze was fixed on Jimmy.

Maggie smiled. 'Is she always like that? Jolene I mean?'

'Pretty much, but you get used to it. I've been here more than three years now and she's not changed one bit. In fact, she's got worse if anything.'

'She was a bit cruel to that bloke,' Jimmy said. 'I had to look away at one point, I thought he was going to hit her.'

'Who Harry? Yes, she's often a bit hard on him but then again between you and me he is actually a bit useless. There's one or two she often picks out in that way. Generally they're fairly new to the team and haven't realised the standard of work Jolene expects from us all. She hates anything sloppy and isn't slow to say so.'

'Worth knowing Emily,' he said, smiling back at her, 'but it's a bit cruel to do it in public like that. I doubt whether it has the desired effect. More likely to piss someone off rather than motivate them, that's what I would say. Even the army has chucked that sort of stuff in the dustbin now.'

Emily. Maggie looked at him, half-amused, half-puzzled. Generally her colleague was oblivious to such obvious attentions from women, and goodness knows he got plenty of it. But his ill-fated relationship with the seductive Swedish country singer Astrid Sorenson, which had wrecked his marriage to his adored Flora, had succeeded in immunising him against the charms of even the most ardent admirer. Yet here he was now, addressing this woman by her name and being almost chatty with her too, which was very much not his normal style.

And then it struck her. *Slim, beautiful and red-headed*. From a distance, you could easily mistake them for sisters, Emily Smith and Dr Flora Stewart, although on first acquaintance, the former did not quite project the same warm intelligence that made his estranged wife so stunningly special.

'So you were in the forces Jimmy?' Emily asked, fixing him with a steady gaze. 'That must have been interesting. How long did you serve?'

Blooming heck, Maggie thought, grimacing inwardly, does she think she's on a first date or something? Before Jimmy could answer she said, 'Emily, when Jolene interviewed us, she told us about the harassment she had been getting. She said she'd rather we heard it from her directly rather from the office gossip. I just wondered, does everyone in the team know what's been happening?'

Emily returned a look which telegraphed her annoyance at being interrupted. 'What? Well yes of course, nobody talks about much else.'

'And are there any theories as to who's behind it and why they're doing it?' Maggie asked.

She shrugged. 'Yeah, well it's quite obvious why it's happening, isn't it? The woman's a bloody nightmare to work with. Everybody hates her, I'm pretty sure of that. As to who, well of course there are plenty of theories. Poor Harry for a start, the stick she gives him, I'm surprised he hasn't stuck a knife in her by now. And Lily Wu, she was another victim of her tongue. Some of the things Jolene says to her are nothing short of racist, and that's not just my opinion, everybody feels the same.'

'Like what?' Jimmy asked.

'Like slanty-eyed fuck-wit?'

'Flipping heck,' he said. 'So she's a real people person then, our Jolene?'

Emily nodded. 'Yeah, big-time. But remind me, what exactly is it you guys do again? Investigators, is that what the witch-bitch said?'

Maggie noted the non-too-subtle change of subject and wondered whether Emily Smith had already seen through their cover story. Maybe not, but it still probably wasn't a good idea to ask any more questions for a while. However the casual use of the derogatory nom-de-plume could not go without comment. Feigning surprise, she asked,

'Witch-bitch, is that what they call her?'

'Sorry, that just slipped out,' Emily said, her tone mildly apologetic. 'I know it's horrible, but yes, that's what everyone calls her. It's not nice I know, but unfortunately it just seems to fit.'

Maggie laughed. 'Well I'd better make sure I don't repeat it in her presence. But yes, you asked what we do and you're correct, we are investigators. It's all pretty boring stuff, nothing like on the telly.'

'Aye, no guns,' Jimmy said, directing a smile at Emily. A smile, Maggie observed, which had a nauseatingly melting effect on its recipient. But then she reflected that pretty Miss Smith might well turn out to be useful to the investigation so she shouldn't complain too much.

She said, 'In this case, we're looking at the background of the guys behind that Bahamas investment fund that will be taking a twenty-five percent stake. To make sure the source of funds is all legitimate. And specifically that there's no Chinese government money behind any of it.'

'And before you ask,' Jimmy said, 'the directors are based here in London so we won't be doing any fancy trips out there, worst luck. It's all spreadsheets and statements. Dull as a dull thing that started dull and got duller. If you can follow that.'

'Sounds *very* dull,' Emily laughed. A laugh which in Maggie's opinion was more enthusiastic than Jimmy's lame attempt at humour really merited. 'But listen, I'd best get upstairs to my office before Jolene sees me. She doesn't really like me loitering around the fee-earning staff. But I hope to see you around.'

It was quite obvious to whom her closing remark was directed.

Chapter 5

Frank had come into the office that morning fired up with an indignation which was alien to his normal easy-going manner. But then again the news, conveyed to him in an emoji-festooned WhatsApp from his wee forensic officer mate Eleanor Campbell, was grave. Never mind that his next case had been handed down to him from the highest level of government and was likely to prove both challenging and interesting. This new matter was so damn serious that everything else would have to wait.

A war cabinet had been hastily formed comprising himself, Eleanor and Ronnie French, the Met's laziest detective constable currently languishing in the career backwater that was Department 12B. Now refreshments had been down-loaded from Atlee House's high-tech vending facilities and the threesome were gathered in the little meeting room he had commandeered for the duration of the Parrish case. The first session was about to begin, a quick five minutes before they got back to their day jobs.

'Is it true boss?' Ronnie kicked off, 'that they're shutting Atlee and shunting us back to Paddington Green?'

'Seems that way,' Frank said, his tone gloomy, 'but it's Eleanor who first blew the whistle on it. How did you find out about this Eleanor?'

'It was Abu. He works in central accounts and he saw a memo about it and thought he should like message me right away.'

Frank smiled. He knew this was how she worked, through a diverse network of informants, collaborators and subject-matter experts tucked away in every corner of the organisation and beyond, and all who seemed to have only first names.

'Big thanks to the boy Abu then,' he said, giving a thumbs-up. 'And has this mate of yours said what's prompted this? Because I always thought our wee department was far too unimportant to be on anyone's radar.'

'I think I might know,' Ronnie said, nodding sagely. 'I seem to remember one of them organisation e-mails we got a few months back. It was telling us we were getting a new Head of Finance, some geezer who used to be at the Home Office if I recall right.'

Aye that would be it, Frank thought. Some new guy trying to make a name for himself by shaving a few quid off the accommodation budget. The guy probably didn't even know that just six months earlier the Met had spent nearly fifty grand doing the place up, with a pastel paint job, new carpet tiles and the fancy vending kit Frank and his pals loved so much. He knew that Eleanor for one would be devastated if she was forced to move back to her proper office over at Maida Vale labs, where she would be mandated to attend team meetings and submit weekly reports and fall in line with all the other organisational crap that she hated so much. Down here in the bowels of Atlee she was able to concentrate one hundred percent on her work, and if some head-office efficiency wonk had taken the trouble to get off their arse and observe her performing that brilliant work, they would see the Met was getting about ten times the value from her by allowing her to do so. But of course, that wouldn't show up on any of their stupid spreadsheets. And as for his own little rag-tag Department, hadn't it been a deliberate policy that the motley collection of misfits, has-beens and never-had-beens should be tucked away out of sight of the brass? Looking at Ronnie French reminded him why. Fat, scruffy and lazy, and with less than twelve months until he picked up his ill-earned pension, he was never going to feature in one of these glossy 'about us' brochures that the Met like to publish from time to time. If an Assistant Commissioner saw Ronnie French lounging at a desk over at Paddington Green, they'd ask a cleaner to tidy him away.

'So what are we going to do about it guv?' Ronnie asked, interrupting Frank's train of thought.

'Don't know Frenchie, but we've got to do something. Let's all have a think and we'll re-group in a few days, see where we've got to.'

Ronnie responded with a look of disappointment, clearly expecting better from his boss. Frank knew it was thin gruel, but it was all he could think of at that moment. But then he looked over at Eleanor and smiled as he recognised the expression on her face. He'd seen that expression of steely determination many times before and knew that invariably it led to good things.

Eleanor had a plan.

*****

The reason Frank didn't have much of a plan himself was because he'd been a bit blindsided by the whole matter. The thing was, it seemed impossible that his boss DCI Smart wouldn't have known about the Atlee House closure proposal, so why hadn't she told him about it before? He'd thought about asking her straight out, but then thought again. Liking and respecting Jill in equal measure, he'd decided he didn't want to do or say something rash, something that might irretrievably damage their excellent relationship. So for now his plan, if it could be called that, was quite simple - do nothing for a few days and see if she eventually got around to telling him. In the meantime, he could relax a bit in the knowledge that Eleanor and Frenchie were up to speed with the situation. Both, he knew, were going to move heaven and earth to make sure their nightmare didn't come true, and so there was every chance the problem might be solved without him having to lift a finger.

At least that would allow him finally to concentrate on the Parrish affair. He'd a chance to do some basic research on the guy's back-story in the last day or two and had taken the trouble to scribble the basics onto the little white-board that hung on the wall in a corner of the meeting room. Now he lounged back in his chair and refreshed his knowledge, which had been easily obtained due to the fattening out of Parrish's Wikipedia profile as a result of his recent fame. Fifty-two years of age, he had been born and raised in Dundee, coming from a modest background, father a factory worker, mother on the tills at M&S. That interested Frank particularly, because he hadn't realised the guy was a fellow Scot.

The boy had obviously been bright and had made it into Glasgow University, initially studying Physics before switching to Medicine after a year. He'd been socially active too, a member of the drama society and two political parties, all of which Frank found interesting. It was as if the working-class boy was desperate to shake off his roots, to fit in with those who would have been considered his social superior, and he wondered if it was that need for acceptance and recognition which drove his craving for the knighthood. There was no evidence that he had continued his interest in either show-business or politics after taking his degree. On graduation, he'd continued his training in Scotland, spending ten years at the Glasgow Royal Infirmary where he had made rapid progression up the career ladder. A consultant by his early thirties, he'd then done a short stint at Addenbrooke's in Cambridge before moving to London and his present position as head of surgery at Guy's hospital.

The guy obviously had talent, but that did not extend to an ability to hang on to his wives. Old James obviously liked the ladies, being on his fourth other half, and it was the tragic fate of wives two and three that had led to Department 12B being rostered to the case in the first place. Wife number three, Petra, was the one who had drowned in the treacherous waters of Loch More whilst Kelly, wife number two, had seemingly taken an overdose of some sort, a method of suicide that seemed an anachronism, straight out of the pages of an Agatha Christie novel. He wondered if Parrish's current wife Dawn, an identikit blonde nearly fifteen years younger than him, ever feared the same fate would befall her too given her husband's track-record.

But usually in a case it made sense to start at the beginning. Wife number one, Jolene Parrish, didn't get much of a mention on Wikipedia but then again that marriage had apparently lasted less than eighteen months and that was twenty-five years ago. But it did list a maiden name, Johnson, and the fact that she had been a law student. Interesting, that.

He picked up his phone and scrolled through his contacts, although this was the one number he had committed to memory. *Maggie Bainbridge*. He could feel his heart give that stupid little skip that it did every time he thought of her.

'Hi Maggie, it's Frank. Look, if you're free on Saturday I'd really love to take you out to dinner.' That's what he wanted to say and that's what he ought to say but he knew he wouldn't. The time wasn't quite right, not when he had still failed to exorcise the agony of what had happened with him and Mhari all these years ago. Jimmy had said umpteen times that he was being a complete idiot and really ought to get some therapy before it ruined his life forever, but then who was he to talk, the brother who was still totally screwed up because of his estrangement from the beautiful Flora? The truth was they both could do with some help. With a wry smile he wondered if maybe they could find a psychoanalyst who did a two-for-one offer.

'Frank, lovely to hear from you.' Her voice was bright and the sentiment sounded sincere, causing his heart to give another stupid little jump. *'How are you?'*

'Aye great Maggie,' he lied. 'Listen, you know we were joking about that name in the pub the other night and what a coincidence it would be if your Jolene turned out to be my Jolene? Well, it turns out mine was actually a law student would you believe? Jolene Johnston was her maiden name. I don't suppose you know yours by any chance?'

'No, but do you have a picture of her? That would be just as good. Or you could just google it, see if there's any photos on-line. Type in Jolene Johnston and then click Images.'

'Oh aye, I could do that right enough,' he said, embarrassed that he hadn't thought of it himself. In the background, he detected the clattering of a keyboard.

'Actually I've just done it,' he heard her say. *'Google's got facial recognition matching and I've punched in our Jolene Cavendish as a third cross-reference, so it should come up with something I should have thought.'*

Not for the first time, he cursed his lack of savvy in matters technical. He couldn't even use the 'I'm old' excuse because he wasn't that old and besides Ronnie French, nearly ten years his senior, was an IT genius in comparison. The truth was Frank hadn't bothered to keep up, being content to rely on wee Eleanor Campbell to take care of all that sort of stuff for him. Perhaps he should go on a course. If he could fit it in between the psychotherapy sessions that was.

'It's her.' He could hear the excitement in her voice. *'No doubt about it. And that's very interesting. Very interesting indeed.'*

'What? What've you found?'

'I'll send you a link.'

'Oh aye do that,' he said, hoping she wouldn't spot his unease, 'but maybe give me the edited highlights in advance?'

He heard her laugh. *'Yes, all right then. So I found this picture on the internet. It says it's from the social pages of the Glasgow Herald, whatever that is.'*

'The Herald's for the Glasgow toffs. Us plebs read the Record.'

'Right. Well anyway, it was taken at some civic or university do or other. It's captioned Glasgow Grads Stage Third-World Fundraiser.'

'A charity do then?'

'Yes, looks like it. There's a couple of guys in the picture wearing evening dress and the women are in their party frocks. Hang on, let me read the article and see if it names names.'

The line went silent for a moment, he imagining her searching for her reading glasses before peering intently at the screen. And then, just a few seconds later, he heard her laugh.

'Well well, now this is something. Dr John Paton, Mr Peter Clark, Councillor Annand Singh and...' She hesitated for a

moment before giving a chuckle. *'Dr James Parrish and Mrs Jolene Parrish.'*

'Christ,' he said, the exclamation involuntary. 'So your Jolene *is* my Jolene then.'

'Definitely. She's not changed much in twenty-five years. But never mind that. So I'm guessing the guy you're investigating is James Parrish, that surgeon who worked on the Portman girl?'

He laughed. 'Aye, you've cracked it Maggie. But please, keep it to yourself. As I said, the mission's top-secret. Hush-hush government business, right from the top.'

'I'm a detective, what do you expect? And of course I'll keep it a secret.' Then he heard her voice take on a serious tone. *'But listen Frank, you really need to see this photograph, you really do.'*

'What do you mean?'

'You'll know when you see it. I'll send it to you now. Because I'm thinking there's someone else in the photograph you might want to track down too. A woman.'

'Really?' he said, puzzled. 'So what's her name then?'

'That's the thing, it doesn't say. Let's just call her the mystery blonde, shall we?'

'But no name.'

'No. But of course...'

'... I could do a recognition search, see if it comes up with anything on her.' He tried not to sound smug but was unsure if he'd succeeded.

'*You mean you'll get Eleanor to do it*,' she said.

He laughed. 'Ooh cruel. But absolutely spot-on. It's called delegation if you must know. An important skill for a leader.'

'*If you say so. But listen, I'm in this big open-plan office here and they don't like us taking personal calls so I'd better push on. See you down the pub on Thursday*?'

'I'll be there.'

'*Great. Looking forward to it.*'

Not as much as I am, he thought.

Chapter 6

Maggie wasn't surprised when Jolene wasn't ready for them when they turned up for their ten o'clock appointment. She'd seen the same behaviour plenty of times before, both when she was a salaried drone at this self-same firm and then when she'd moved on to Drake Chambers. There was a certain type of character in these big law firms, so terminally self-absorbed that they thought they had the right to treat the diary commitments of others as purely advisory. *I'm much more important than you* was the message, deliberate or otherwise, and generally it was the ones who wanted to appear more important than they actually were who were the serial offenders. To Maggie, it was either a symptom of chronic self-doubt or else simply revealed that they were a complete arse. She wondered which category Jolene Cavendish fell into, suspecting the latter without being completely sure. No doubt time would tell.

Jimmy was passing the time in mild flirtation with the young girl who occupied the desk just outside Jolene's office. A comically-overlong engraved name plate identified her as *Kylie Winterburn Personal Assistant to Miss Jolene Cavendish LLB*. In what way Miss Cavendish needed personal assistance was not specified. The girl was young, barely into her twenties Maggie guessed, and not conventionally beautiful, but with a dark complexion partly obscured by a mop of tight jet-black curls which gave her a quirky attractiveness.

'Miss Cavendish is tied up on a call,' she had explained, 'an international call,' the latter presumably added as a justification for the delay. Her accent was pure East End but with all the consonants carefully placed where they should be, as if she had been having old-school elocution lessons and only recently graduated. She reminded Maggie of the Downing Street secretary character from *Love Actually*, whom the Prime Minister, improbably played by Hugh Grant, equally improbably falls in love with. Martine McCutcheon, that was the name of the actress, loveable and charming and a former star of the *East Enders* soap-opera on the revered British Broadcasting Corporation. Like Emily and Flora, Kylie and Martine could have been sisters. Then she remembered to her dismay that the film was approaching twenty years old. So mother and daughter would be more like it, with all due respect to Miss McCutcheon.

Back in the present, she realised that Jimmy was speaking to Kylie.

'I've heard she's got a nickname,' he was saying, a mischievous grin on his face. 'It's not very complimentary is it?'

The girl looked at him uncertainly. 'Yes, well I haven't been here that long so I don't know anything about any of that. And even if I did, I wouldn't tell you.'

'Quite right,' Maggie said, jumping in. 'Office gossip is so awful, isn't it? But all these horrible things that were left on Jolene's desk. You must feel terrible about that I suppose?'

'What do you mean?' the girl said sharply. 'Why should I feel terrible about it?'

'Well you're her kind of guardian I'm guessing?' Jimmy said, cottoning on to where Maggie was going. 'I should have thought nobody gets past you without you knowing about it.'

She gave him a haughty look. 'That's right, and nobody did, I can assure you of that.'

'But *somebody* must have,' Maggie said, lowering her voice and adopting what she hoped was a sympathetic tone.

'They were all here when I got in,' the girl replied, sounding upset but defensive at the same time. 'Every time. That witch's hat and that disgusting baby doll and all that other stuff. Someone must have come in especially early to have done it. Before I arrived. And I'm normally in just after seven,' she added, answering the question that Maggie was about to ask.

'Any ideas who might be responsible?' Jimmy said.

'I should have thought that would be obvious,' she replied, giving them a supercilious look. 'Everybody around here will agree with me.'

Maggie was about to ask her to elaborate when the office door behind her opened abruptly.

'Come,' Jolene said in a loud staccato bark that everyone in the open-plan office would be able to hear. No *sorry I'm late* or *sorry I kept you waiting*. 'Take a seat,' she said, gesturing towards the little conference table that sat in a corner of her spacious office. It was furnished in a strikingly austere fashion which Maggie thought would have made a depressing workspace if someone had not gone to the trouble of lightening the atmosphere with an array of glossy house-plants. A small pink-painted tin watering can sitting on Jolene's desk suggested that it might be she who was the green-fingered custodian of the botanic display.

'So, you're Asvina's little detectives are you? I must say she thinks a lot of you.' There was something about the way this woman almost spat out her friend's name that made Maggie wonder whether she should revise her early opinion of her, thinking that perhaps it was a self-confidence issue after all. Then again Asvina Rani, not yet forty and with supermodel looks, a perfect family and a stellar career was going to make any woman feel inadequate. Jolene too of course had done very well in her career, but she was older and did not share her rival's beauty. But at least there was something the two senior lawyers had in common, something way more important than work.

'When is your baby due?' Maggie asked, with a kindly smile. 'Not too long now if I'm any judge.'

Jolene seemed to soften for a moment. 'I'm thirty-three weeks so you're right, not long now. Almost exactly the same as Asvina, although of course this is my first.'

'Gosh that must be exciting,' Maggie said, whilst thinking that it must be pretty scary too. It was true that women were having their children much older these days compared with their mothers and grandmothers, and she herself had been thirty-six when she had her beloved Ollie. But Jolene Cavendish was probably a decade older still, where the risk of complications grew if not exponentially then certainly with a steep upward gradient.

'And what about your husband?' Jimmy said guilelessly. 'Is he looking forward to the sleepless nights?'

She gave him a sardonic look.

'There is no husband.'

'Sorry,' Jimmy said, sounding flustered, 'I didn't mean to presume. Your partner...'

'No partner either I'm afraid. I was married twice before, one of whom provided me with my present surname but nothing else worthwhile. There is of course a biological father, courtesy of a very expensive and discreet service, but I'm at the stage of my life when I no longer need a man in my life, thank you very much.'

'Yes, they're a lot more trouble than they're worth,' Maggie said, suddenly anxious to lighten the atmosphere after Jimmy's *faux pas*. 'I don't have one myself and I'm getting along just fine.'

And in her case, she reflected, it was true, more or less. Her marriage to Phillip Brooks had been a disaster and she knew now that it was simply the unrelenting pressure of that biological clock ticking away that had ever persuaded her it had been the right thing to do. Now it was just her and wonderful little Ollie, only eight years old but wise beyond his years. Except of course, there was Frank Stewart hovering in the background, sweet but bloody useless it seemed in matters of the heart. Once again she resolved to tackle Jimmy about it and this time she would insist on an answer. Surely something had happened to Frank, something in his past that might explain his infuriating reticence? She was bloody well going to find out if it was the last thing she did.

But this revelation from Jolene had come as a complete surprise. Asvina obviously had not known about it and she wondered why she had not been told, although of course there was no reason why Miss Cavendish should share details of her private life if she didn't want to.

'We didn't know about that,' Maggie said simply.

'I know, it's not something I wanted to broadcast. I thought it would just provide more ammunition for whoever is behind this vile campaign. But then it occurred to me that it was something you ought to know about. In case it was relevant to your investigation.'

'Do you think it could be?' Jimmy asked.

'I don't know. Perhaps. But isn't that for you to find out? You're the detectives.'

God, thought Maggie, the woman really knows how to win friends and influence people, but she decided to let the barb pass without comment.

'Yes well thank you for letting us know Jolene, it may very well be relevant but obviously we can't say one way or the other at this stage. But if you don't mind, we need to ask you a few questions to get some background on what has been happening. Dates mainly, and also any ideas you have about what's behind all this.'

'If you must,' Jolene said.

'We must,' Jimmy said, shooting her an apologetic smile. 'Sorry. But we'll be gentle with you, I promise.'

Maggie thought she saw a flicker of a smile cross her face. It seemed even witch-bitches struggled to remain immune from Jimmy Stewart's easy charm.

'So Jolene,' she began, 'when did all this start? If you could be precise as possible it would be helpful.'

'As if I could forget,' Jolene said. 'It was a Wednesday, May the eighteenth. We were up against a tight deadline and I'd got in just after six-thirty to get a head start.'

'That was the witch's hat?' Maggie said.

'Yes it was. It didn't bother me, not at first. A couple of days later they left a broomstick and I know the nickname they have for me of course, so I thought it was just some stupid practical joke or dare. But then it began to happen again and again and became much more horrid.'

'What do you mean, more horrid?' Jimmy asked.

'Messages were left on my desk, horrible messages. *The witch-bitch must die. Live in fear.* And a lot worse besides. Then of course there was that ghastly baby doll. That was really sick.'

Maggie nodded sympathetically. 'Yes, that must have been particularly upsetting.'

'And all these things, they were there when you came in in the morning?' Jimmy asked.

'Mostly, but not always. Two of the horrible notes were on my desk when I came back from meetings.'

'So that kind of suggests that it must be somebody in the team who's responsible,' Jimmy said, adding hastily, 'Just thinking out loud.'

'Well of *course* it's one of the team,' Jolene said, her tone dismissive. 'Who else could it be?'

'I suppose it could be a visitor or even an intruder,' Maggie said, 'but I agree, that's highly unlikely. But anyway, I think after a while you decided to bring it up with Rupert Pattison, didn't you? He's the Managing Partner if I remember correctly? Your boss.'

'Yes I brought it up with useless Rupert. As if he gives a damn about what's been happening to me.'

'But I understood from Asvina that he was worried for you. He wanted to get the police involved.'

'Worried?' Jolene said. 'Yes, he was worried all right but not for me, only for the precious reputation of the firm.'

Maggie nodded. 'Well, yes I could see why he might think that way, but this is definitely a case of criminal harassment, so bringing in the police would have been quite understandable.'

She shot back her response. 'No police. I spent ten years in criminal law and they're utterly useless, each and every one of them. That's why we hired you two.'

Maggie wondered with some amusement how Frank would react when she told him how totally his profession had been trashed in just one sentence by the woman who shared her name with Dolly Parton's famous *femme fatal*. If nothing else, it might stop him humming the bloody annoying tune. But the truth was, this was without doubt a criminal matter, and it came to her that maybe there was something else behind her client's reluctance to get the police involved. That was something that no doubt would emerge later in their investigation. But now, she needed to ask the obvious question.

'So Jolene, what do you think this is all about? Why are they doing it, whoever's behind this?'

She gave a half-smile. 'I haven't the faintest idea. Professional jealousy or someone with an imagined grudge or just some sad person who thinks it's all rather hilarious. As I said, I really don't have a clue.'

It wasn't very helpful but Maggie sensed they were unlikely to get much more from her. Instead, she decided to bring up the other little matter that Asvina had asked them to help with.

'I think the firm is very concerned that this whole episode might make you question whether you still want to work at Addison Redburn.'

'Yes, I wondered when that might come up,' Jolene said, giving them a sardonic look. 'He's beside himself I suppose, our Mr Pattison, worried about all that big fat fee income sailing out the door. And before you start prying, it's none of your business what my plans are. I hope you understand that.'

Except of course, it *was* their business, in fact it formed the major part of the brief they had been given when taking on the case. But Maggie couldn't tell her that, not right now at least. Instead she said,

'Yes, well of course we *do* understand that, but I know that the firm would be very sorry to lose you. But you're right, it *is* none of our business and we've plenty to be going on with your harassment matter. So just a final couple of things spring to mind in that regard.'

There was no point in beating about the bush, she just had to come right out with it.

'Look Jolene, this witch-bitch thing. It's not very nice I know, but I understand you've had the nickname, if that's what we should call it, for a number of years now.'

'So it seems,' Jolene said, giving a half-smile. 'I take it as rather a compliment if you want to know the truth.'

Jimmy gave her a look that said *I quite believe it.*

'The point is,' Maggie continued, 'that makes it quite likely that whoever's behind this is relatively new to the team, since the incidents only happened quite recently. So it would be good to get a list of newish team members, perhaps ones that only started in the last six months or so.'

'There's a lot of turnover,' Jolene said, 'but Emily can help you with that.'

'Is that Emily Smith?' Jimmy asked.

She smiled at him. 'Oh you've met have you? Why am I not surprised at that? But yes, she's our department's Human Resources manager, she'll have all the details. But you said there was something else?'

'Oh yes,' Maggie said. 'I wondered, did you keep everything they sent you?'

'Of course. The notes are in my desk drawer and the hat and broomstick and that...that horrible doll are in my cupboard. What, are you going to examine them all with your big magnifying glass?'

Maggie couldn't quite decide if this was an attempt at a joke or a sly dig. No matter, she'd learnt a long time ago you didn't have to like your clients and in fact it was often better if you didn't.

'Well perhaps. I just thought it would be useful.' In what way it might be useful, Maggie was not sure, but she had learned you had to start with the evidence, such as you had, and see where it led.

'Yes, well you're the *experts* I suppose.' It wasn't quite an insult but it wasn't far off. And evidently the meeting was now over, as Jolene picked up a plastic document folder that had been sitting in front of her, unsnapped the cover and emptied the contents onto the table. 'Right, I've got to get on with this if you don't mind. So take these horrible things away with you and let me know as soon as you've found anything.'

She nodded towards the watering can.

'Oh and Jimmy, you wouldn't mind dropping a spot into that cheese-plant on the way out, would you?'

*****

After the meeting they had returned to the main office, whereupon they'd spent a frustrating five minutes trying to find a desk. Jimmy, carrying all the items of evidence that Jolene had given them, was getting particularly exercised about it despite Maggie trying to explain the concept of hot-desking to him.

'So there's more desks than people?' he said, perplexed. 'God, it would really piss me off if I came in one morning and couldn't find one.'

'I think you mean more people than desks,' she said, laughing, 'and as for getting pissed off, you mean like you are now?'

He gave an apologetic smile. 'Aye sorry boss. But it does seem really stupid to me, the whole idea of it.'

'Yeah, it probably is but look, here's one here free. Grab another chair and we can have a quick sift through this stuff she gave us.'

'Sure.'

Maggie watched as he dumped the items on the desk and spread them out. The witch's hat and the broom were cheap and flimsy, the kind of things that you bought the kids at Halloween. The baby doll was different, eerily realistic and obviously expensive, but the fact was it would be well-nigh impossible to trace the provenance of any of it. Whoever had bought these would have had no trouble finding them online, delivered next day to their door. She could see from his expression that Jimmy was thinking the same thing.

'None of this really helps us Maggie, does it? You could get this stuff anywhere. Not unless we can get them checked for DNA or fingerprints and then get samples from everyone in the office.'

She knew he wasn't being serious. 'No, it's not as if it's a murder case or anything, so even if the police got involved, they're never going to commit that level of resource to it.'

'Agreed,' he said. 'So what about these notes? Anything in them?'

She spread the sheets across the desk, eight of them in all. The messages had been printed landscape in a large font, black ink on normal computer paper. The sort of thing anyone could knock up on a word processing program in half a minute.

'Identical style, so probably done by the same person would you think?' Jimmy said.

'Looks like it,' Maggie agreed, 'and whoever's done it definitely doesn't like Jolene, that's for sure. Some of these are pretty nasty.'

Jimmy nodded, then pointed to a particular sheet. 'See that? *You will die by our hand.* Does that mean there's more than one person involved?'

'What?' she said distractedly. 'Yeah, perhaps.'

But she wasn't really listening. Because she had noticed there was one note that was different from the rest, this one not containing an overt threat but a message that was no less chilling. She picked it up and thrust it under Jimmy's nose.

'See this? This is what it's all about, I guarantee it.'

I know what you did.

Chapter 7

It seemed that Jolene must have got in touch with Emily Smith directly after their meeting, because barely thirty minutes later she turned up at their desks, a slim buff folder in her hand. To be absolutely precise, she turned up at Jimmy's desk, eyes sparkling and beaming a smile. But it wasn't just that which caused Maggie to give a double-take. Because the elaborate plait had gone and now Emily's strikingly-coloured hair cascaded down in wild ringlets, perfectly framing her beautiful face. It was apparent she had also managed to fit in a visit to the ladies' room, because her eyes were now lined in a delicate pale blue and her wide mouth wore a shimmering pink gloss lipstick. It was the sort of look, Maggie reflected, that she herself would aspire to before a big night out. But there was no disputing the effectiveness of the efforts the woman had made. Emily looked fantastic.

'Jolene said you were interested in recent starters?' she said. 'My responsibility is only for the Contracts teams, I don't do Family Law or anything like that so I don't have their newbies although I can get them of course if you need them. But I was wondering why you were interested?'

There it was again, the second time Emily had dropped an innocent-sounding question into the conversation. But then Maggie wasn't surprised, having already figured out that asking for the information was bound to arouse suspicions as to their real objective. Luckily she had anticipated the risk and had an answer ready.

'Well I know it sounds far-fetched Emily, but it's not unknown for the other party to try and plant someone in the team, to get inside information on our side's tactics. So it's just something we like to check out and then eliminate from our enquiries.'

The explanation seemed to satisfy her. 'I hadn't thought of that but I suppose it makes sense.' She placed the folder on Jimmy's desk and opened it. 'Fourteen new starters in the last four months. A young associate only lasted two weeks before she decided to quit, which leaves thirteen.'

'Bloody hell, that's unlucky thirteen as far as we're concerned,' Jimmy said. 'I mean, any one of them could be a plant. And we haven't got much time.'

Maggie smiled at him, impressed with how authentic his concern sounded.

'Mind if I take a look?' she asked, reaching over for the neatly-typed list without waiting for a reply. It listed name, age, job title, salary and previous employer, these in the main being firms that Maggie recognised from her own time in the profession.

'That's a lot of people to take on in such a short space of time,' she mused. 'It must have kept Jolene busy, on top of everything else she had on her plate with the deal. With all these interviews and whatnot.'

Emily grimaced. 'You think so? Actually she was barely involved at all. Too busy with all the contract stuff. It was a crazy time, we were desperate for heads and the recruitment agencies were firing a ton of CVs at us every day. So mostly it was down to me. Interviews, chasing references, agreeing start dates, everything. It was exhausting actually.'

Maggie smiled to herself. She'd seen it herself when she was a junior, the crazy rush for staff whenever your firm landed a massive matter. Gesturing at the list she said, 'Well I must say you've done well to get this many through the door.'

But then about halfway down, an entry caught her eye.

'Harry Newton?' she asked, struggling to conceal her surprise. 'Is that the guy...?'

Emily nodded. '...that Jolene was bloody horrible to? Yes it was.'

'I'm glad you said it, not me,' Jimmy said, 'but by the look of him, we kind of assumed he'd been around a while.'

Maggie had spotted something else too. 'Thirty-four thousand? I can't believe that's the going rate around here. Isn't that very low, even for an associate?'

'Yes, it is. But you see...' Emily hesitated, as if wondering if she should carry on. '...there were special circumstances, so he was happy to accept the salary we offered. I'm sure you'll understand the details must remain confidential between the firm and the member of staff.'

She looked uncomfortable and Maggie suspected what was now racing around her head. Was this guy really who and what he claimed he was? What if he was a spy, happy to take any salary to get through the door? What if I've messed up with his recruitment?

'The old data protection act is it?' Jimmy said, taking on a serious expression. 'I don't think the firm would thank you if our Harry turns out to be concealing something, act or no act.'

'Well, I'd be surprised if that was the case,' Emily said. 'I mean, if Harry really is a spy. But anyway, I guess that's for you guys to work out.'

Maggie gave a mock grimace. 'Yes it is, worst luck. But thank you for getting this to us so quickly Emily. And if we needed any more details about any of these guys?'

'I've got everyone's CV. You'll find me one floor up and of course I'll be happy to help you in any way I can.'

As she said it, she fixed her gaze on Jimmy. Then to Maggie's amusement, she saw their eyes meet, like a pair of B-list actors in some cheap romantic movie.

*****

'Thirteen suspects eh?' Jimmy said, stirring his coffee with a wooden spatula. 'That must be some sort of a record, even for us.'

They had been pleased to discover the Addison Redburn tower-block had a coffee shop cum restaurant on the top floor, its windows east-facing meaning the views, though still impressive, were out across the lower Thames estuary rather than the more impressive cityscape afforded to those offices, like Asvina's, that faced west. The office grapevine had suggested that Jolene Cavendish did not approve of her team sloping off there in office hours, but as Maggie reasoned, this was their first day, so how could they be expected to know that?

'Well at least we've got some,' she said, 'which is better than having none at all. Obviously. And Emily Smith seems very helpful.'

She was amused to see him blush. 'Aye she is,' he mumbled. 'Very helpful.'

'And very pretty too,' she said, teasing. He gave her a look that said *don't push it*.

She took the new starters list from the buff folder that Emily had given her and laid it on the table, as if hoping some magical inspiration would jump up from the page. Alongside it she laid one of the poison pen notes, the one that interested her the most.

'*I know what you did.*' She read it out loud, her brow furrowed in concentration. '*I know what you did.*'

'Is that what this is all about then?' Jimmy said. 'Something in Jolene's past, something connected to one of these new guys?'

'Yes, well you know the old saying, about your past sins always catching up with you. It would be a good place to start anyway.'

He nodded. 'Agreed. Thing is though, Jolene didn't mention anything along these lines, you know, if she'd worked with any of these people in the past or anything like that.'

She smiled. 'Yes, but we already know what sort of woman she is, don't we? The welfare of her junior staff is not exactly her primary concern and it's perfectly possible that one of them worked for her in the past without her remembering.'

'Or even knowing,' Jimmy said.

'Exactly. So maybe if we knew who she's worked for before, we might find a connection. Perhaps someone she's slighted who's now looking for revenge.'

'Or even try the obvious ones first,' Jimmy said. 'No offence boss, but remember what Emily said. That guy Harry, obviously, and there was that woman Emily mentioned, wasn't there? Chinese she said. Is she on there?'

Maggie scanned the list. 'Lily Wu, I'm guessing. Senior Contracts Associate. Thirty-six years of age.'

'So what's the plan? Divide and conquer? We just want to make initial contact with them, establish a connection. No heavy questioning to start with.'

She nodded. 'Makes sense.'

She was just about to say who should take who when she remembered the conversation they'd had several months earlier, when he'd made it plain he was no longer willing to be cast in the role of honey trap. Except that wasn't how he'd put it. 'I'm fed up being used as a sex object' was what he'd actually said, causing her to laugh out loud. But she'd got the message and now was careful to balance out his assignments more evenly.

'So I'll tackle Lily and you can do Harry, if that's ok?'

'Fine boss,' he said. 'But any ideas how we should broach the subject? We're supposed to be undercover after all.'

She laughed. 'Casual conversation. You can do that, can't you?'

'I suppose.' But then to her surprise he said, 'although I'm thinking it might be worth swapping. Because that guy looks as if he might need a shoulder to cry on.'

*****

Maggie found Harry Newton at his desk, sleeves rolled up, eyes half-closed and chewing on a cheap ballpoint. Out of habit, she snuck a glance at his ring finger. He wasn't wearing a wedding band but he was too good-looking to be one of these live-with-his-mum bachelors. When she'd studied him earlier, during that stand-up altercation with Jolene, she had thought he looked a bit of a jack-the-lad, the sort who enjoyed playing the field but bolted at the first sign that any woman might want more from him than just a casual affair. But then she pulled herself up short, because what was this sub-Sherlock Holmes deduction based on other than his semi-permanent scowl and bad-boy good looks? And anyway, what relevance did that have as to whether he was Jolene's harasser or not?

It was approaching midday so she assumed that he had met the eleven o clock deadline Jolene had so publicly imposed upon him. Or perhaps not. Sensing her presence, he glanced up and gave her a sullen look.

'She didn't like it,' he said, nodding towards his computer screen. His tone was semi-resigned, as if this latest rejection hadn't been unexpected. But he didn't seem too concerned either.

'She seems like a tough cookie,' Maggie said, choosing not to answer his question immediately. 'Over-compensation that's what I reckon. For being a woman in a man's world.' Inwardly she gave a curse, because what right had she to offer an opinion having only known Jolene five minutes? That was the problem with casual conversation. Sometimes it took you places you didn't mean to go. Still, empathy was never a bad thing.

'But she still shouldn't have spoken to you like that,' she continued. 'It would really piss me off if she did it to me.'

Which gave her the opening to ask the question she needed to ask.

'Do you think there's any reason why she picks on you in particular?'

He sneered. 'Who knows, maybe she just doesn't like my face. Anyway, what's it to you?'

The tone was borderline-menacing, his meaning clear. *Back off*.

'Sorry,' she said, smiling. 'I'm just a nosey-parker, it comes kind of automatically with the job I'm afraid. I didn't mean to pry, honestly.'

'Well *don't*,' he said sharply. 'Anyway, what is it you want? I haven't got time for casual conversation.'

'It is a quick one,' she said, thinking on her feet. 'I was wondering if any of these drafts you are doing are for that Bahamas-based corporation. My colleague and I need the names of the directors so that we can check out their bona-fides. We're looking for Chinese links of course, not that they will be easy to spot.'

He shrugged. 'They're listed as signatories in one of them. I'll email you their names. I don't remember seeing anything Chinese-sounding though. Is that it?'

'That's great,' she said, shooting a smile which wasn't returned. 'Great.'

And that was it, end of conversation, a conversation lasting barely a minute and as far as Maggie was concerned, one that had not really achieved anything. Except there was just something about that sneering answer he had given to her question. *Maybe she just doesn't like my face.*

Because she couldn't help thinking it sounded just a little too pat. She didn't know what, but there had to be something more to it than simply how he looked.

*****

Jimmy had always known that it wasn't really his thing, this small talk stuff. It wasn't that he was exactly shy, but after a near ten-year stint in the army, you learned to be economical with words when giving out orders and the habit had stuck. That was especially true in the bomb squad, where verbal precision was absolutely vital when you were helping one of your crew disarm a Taliban IED. But that was a different life and now it seemed an age ago, although it was barely three years since he'd got out, an exit that had just about saved his sanity. Because his mental health had well and truly been shredded after the shooting of that young female soldier in Belfast, a shooting that had happened right in front of his eyes and a shooting that had been unquestionably his fault. He still thought about it every day, how could you not, but at least the nightmares that had shook him from sleep night after night were thankfully fewer. Now he had a new life, as an unlikely private detective in the employ of Maggie Bainbridge, a life path he hadn't foreseen when he'd hung up his uniform for the last time. But the fact was, he'd come to love his new profession and he'd come to love Maggie too. Not in a fall-in-love-and-live-happily-ever-after way of course, that was never going to happen, but he had come to realise quite early in their relationship that she was quite simply the nicest person he had met in his whole life. Now, it was impossible to imagine a future without her, and perhaps, if his brother Frank ever got off his backside and did something about it, he might even end up her brother-in-law. Which would be nice.

Such were his thoughts as he wandered semi-aimlessly around the open-plan office. To a detached observer it looked as if he was searching for a vacant desk, but in reality what he was doing was looking for Lily Wu.

'Chinese origin, obviously, and quite a bit overweight,' was how Emily Smith had described her, rather unkindly he thought, but it did make identification straightforward. And when he finally spotted her, by great fortune there appeared to be an unoccupied desk right next to her. This was the kind of small-talk that anyone could do.

'Excuse me, is this desk free do you know?'

She smiled at him. 'Looks like it, but you have to scan the QR code with your phone to be sure.' With some amusement, he recognised the accent. Not so much Wuhan as Wolverhampton.

'Ah right thank you,' he said. 'I'm Jimmy by the way. Just started today so it's all a bit new for me, all this hot-seat stuff and the like.'

'I'm Lily. Nice to meet you. You're one of the investigators aren't you? I saw you at Jolene's stand-up meeting. When she introduced you and your colleague.'

He nodded. 'That's right, I am. But God, that was quite a crazy show wasn't it? That poor guy Harry getting all that stick and everything. Tell me, is she always like that?'

'Pretty much. I've been on the end of it myself. I don't think it's anything personal. It's just the way she is.'

'Good to know,' he said. 'But I'm aiming to keep a low profile, just in case she's got something against Scotsmen in particular.'

He found it interesting that she had mentioned about being on the end of one of Jolene's public barbs. Outwardly unconcerned, there was no doubting an edge had appeared in her voice as she said it. Maybe it was nothing personal, but that didn't mean she liked it.

'No, just people in general I think,' she said, 'but especially men.' He couldn't work out if it had meant to be a joke, causing him to struggle to come up with a response. But it seemed that Lily meant to continue.

'You know she's pregnant, don't you?'

'Hard to miss,' he said, thinking what a minefield that whole pregnancy thing could be. Because it had just occurred to him that Lily Wu, rather than being simply a bit podgy, might be expecting a child herself. She wasn't wearing a ring but that didn't mean anything nowadays. Nowadays? It hadn't meant a thing for about forty years.

'I was desperate for a child when I was married,' she said, 'but it never quite worked out. We spent a fortune on IVF but they don't give you any guarantees do they? My husband was much older than me, and when they eventually diagnosed that the problem was with him, well he found it hard to deal with.'

Jimmy gave her an awkward look, unsure how to react or what to say. Too much information was what came to mind, but you couldn't very well say that to someone you'd only met two minutes earlier. Fortunately, Lily had more to say herself.

'That screwed our marriage of course, and it screwed up my studies too. I was at Birmingham Uni doing law, and of course it was probably stupid of me to think I could have a proper family life at the same time. My parents were angry with me for getting married so young and in the end I didn't get anything like the degree I should have had, I was too much all over the place. In fact, I was very lucky to scrape a Third which didn't go down well with my folks. They had such high expectations of their only daughter you see.'

'That's interesting,' he said, that being the first thing that came into his head, but he was being sincere. He wondered if she was going to continue with her potted life history, and wondered too if she did this with everyone new that she met. He knew it was a bit of a cultural stereotype, but he guessed she might be the offspring of first generation immigrants, perhaps from Hong Kong or Taiwan or maybe even mainland China, and if that was the case, it was no surprise that she had disappointed her mother and father both by marrying so young and by her academic failure. Hot-house parenting, that's what they called it, but it was driven from love, the desire for their kids to get opportunities that had been denied to them. In actual fact, he and his brother Frank had suffered a bit of hot-housing themselves, the old man keen that his sons should follow him into the legal profession. Frank in characteristic fashion had told their father to get stuffed, opting for a career in the police force. He himself had reluctantly succumbed, taking a law degree at the University of Glasgow, before he too rebelled and joined the army. Academically he'd done ok, bagging a half-decent upper second, but he knew right from the start that the law wasn't for him. Mind you, he was forever grateful that fate had persuaded him to stick it out, otherwise he would never have met Flora McLeod in his final year. Another marriage that had ended up screwed, and god knows he only had himself to blame for that one.

Lily looked as if she was about to continue her autobiography, when out the corner of his eye he clocked the imposing presence of Jolene Cavendish, clearly heading in their direction and wearing a scowl.

'Do you think I'm paying you for this idle chit-chat?'

She tossed a thick ring-bound document down onto Lily's desk. 'This is shit and it's your shit I believe. So it needs a total re-draft and I need it by close of play tonight. Understand?'

'Yes Jolene,' Lily said meekly. 'I'm sorry.'

'And maybe you should re-draft your CV whilst you're at it. Honestly, I've no idea where Emily drags them up from.'

Involuntarily, Jimmy could feel his hackles rising. Maybe Lily needed to arse-lick this ghastly woman to keep her job, but he didn't. So he wasn't going to take any crap from her, client or no client.

'That's a bit unfair,' he said, getting to his feet. 'It was my fault. I was looking for one of these daft hot desks and didn't know how the system worked. So I interrupted her. She was only trying to help me.'

For a moment, he feared he'd made a boob, finding himself wondering what Maggie was going to say when she learned they'd been blown off the case on their very first day. But just as he was thinking about back-tracking, Jolene responded.

'Very well, but you need to understand we're totally deadline-driven around here. Time is money. Please don't forget it.' And without another word, she swept off to find her next victim.

'Thank you,' Lily said. Her face was flushed and her voice trembling. 'The trouble is I'm a bit out of my depth here and I think Jolene's worked it out.'

'Och I'm sure that's not true,' he said. But he could see how it might very well be. Bullies always seemed to be able to pick out the weakest, it was how they worked. There was the guy Harry, still in a relatively junior position after years in the profession and now Lily, who seemingly flunked her law degree but somehow still landed a job as an Associate at prestigious Addison Redburn. Could she be the person behind the campaign of harassment? On the face of it, it didn't seem likely. She was way too meek and deferential and certainly outwardly at least, seemed to bear no obvious grudge towards her boss. But the thing was, if you were intent on revenge, you would probably take care to disguise the fact from the outside world. Something to talk through with Maggie, to see what she made of it.

So that was it, contact made with suspect number two. Two down, just eleven to go. This wasn't going to be easy.

Chapter 8

After a couple of days of will-I, won't-I, Frank had at last decided to ask Jill Smart straight out about the Atlee House situation. Actually, he wondered if she might be about to pre-empt his question, because out of the blue she'd gathered all her direct reports in a meeting room at Paddington Green nick for what was described as an organisational announcement. The email had simply said *be there*, with no hints as to the subject matter, leading to inevitable speculation amongst the participants. The Met's Commissioner was still getting daily stick from the media about her force's failure to catch the perpetrator of the Freja Portman acid attack, and Frank wondered if she was about to announce her resignation as a result. Not that it would be any great loss to the city or to the force, that was his very non-PC opinion. The Home Office had been anxious to tick all the equal-opportunity boxes when they appointed her, but unfortunately they forgot to tick the competence box too.

And then another thought struck him, a thought he didn't like one bit. What if it was in fact DCI Smart who was throwing in the towel? She loved nothing more than riding the waves, if that's what it was called, escaping down to the south-west at every opportunity, and had often joked about opening a little cafe in some little surfing hotspot down there. What if she had decided to turn her dream into reality? But no, that was nonsense. Jill was just forty, already a DCI and tipped to go higher. She could continue gliding up the ranks then take retirement at fifty along with a nice fat pension. With that, she could move to Cornwall and surf to her heart's content.

There were six of them in the room not counting Jill, all DI rank including his old mate Pete Burnside. He'd exchanged a couple of texts with Pete before the meeting, but all they had concluded was it must be something fairly serious for her to go to the trouble of getting them all together.

But the truth when it came out was a hundred times worse than either of them were expecting.

'Right,' Jill said, 'we might as well get straight down to it. You know of course our glorious leader Dame Amanda is under some serious pressure from the media and the politicians. There's the Portman debacle and now the latest crime stats are showing muggings and stabbings up thirty-two per cent.'

'A tsunami of violence ma'am, according to the Chronicle.' The voice was lugubrious, belonging to DI Lauren Platt, who Frank didn't know too well but who he knew headed up one of their undercover fraud teams in the City.

Jill smiled. 'Yes, very helpful Lauren. So we all know what happens when the violent crime stats shoot up, don't we?'

With a feeling of alarm, Frank foresaw what was coming.

'Come on ma'am, you can't be serious, surely? No way.'

'Yes, I'm afraid so Frank. More bobbies on the beat, the perennial battle-cry when things are going tits-up. So at 5pm this afternoon, the Commissioner is going to announce to the media that starting immediately, forty percent of the force will be deployed in uniform. A visible police presence to make us all feel safer, that will be the mantra. And in case you're all wondering, yes, that is to include senior ranks too.'

Burnside gave a sardonic laugh. 'So by my calculation, that means two-point-four of us have to hop off home and get changed right away.'

'Nah mate,' Frank said. 'There'll be rounding up of the figures so that will mean half of us.'

There was an audible groan around the room. Then Lauren Platt said, 'Well me and my team will have to be exempt. I mean, uniforms tramping all over the big financial institutions? How's that supposed to work ma'am?'

Jill gave her a stern look. 'No exemptions I'm afraid Lauren. And anyway, I would have thought there were more muggers and crooks in that square mile than anywhere in our patch. Might make them think twice before ripping off the next old granny.'

That brought a laugh from everyone, including Lauren Platt herself.

'Aye and don't worry Lauren,' Frank said, giving a shrug. 'It'll all have burnt itself out in a month or two when the next cock-up comes to the media's attention.' He'd been through more of these panic-driven top-down initiatives than he'd had hot dinners, and already he was thinking on the bright side. Like seeing how Ronnie French was going to react when he told him he was going to be back in uniform.

'We'll all be fine, won't we guys?' he said, looking around the sea of gloomy faces. 'And some of us, although I say so myself, look pretty sensational in uniform.'

'Some more than others,' Jill said, laughing. 'So everybody happy with that?'

She didn't wait for a reply. 'Good. So off you go and make it happen. And no excuses, ok? Because I'll be checking.'

Accompanied by a few more groans, the team began to disperse. Then, just as Frank was contemplating how he was going to frame the Atlee question, Jill said, 'Frank, would you mind hanging around for a few minutes?'

He smiled to himself. So, as he'd thought, she knew already.

'Look Frank, I didn't want to do this on the phone. As you might know, we've got a new guy heading up Finance. He's been parachuted in by the Home Office with an efficiency mandate.'

Frank gave her a smug look. 'Aye, dangerous guy, but we get one of those nearly every year. And before you say anything ma'am, the jungle drums have been beating, so I already know about the Atlee proposals. I am a detective after all. And if you ask me, it's really dumb given all the money they spent doing the place up.'

To his surprise, there wasn't even a hint of a smile from her.

'Well, so you'll know it's worse than that?'

'What do you mean?' Already, he could feel his heart sinking as a sixth-sense told him where this might be going. 'Come on.'

'Yes, I'm afraid so. They want to close down Department 12B. It costs more than a half a million a year to run and I'm afraid they see it as an easy target.'

He was about to vent but then bit his lip, realising there was no point in shooting the messenger, especially since he couldn't be sure where the messenger stood on the matter. There was no denying Jill Smart had been hugely supportive of the department in the two years it been under her jurisdiction, but he also knew that her career was the most important thing she had in her life, and everything she did was viewed through that prism. Right now he knew she would be weighing up the situation without emotion. For her, it would be a simple rational decision. *Fight or flight*. Fight if it's beneficial to my career, give in gracefully if it isn't, and he wasn't sure there was much he could say that would influence her decision one way or the other.

But that didn't mean he wasn't going to give it a try.

'But half a million is not even a piss in the ocean in the scale of things ma'am. Not compared with all the good work we've been doing.'

She shrugged. 'I agree Frank, but it's the bean-counters that need to be convinced, not me. But look, it's only a proposal at the moment, the budgets don't get finalised for another month or two. And in case you're worried Frank, your job's completely safe. There'll always be a position for you in my team.'

'Great.' He hadn't meant for it to sound disrespectful but it came out that way.

She gave him a sharp look. 'Things change all the time in big organisations, you should know that. Obviously I'll be fighting your corner but there are no guarantees.'

'Aye brilliant.' He realised that he was now acting like a sullen teenager and made a concerted effort to pull himself together. 'What I mean is, I understand that ma'am and I'm sure you'll do everything you can.'

But he wasn't sure, he wasn't sure at all. Because the fact was DCI Smart's gilded career voyage would continue on its serene path regardless of the outcome, whilst for himself and his little gang of Atlee House outlaws, the seas ahead looked decidedly choppy.

The was no two ways about it. As soon as he got back to Atlee, Department 12B was going onto a full-on war footing. *Code red*.

*****

The couple of hours he'd expended simply staring at the whiteboard in the commandeered investigation room had spectacularly failed to come up with any Eureka-like revelations. There would be something, there always was, something that would prove critical to the Parrish case, but right now it was remaining hidden and out of sight. But then again it was early days, and Frank knew you always seemed to be floundering around aimlessly at that point in the investigation. And actually, now that he came to think about it, there was one tiny little morsel of information that had aroused his curiosity.

It had been interesting, that telephone conversation with Maggie Bainbridge, when they'd uncovered the twenty-five-year-old photo of Parrish with his pregnant wife. His first wife that was, Mrs Jolene Parrish nee Johnson, who it turned out was the self-same woman who was being subject to a campaign of harassment at the fancy City law firm where she now worked. And who once again was pregnant it seemed, even he knowing that late forties was old for motherhood. Was this pregnancy another crazy coincidence, or was it somehow relevant to his investigation? The truth was, it was too early to tell. But he could see why Maggie had got so excited about the photo. There was Jolene, looking about six months gone, scowling in the background as a striking blonde schmoozed up against her husband, doe-eyed yet seductive. Was this early evidence of Parrish's modus operandi he wondered, a blueprint the surgeon had subsequently followed when moving on to wives two, three and now four? Lining up the new model whilst the old one was still in his possession so to speak? If he was doing this whilst his wife was pregnant, then it spoke volumes for the sort of man he was. And then he remembered the almost eight-year gap between him divorcing Jolene and his next marriage. Whoever this woman was, he hadn't ended up marrying her. But as Maggie had pointed out, the article from the Herald hadn't named her, and Eleanor's facial-recognition sweep had drawn a blank as to her identity. No matter, it probably wasn't going to be more than a footnote in the case. He reminded himself that the priority was Petra, the wife who had drowned in circumstances suspicious enough to warrant a national newspaper investigation.

He was interrupted by the meeting room door being barged open and smashed against its floor-mounted stop. Through the doorway sprang DC Ronnie French, his face wearing a thunderous expression.

'It is true guv?' His voice was almost plaintive. 'Is it true?'

Given recent events, Frank had a lot of choice in working out what Ronnie might be talking about. So he decided to hedge his bets.

'Is what true Frenchie? What are you asking me?'

'That we're all going back to the uniforms? Is it true?'

Frank laughed, relieved that he would be able to broach the subject of the department's threatened demise in his own time.

'Aye, afraid so mate. But don't worry, I've got a wee plan, so it won't be too bad.'

Ronnie gave him a suspicious look. 'No offence guv, but I've been on the wrong end of some of your wee plans before.'

'Cheeky swine,' Frank said, his tone affectionate. 'We're going to have a rota, that's all, and before you ask, yes, I'm including myself. So there's what, seven or eight of us in the department? That means at most three in uniform at any one time. And we'll round ours down to two because there's plenty of arse-licking fast-track Inspectors who'll be rounding theirs up so's they look good.'

'And there's Wayne too don't forget,' Ronnie said, evidently warming to the direction Frank was taking this. 'Wayne can't wait to get *back* into uniform I'll bet.'

Frank grinned. 'Aye that's true enough. Maybe I can tell him it's the first stage in him getting back behind the wheel again.' Dave 'Wayne' Rooney was the newest and youngest member of the Department 12B squad. Not yet thirty, he had been a PC in the Traffic division for less than nine months before a spate of spectacular smash-ups, writing off three expensive pursuit vehicles in as many months, ended his carchase career. Now he languished in Atlee House, pushing a pen and longing for the day when he could get back behind a wheel and floor the accelerator once again.

'So that means just one of us at any one time, and only once every six weeks or something like that. How's that for a plan?' Frank wasn't too sure of his arithmetic, but then again, he wasn't exactly sure how many of them were in the Department in the first place. No matter, it was there or thereabouts.

'And just to show leadership, I'll go first,' he said. 'Assuming I can fit into it that is.'

'And I'll go last,' French said. Frank gave him a sardonic look. Frenchie had been on the force long enough to know that these initiatives had a track-record of soon blowing themselves out. He'd be hoping the whole idea would be canned before his turn came round. For a moment, Frank wondered if this was a good time to tell him it was the whole existence of the department that was threatened and not just their tenure at Atlee, but decided against it. But then Ronnie brought up the subject himself.

'You know this Atlee thing guv? Well, I've been thinking.'

Frank laughed. 'New sensation for you Frenchie.'

'Cruel guv, cruel. But seriously, me and Eleanor have been chewing the whats-it and we've got an idea. Well to be fair, it was actually her idea.'

Frank had seen the look on the forensic officer's face when he'd first told them about the plan to close down Atlee. Now he suspected that one of her many informants had leaked to her the proposal to shut down the department, and she'd obviously decided she needed to recruit Ronnie to help with her scheme, whatever it was.

'But the thing is guv, I don't think I can tell you what it is. See, I wouldn't want you implicated, not in your position.'

'What, so it's something dodgy?' Frank said, frowning. Not that there was any need to ask the question, because with wee Eleanor Campbell and Frenchie in this together, there was no way it would be kosher.

'Nah nah guv. Not dodgy, let's just call it sensitive. See, I figure it's ok if an ignorant ragged-arsed DC like me tramps over someone else's investigation, but maybe not so good when it's a DI like yourself. And DCI Smart might not be too happy either.'

'I'm not sure I like the sound of any of this,' Frank said, giving him a searching look, 'and I don't want you to get yourself into any bother.' But of course when he thought about it properly, he didn't really have to worry too much what happened to Ronnie French. With a career record that was already a desert of under-achievement, there wasn't much his useless DC could do to make it any worse.

'So this plan of yours Frenchie? There's nothing illegal that I need to worry about?'

'Nah guv, all straight and above board, honest. And you can ask Eleanor if you don't believe me.'

'And if I do ask her, will *she* tell me what you're both up to?'

French shook his head. 'Nah guv, no chance. But honest, it's one-hundred and ten percent straight down the line. Totally pukka. Nothing for you to worry about.'

He had to admit, it sounded convincing and for once where Frenchie was involved, Frank was convinced. Maybe the future, Atlee and 12B-wise, wasn't quite so bleak after all.

Chapter 9

It had been a stressful Tuesday all-and-all, and although it wasn't yet three o'clock Frank was already planning an early escape to the Old King's Head where he would find a quiet table and sink a restorative pint or three of his favourite Doom Bar. Thursday night was his normal pub night, the night of his weekly get-together with Maggie and Jimmy, but he couldn't wait that long given the crap he'd been through that morning. It had all started with a phone call from DCI Jill Smart, she responding in turn to a heated call she'd evidently had with Sir Patrick Hopkins of Her Majesty's Government.

'They're bringing it up in the House,' she had said. 'I mean the Opposition. In Prime Minister's Questions. About the Parrish knighthood.'

He'd responded sharply, saying he didn't give a stuff about what anyone was asking the PM, but Jill was adamant.

'Apparently they've got wind that there's some problem with it and they're asking the PM to come clean. Will he or won't he be getting one, that's what they will be asking. And to make matters worse the Chronicle is headlining tomorrow with *PM Set to Block Parrish Honour*. The Opposition have leaked it to them of course. It's all kicking off big-time.'

'So?' he had said, not meaning to be disrespectful but managing to be so.

'So we've now just got three weeks to sort it all out,' she had said, before abruptly hanging up.

It was a ridiculous timescale, and for the remainder of the morning he'd sulked and thought about just quietly handing in the towel, resolving to do another couple of days of relaxed googling to see if anything iffy came up about Parrish and then giving the guy a clean bill of health. Then the PM could announce the bloody knighthood, the Chronicle could rejoice in the success of its campaign and everybody would be happy. Except it wasn't as simple as that, it never was. Because with that sword of Damocles hanging over Department 12B, it would only take one foul-up on their part to seal the deal. If some bad news about Parrish was to subsequently emerge, it would be 12B that would get the blame. Besides which there was the little matter of professional pride. It had hurt when the brass had sent him off to exile after his little altercation with the gigantic pile of uselessness that was Detective Chief Superintendent Colin Barker, and since that day more than two years ago, he had dedicated his working life to proving them wrong. The Alzahrani case, those Leonardo murders, that business with the young kids who had seemingly killed themselves. He was proud of his achievements on these investigations and how the department had built a reputation the length and breadth of the land. *Damn.* Much as he would have liked to dump the whole bloody thing in the nearest waste-bin, he knew that just wasn't an option.

By early afternoon, his spirits had revived somewhat, principally when he recalled he had a scheduled meeting with Eleanor Campbell later that day. At one minute past three precisely she turned up at his desk, her frosty demeanour confirming what he already knew. That she had been less than happy with the assignment he had set her.

'I'm a *forensic scientist* in case you didn't know,' she said as she tossed a transparent document folder on his desk. 'This is a job for an information analyst. And in any case, I don't know why you can't learn to do this stuff yourself. It's simples-ville, even for you.'

Why have a dog and bark yourself was the response that sprang into his head, but wisely he kept the thought to himself. And she was right of course, the Met was stuffed with civilian IT experts who could have helped him in his information search. The problem was, they were all hidebound by procedures and protocol, asking for data protection declarations and case summaries and cost justification forms before they would lift a finger. It took a bloody age to get them engaged on a case and by comparison Eleanor, though not averse to a little bureaucracy herself, was a free spirit. As long as there was a case number, she just got on and did it. Which is why he was going to move heaven and earth to stop her being removed to Maida Vale labs, where she would be outside his sphere of influence.

'I value your genius Eleanor,' he said, smiling. 'Anyway, how's your Lloyd?'

She gave him a mistrustful look. 'Why? What's it to you?'

'Nothing, nothing, just like to ask. No wedding bells yet?' As soon as it left his lips he knew it had been a mistake. 'Only joking,' he added hastily.

'He hasn't asked.' By her thunderous expression, he could tell the conversation if not curtailed would be entering dangerous territory.

'Aye well, marriage is way over-rated, that's what I found.' He leaned over and picked up the folder. 'So what is it you've got for me here? Anything interesting?'

'You asked me to get some dates and stuff about these women. I got some dates and stuff. I don't know if it's interesting or not.'

He could sense one of her diva-actress moods coming on, the kind which generally led to her metaphorically tearing up the script and storming off the set. That was always a bit of an inconvenience if there was anything else that you needed her to do, which he usually had. So as normal, he was prepared to swallow his pride and grovel.

Beaming her a smile he said, 'Very nice work Eleanor, and I'm really grateful.' He took the first sheet of paper from the folder and scrutinised it. 'So what have we here?'

'It's like a timeline,' she said, her tone scathing. 'I did it in a spreadsheet. It shows dates and events, everything I could find in my data mining.'

He wasn't sure what data mining was, but knew if he asked he would be at the end of one of her lengthy and technical explanations, which he knew he wouldn't understand anyway. Fortunately, it seemed she was planning to provide further details unprompted.

'So I ran a web-bot through the registers of births, marriages and deaths, obviously, then some national census stuff, then the university's on-line matriculation and graduation records, then their hospital's staff website and then I linked them together using their maiden names and their married names....'

He nodded as he interrupted her flow. 'Good stuff Eleanor, exactly what I would have done myself. That's what I've always thought about these web-bots. You can't beat them. Fabulous things. Always keep a few in my toolbox at home.'

Unexpectedly, she laughed. 'Yeah right. You've no idea what a web-bot is have you?'

'Not a clue. Do I need to know?'

She shrugged. 'No. In fact, it's best you don't. 'Cos Zak loaned me some military-grade web crawlers that are still in beta.'

He knew of Zak from previous cases. A spotty youth who appeared barely out of his teens, he was a backroom whizz over at MI5 or MI6, he couldn't remember which.

'All hail Zak then, he's a good lad. So what do we have?'

'So I started with the Kelly woman,' she said. 'That was this Partridge guy's second wife, right?'

'Parrish. His name is Parrish. And aye, she was his second wife.'

He scanned Kelly's entry, speed-reading to pick out the key points, trying to form an overall picture of her short life. Kelly Elizabeth Mann, born Norfolk in 1975, which would have made her twenty-eight when she married Parrish in 2003. Five years younger than her husband, not a huge age gap. Graduated with a nursing degree from Cambridge University in 1996, and then on to Addenbrooke's Hospital in the same city, where she was following the psychiatry path, at the place to where James Parrish had recently moved from Glasgow, taking up a surgical consultant post. He guessed that's where they met, a real-life enactment of the trashy nurse-doctor romantic novels that his mother loved so much. And then, nothing of any significance until her death in 2008 at the tragically young age of thirty-three. An excerpt from the Coroner's report cited an overdose of a prescribed anti-depressant as the cause, but had left the verdict open as to whether it had been taken accidentally or deliberately. Eleanor had dug up some local press photographs from the funeral, and he wondered if somewhere in that group of unnamed mourners the image of his next wife might be found.

'And what about wife number three Eleanor?' he said, pointing at the sheet of paper. 'This is... this is what we've got?' Just in time he'd checked himself. This is *all* we've got is what he nearly said, and with a questioning inflexion too. She wouldn't have liked that, an innocent slip of the tongue that would have inevitably triggered strike action. Luckily, she hadn't seemed to notice. He glanced at the screen, picking out the top line. Petra Wallace, born in Stirling in 1980, which made her five years younger than her predecessor.

'She was a lady or something,' he heard Eleanor saying, 'or at least her father was a sir. I found something about him and look, it's there in the spreadsheet.'

Well well. He'd heard of Sir Bruce Wallace of course, an entrepreneur who had made his pile out of carpets, if that wasn't a pun too far. Everyone in Scotland knew Sir Bruce, chiefly from the cheesy TV adverts he fronted himself. Later, he had been knighted for the foundation he had set up, which if he remembered correctly was all about helping Scotland's children escape from a life of poverty. Frank vaguely recalled the guy had bought a country estate not far from Lochmorehead, more or less next door to the Ardmore place owned by the Macallan family. It seemed his only daughter had been a smart girl, Petra winning a place at Cambridge University where she took a first in Business Administration. After graduation, she went to work in the NHS, first in London before moving back to Cambridge in 2007.

'Interesting that,' he said. 'Look, she worked at Addenbrooke's too. One of these NHS managers that everyone likes to bad-mouth. Head of Resourcing for Surgery and Psychiatry, whatever the hell that is.'

Whatever it meant, it seemed highly likely that Petra Wallace and James Parrish would have come across one another in the course of their work. Was that where it started he wondered, when the ambitious social-climbing surgeon discovered the multi-millionaire's daughter and decided that was a future he would quite like to have? And a future with a beautiful woman ten years younger than himself, itself a prize to savour and no doubt to boast about too?

And then she had died.

'There's like tons about her drowning,' Eleanor said. 'I think it was because her dad was famous mainly.' She took two more pages from the folder and spread them on his desk. Images of newspaper front pages, with photographs of the dead girl accompanied by lurid headlines. *Wallace Girl Drowns* and *Tragic Petra Victim of Loch More Tides*. But then, published a couple of days after the incident itself, there was one that jumped out at him. *Petra Drowning No Accident Claims Witness*. Below the headline was printed the name of the reporter who had evidently written the piece. *Katherine McNally*. This would be the reporter that Sir Patrick and his snotty assistant had mentioned during that meeting with Jill Smart up at Portcullis House. It was already obvious that this McNally was the first person he should talk to, and he guessed she wouldn't be too hard to track down. And then he remembered. Katherine McNally, now of the BBC, one of the super-smart rota of female presenters of *The News Tonight*. No, it wouldn't be hard at all to track *her* down.

'So what about the current Mrs Parrish. What do we have on her?' The question was rhetorical, because his eyes were already focussed on the lower rows of Eleanor's spreadsheet. On the column headed *Date of Birth*. No surprises there then. Dawn Parks, apparently a columnist with a national newspaper although Frank had never heard of her, was born in 1985, making her a neat five years younger than the drowned Petra. God, what was it with this guy? It was as if he viewed his wives like his cars, trading them in when they were approaching forty, except it seemed he favoured scrapping them rather than swapping them. There was no evidence of a connection to Addenbrooke's or Guy's so if she knew him before the death of Petra, which would have been in line with his normal MO, that would have to be the subject of a separate line of enquiry. What they did know, as evidenced on the spreadsheet, was that they had married in January 2014, barely eighteen months after the tragic incident on Loch More. Which meant that Mrs Dawn Parrish had now been in post almost eight years, which made her quite the survivor compared with her predecessors. Her story was interesting, but probably not a priority for now. He had to keep reminding himself that this wasn't a real case, insomuch as any evidence he uncovered wouldn't have to jump any CPS hurdles before going to court. He just had to find something solid that could be put in front of the Prime Minister and his lackey Sir Patrick. It was they who would be both judge and jury.

'Well that's all good Eleanor,' he said, now wishing to manoeuvre the meeting to a conclusion, 'and plenty to get our teeth into. As I said, really nice work on your part.'

She gave a modest shrug. 'It was technically interesting. And easy.'

'The magic of the web-bot eh?'

'Yeah, if you like.'

As she got up to leave she suddenly spoke again, her voice a mixture of curiosity and seriousness, a mix he had never heard from her before.

'You said marriage is over-rated.'

He shrugged. 'Did I?'

'You did. So were you like married Frank? Is that how you know?'

She said it in a way that was non-intrusive, as if she was really asking for advice. Perhaps she was, but he was surely the least qualified person in the world to give it.

'Nearly,' he said. 'Close but no cigar.'

She frowned. 'What does that mean?'

He didn't answer. He *couldn't* answer. *Close but no cigar.* Aye, no wife and no nice wee house and no kids either. Every day he wondered what Mhari was doing now, more than fifteen years after she'd stood him up at the altar.

He bore her no ill will, not really. He just hoped that like him, she was having a shit life.

Chapter 10

They were back in their little serviced office off Fleet Street, where Maggie was struggling to process a startling item of stop-press news that had just came in. For it seemed Jimmy was to go on some sort of a date with Emily Smith, the beautiful Human Resources manager at Addison Redburn.

'She just asked me, straight out,' he said, his tone apologetic as he explained the circumstances that had led to the assignation. 'She said she's really into the environment and all that stuff and wondered if I might like to come along, that was all. Oh aye, and she suggested we might grab a bite of dinner beforehand.'

'And you said yes.' It was meant to be said with humour but came out a little censorious.

'Well aye,' he said, looking puzzled. 'I mean, it's not a conflict of interest or anything is it?'

'No no, it's just...'

She broke off, uncertain where she had been planning to go with the conversation. *It's just what?* It wasn't as if she was jealous on her own account, because although she was very well aware of Jimmy's attractiveness, she knew there could never be a romantic attachment between them. And it wasn't just because of their ten-year age gap. It was deeper than that, driven by the powerful friendship that had developed over the two years they had worked together. She had come to realise that she valued that friendship more than almost anything in her life and so would never do anything to jeopardise it. But there was something else too. As well as a friend, she saw herself as his protector, with a specific mission to spare him any more hurt in matters of the heart after his devastating break-up with Flora. And, taking it a stage further, to be the balm that soothed and repaired that relationship if it was at all possible. Yes, that was where the *just* came from. In the time he had known him, she had never seen him look at a woman the way he looked at Emily Smith. It was as if a switch had suddenly been thrown, a realisation that he could never have his old life back and it was time to move on. But when Maggie thought about it a bit more, she realised she ought really to welcome this development. Jimmy had been really down, so much so that he had taken to drinking, to an extent that had dismayed both her and his brother. Now, he seemed to have regained some of his old zest for life, and if she was honest with herself, she wasn't sure that she liked it. Jimmy had been her rock when her life was coming apart at the seams and she had since been determined to repay that debt in any way she could. In her mind, that had always meant getting him back together with his adored wife, but now it seemed she might have to rethink her strategy.

'No, of course it's not a problem,' she said, wondering how convincing she sounded, 'and she seems nice. I just don't want you to get hurt, that's all.'

'Well that's all right then,' he said. 'It's quite a big event, the first time Freja has spoken in public since that horrible acid attack. It'll be interesting to see how she is.'

'She's going back to the very room where it happened, isn't she?' Maggie said. 'As a kind of show of defiance.'

He nodded. 'That's right. If anything, I think the attack's strengthened her resolve. Fair play to her. She's a bloody brave girl.'

Then out of the blue he said, 'Nothing to stop you coming along of course. Emily knows one of the organisers and I'm sure she could get you a ticket.'

Involuntarily she found herself convulsing with laughter, causing him to shoot her a frown. She couldn't tell if it was with puzzlement or disapproval.

'Well it's very nice of you to think of me,' she said, 'but I'm fairly sure Emily wouldn't have been expecting you to be bringing along a chaperone when she asked you along. And besides, I thought you said there was some cosy little dinner for two scheduled into the programme.'

He gave a good-humoured sigh. 'She only said we might grab a bite to eat. It's *you* who's turned it into a cosy little dinner. But anyway, I thought we'd sneaked off from Addisons to talk about the case in private, not to talk about my non-existent love life?'

She grinned. 'Yes, you're right. As I recall, you were going to talk to the lovely Emily about the background of some of the new recruits?'

'Aye, that's correct,' he said, ignoring her teasing, 'and I did manage to get ten minutes with her yesterday and got some information that might at least give us a start. And before you ask, I don't think I gave anything away. She still thinks we're looking for a spy in the nest so she was quite happy to give me the info I needed about the recent starters. Although obviously she couldn't tell me too much detail, with confidentiality obligations and all that.'

'Sure, of course. So what have you got? Anything?'

He shrugged. 'I don't know. Maybe. So I asked about Jolene first, and it turns out that she started her City career at some place called Fortnum Price, which apparently is another well-known outfit. She did more than fifteen years there and made it to partner, before joining Addisons five years or so ago.'

'I know them,' Maggie said. 'One of the big six firms, very well respected.'

'Aye, so here's the thing. Four of our thirteen also worked there at one time or other.'

'Interesting.'

'More than that,' Jimmy said. 'Because that four includes Harry Newton and Lily Wu.'

Maggie raised an eyebrow. 'Now that *is* interesting.'

'Not only that, it seems that there was some overlap in times with all four. What I mean is, they all worked at this Fortnum firm at the same time as she did.'

Maggie pursed her lips as she thought about what this might mean for their investigation. Narrowing down the long list of possible suspects to four could be considered progress, but really, was it? It all hinged on their theory that it was someone with a past connection to Jolene who was responsible for the harassment, but the fact was, that theory had more holes in it than a lump of Gorgonzola. Then something sprang to mind, or rather someone. Someone from her past that she hoped she'd never have to think of again.

'They've got a big criminal practice, in fact it's probably what they're best-known for in the profession. My old place Drake Chambers used to get a ton of work from them.' And all of that work went through the sticky hands of Nigel Redmond, the scumbag clerk of chambers. If anybody knew the inside story of what went on in Fortnums, it would be him. *Worst luck.*

*****

She knew Redmond wouldn't just agree to tell her what she wanted to know over the phone, and sure enough they were less than two minutes into their conversation when he was suggesting they meet for lunch the next day. At least she'd got to choose the venue, deciding in favour of familiar ground. The Old King's Head, scene of her Thursday night get-togethers with the Stewart brothers, was packed at lunchtimes, the noise and bustle denying any chance of intimacy. They didn't like their customers to hang about either, expecting you to order, eat your meal and settle your bill in no more than an hour max. Sixty minutes with Nigel

Redmond was about fifty-nine minutes too long, but to coin one of Jimmy's favourite expressions, she was prepared to take one for the team.

'So *lovely* to see you Maggie.' As he stood up to greet her, a strong scent of aftershave wafted across the table. He'd obviously made an effort, a new-looking crisp white shirt worn with a purple silk tie, his thinning hair combed over his scalp in a vain attempt to disguise his baldness. She guessed he was probably pushing sixty, but even thirty years earlier she doubted he had been any woman's idea of a dream date. Back in her days at Drakes he had always been lurking around her desk, dropping obsequious compliments and generally being a pest. Then it had made her angry but now with the softening passage of time she realised she only felt sorry for him. But that didn't mean she wanted the encounter to last any longer than was strictly necessary.

'Nice to see you too Nigel,' she said, relieved that he hadn't leaned across to kiss her on the cheek as she had half-expected. 'Shall we order? You need to get on with it here else they chuck you out before you even get started.'

She picked up the menu and scanned it quickly. 'Lasagne, side salad and sparkling mineral water please.'

He raised an eyebrow. 'No wine? You always liked a glass, didn't you?'

She smiled. He knew only too well about the aftermath of her meltdown, how day after day she would come into the office nursing a hangover or worse. And looking back, she realised that he had covered for her on more than one occasion when she was in no state to be out of bed let alone at work. For that, she ought to have been grateful, but she wasn't.

'I'd love to,' she said, not insincerely, 'but Addisons has a strict no-alcohol policy. And they reserve the right to test you randomly would you believe? So no wine for me I'm afraid.'

'Addisons?' he said, sounding surprised. 'I didn't know you were back there. That's where you started, wasn't it?'

She nodded. 'Yes it was, but I'm not back as an employee. I'm doing some consultancy work there, with my little investigations firm. That's where the Fortnum Price connection comes in, like I mentioned on the phone.'

He clasped his hands and gave a half-smile. 'Ah yes, Fortnums. A splendid firm. I know them very well naturally. They push a lot of briefs our way of course, as I'm sure you recall.'

A surly waitress arrived to take their order. 'I'm paying, by the way,' Maggie said.

'In that case, I'll have the fillet steak and you won't mind if I have a cheeky little bottle of Merlot to accompany it?' He handed the waitress his menu before waiting for her answer. Not that Maggie minded, since it was all going to end up on her bill to Addisons in any case.

'I sent you a list of four former Fortnum employees,' she said, anxious to get down to business. 'We wondered if you knew anything about them.' Jimmy had argued she should not disclose the connection to Jolene Cavendish so as not to lead the witness and she had gone along with his suggestion. Now it was going to be interesting to see if Jolene's name came up in any of Redmond's revelations.

'I assume you aren't going to tell me what this is all about?' he said.

'No, I'm sorry. It's confidential I'm afraid. I'm sure you understand.'

He shrugged. 'No matter. No doubt I'll be able to figure it out in due course.' He fumbled in his trouser pocket and removed a slip of paper. She saw him screw up his eyes as he struggled to read his own hand-writing, evidently too vain to make use of reading glasses.

'So two of these were just graduate entrants, straight from law school in 2016 or thereabouts. Zoe someone-or-other and a guy called Imran Shahid. Didn't last long, eighteen months for one of them and even less than that for the other one.'

Maggie smiled to herself. They all left law school wearing rose-tinted spectacles, herself included, until the grim reality of life on the bottom rung of the ladder smacked them in the face. Long hours, poor pay, tedious work and being regarded as the lowest form of pond life by your elders and betters. *That* was the reality, as far from the glamour of a John Grisham movie as you could get, and it wasn't surprising that many of them jacked it in after a few months. At least these two had shown some perseverance, evidently hoping that a change of firm might make a difference. She doubted it would have, especially if their motive had been to escape Jolene Cavendish.

The waitress had arrived with their meals, setting them on the table with a casual indifference. Redmond's Merlot, equipped with a screw-top, was delivered unopened and it was evident he was not to be given the opportunity to accept or reject it as might be the case in a more upmarket establishment. He didn't seem concerned, unscrewing the top and pouring himself a generous measure. He took a sip before continuing.

'But as to these other two,' he said, pointing at his list in a conspiratorial manner, 'well that's a different story altogether.' He took another sip from his wine then started on his steak. She looked at him expectantly, waiting for him to speak, but he seemed in no hurry.

'Nice bit of fillet this,' he said, waving his fork in the air. 'How's your lasagne?'

'Very nice,' she said, struggling to disguise her impatience. 'So you've something to tell me about the other two?'

'Maybe, maybe, but what's the rush? Let's just enjoy our cosy little lunch shall we?' He raised the wine bottle and pointed it in her direction. 'Sure you won't have a glass Maggie? I doubt if I can get through all this on my own. So how's your little boy, Oliver isn't it?'

'Ollie. And yes he's fine. And no, I'll pass on the wine thanks.' She could feel herself getting angry but somehow she managed to restrain herself from bursting out a *just bloody get on with it, will you?*

'It's *so* delightful this,' she heard him saying. 'We should do this more often.' *Not bloody likely.* But she knew of course that if the information he had was valuable, he wasn't going to give it up for nothing. There would have to be a trade and the price was her company.

'Yes,' she said, hoping her forced smile didn't look too much like a grimace, 'that would be lovely.' As long as she didn't commit to an actual date, she felt she could just about get away with it.

It seemed that her assurance was enough for him. 'Yeah, so as for the other two individuals on your list, a right pair they turned out to be and make no mistake.'

Maggie could barely suppress her excitement. 'What do you mean, a right pair?'

He took a gulp from his wine glass then relaxed back in his chair. 'Well that Lily Wu for a start. How should I put it? Let's just say she had over-egged her qualifications.'

'How do you mean?'

'Well you know yourself Maggie that Fortnum's only take on the cream of the graduate crop every year. They're very selective and you need a First-Class honours even to get to the interview stage.'

'And she didn't have one?'

'Sadly not. It turned out the poor girl barely scraped a Third, and from the University of East Anglia or Birmingham or some other ghastly place like that. She lied on her application form but I think they were so pleased to be able to tick a box on their diversity spreadsheet that nobody checked up properly.'

Maggie shook her head. 'So what happened to her then?'

Redmond shrugged again. 'I don't know exactly but my mate Des - he's the one who's given me the lowdown on all off this - Des says it all went tits-up for her when someone who was at Uni with Lily joined the firm. Apparently they had previous, this guy and Lily, I don't know what about but anyway, there was no love lost. Whatever the case, this guy was surprised that Lily was holding down a Senior Associate position and grassed her up. They matter went to some HR committee or other, and it was decided she should be sacked. Des said that immediately after the decision was made, she had to clear her desk and then was marched out of the door by security in full view of all her colleagues.'

'Seems a bit harsh,' Maggie said, 'especially if she had been doing an ok job.'

'Yes, that seemed to be the general view amongst the troops according to Des. But apparently the decision was made by some bureaucratic bigwig who had never even met her, and that was it, end of story.' He lifted his knife and made a slashing gesture across his neck. 'Guillotined and no right to appeal either.'

'Harsh,' Maggie said again. 'But your Des, he didn't happen to say who this bigwig was, did he?'

Redmond's eyes narrowed. 'Now I wonder why you're asking that young Maggie? No he didn't, but I suppose I could find out and let you know next time.'

'It's not important,' she said, annoyed with herself for falling into his trap. The trouble was, it would be interesting to find out of it had been Jolene who had ordered the sacking, and the only way she was going to do that was to get the information from her lunch date. Reluctantly she heard herself saying, 'but yes, if you could find out, it might be useful.'

'Yes, I'll try and do that *of course*,' he said, giving her a leering smile that caused her to shiver. 'Anything for you young Maggie. In fact, I'll drop Des a message now, how about that?'

'That would be great,' she said, hoping her relief wasn't too obvious. If Redmond's insider Des got back to him before the end of lunch, she might be able to avoid the follow-up date she was already dreading. In fact, it would be well worth prolonging the agony of this one to get that result. But not too long, because unlike her lovely colleague Captain Jimmy Stewart, she hadn't been trained to withstand torture. But then she thought about it again. *Of course, sly Nigel would already know*. He wouldn't have come to lunch without doing his research properly. But he clearly wasn't intending to give up that precious information without getting a return.

With elaborate exaggeration, Redmond finished tapping the message into his phone then said, 'And now to the last one on your little list. Always keep the best to last, that's what they say isn't it?'

Harry Newton. Jolene Cavendish's kicking boy, the sullen victim of the school bully. And when she had had that brief meeting with him, there was no mistaking the anger in his eyes, an anger that must surely be amplified each time the witch-bitch dished out another humiliation. Now perhaps she was going to find out if there was a connection to his past too.

'That sounds interesting Nigel,' she said truthfully.

'Not just interesting,' he said, rubbing his hands together. 'I think this merits an *extremely* interesting, not to put too fine a point on it.'

'Tell me more.'

'Well if we go back five year ago, let's just say Mr Harry Newton wasn't exactly knocking the ball out of the park, if you'll pardon the expression. He just about scraped through his traineeship and there was some debate as to whether he should be made up to Associate. But in the end the partners decided it would be *another* tick in the box as far as their diversity initiatives went.'

'But he's not black or any other minority like Lily was,' Maggie said, looking puzzled. 'Not as far as I can tell at least.'

Redmond looked at her reproachfully. *'Person of colour* is the non-pejorative term I think you will find. And no, he's not BAME, but he *is* white working class. You won't find too many of *them* in firms like Fortnums.'

'I'm working class too,' she said indignantly, 'as you well know.'

'Ah yes, the sweet Yorkshire mill-town lass. But you were young, female and rather pretty when you applied for a traineeship at Addisons. For that, they always make an exception. Regrettable, but true nonetheless.'

She wasn't going to admit it to Redmond, but deep down she had always known it to be true. But what the hell, you had to play the cards you were given, make the most of your God-given talents even if that only extended to the way you looked. At least he hadn't gone on to make some cringe-worthy remark about how she looked now.

'So, Newton...'

He smiled. 'Ah yes. So they buried him in their Property practice for four or five years, fairly low down the ladder of course...'

Maggie gave a wry smile. 'I know what it's like at the coal face. Long hours and no respect.'

'Quite,' Redmond said, 'but our Harry was doing just about ok-ish. Not pulling up any trees. He worked hard enough but he just didn't have the talent. You get the picture.'

'So he wasn't quite bad enough for him to be pushed out?'

'You could say that,' he said. 'They tried to give him the message by the pitiful annual salary increases they awarded him, but he either didn't get it or else he didn't care. I ask you, what sort of lawyer doesn't care about *money*?'

Maggie allowed herself a knowing smile. Everything came down to money with Nigel Redmond, and he used its lure to keep the avaricious barristers of Drake Chambers under his control. You scratch my back and I'll scratch yours was the way he operated, handing out the juiciest briefs to those who showed him the most respect. The fact that respect was patently fake didn't seem to bother him in the slightest. So as far as Redmond was concerned, a lawyer who didn't care about money must be from another planet.

'But something must have happened,' she said. 'So what was it?'

'Ah, wouldn't you like to know?' he said, taking another sip from his wine-glass.

'Yes, that's why I'm here,' she said, trying to disguise her annoyance at his obvious desire to string out their date as long as possible.

'Come on then Nigel, out with it,' she said irritably. 'I haven't got all day. Tell me what happened.'

'All right, I will,' he said grudgingly. 'One Saturday afternoon, he was observed outside Arsenal's football ground throwing a brick at the window of an opposing club's team bus, whilst in the company of a group of particularly nasty individuals who call themselves the North London Ultras. The name I believe is some sort of twisted homage to a hooligan group associated with an Italian football club. Far right racist thugs that think throwing banana skins at black players is amusing.'

'I've heard of them,' Maggie said. 'So what about Newton? Was he arrested?'

Redmond shook his head. 'In keeping with the light-touch policing philosophy prevalent at the time, he escaped with just a caution. But as I said, he was observed. You see, a senior partner at his firm happened to be a season ticket holder and was there with his young son, as he would be at every home game of course. He recognised Newton amongst the gang and had the presence of mind to take a photograph.'

'Which was bad news for our Harry I assume?'

'Quite,' Redmond said. 'Behaviour likely to be detrimental to the reputation of the firm, let alone the profession. There was a letter on his desk by eight o' clock on the Monday morning dismissing him for gross misconduct. No appeal, no arguments, no compensation, he was out the door. Quite right too in my opinion.'

Maggie nodded in agreement, but then something struck her. After what he had done, Newton would have instantly become persona non grata to any respectable firm in the profession. And yet here he was working at Addison Redburn, dragged on board as part of Emily Smith's panic all-hands-on-deck recruitment campaign for the Hampton deal. Five years on, it seemed he had been given an unlikely chance of redemption.

Her thoughts were interrupted by a loud ping from Nigel Redmond's smartphone.

'Hold on,' he said, giving the screen an exaggerated stare. 'It's from Des. Seems he knows who Lily Wu's boss was. But then he's a good chap is my Des. Knows everything that's going on. Worth his weight in gold.'

'Stop taking the piss Nigel,' she said, half-angry, half-amused. 'We both know who we're talking about here.'

He laughed. 'It's a fair cop. Of *course* I knew who it was you were interested in before you even got here. Jolene Cavendish, isn't it? So is that what you're doing at Addison's then?' he said, fishing. 'Something to do with her? Just putting two and two together you understand.'

There was no point in denying it. 'She's being harassed. My partner and I are trying to find out who's behind it.'

'Yes, I thought as much. Well of course anything I can do to help.'

But she wasn't listening to him anymore, her thoughts churning over what she had learned in the last thirty minutes.

So Harry Newton didn't just *look* like a football hooligan, he *was* a football hooligan and his behaviour had cost him his job at Fortnum Price. But on the face of it, Jolene hadn't been involved in his demise in any way. His would have been a straightforward gross misconduct matter with a clause written into his contract of employment allowing the firm to dismiss him instantly, which is exactly what had happened. Perhaps Newton still bore Fortnums ill-will for what they had done to him, but that was unlikely to be directed against Jolene Cavendish personally. He had been in an entirely different department to her for a start, and Maggie doubted if he would have known who she was, let alone met her in his time at the firm.

As for Lily Wu, Jolene wouldn't have given her dismissal more than a minute's thought. Junior associates were ten a penny, and if this one had lied about her qualifications, then she would have to go. No question of considering how good a job she had been doing or if there were any mitigating circumstances in her personal life, rules were rules and there to be adhered to. What was certain was that although Jolene didn't know Lily Wu from Adam, the reverse was most certainly not true. Lily would have known only too well who was behind her dismissal and it wouldn't be surprising if she bore a grudge about it. And now here she was, like Harry Newton, working at Addison Redburn, and for Jolene Cavendish too. Interesting, that.

Revenge is a dish best served cold. A woman with a reason to hate a former boss, and now more than five years later, here she was with a chance to do something about it. It was plausible, very plausible.

So what of Harry Newton? It appeared his connection back to Fortnum Price might be no more than a coincidence, and perhaps to find a reason for him to be harassing his new boss, you needed to look closer in time, to his current job at

Addison Redburn and to his fractious working relationship with Jolene. The public humiliation would be too much for many people to take, not just a person with a history of violence.

When she got back to the office she would chat it through with Jimmy, and he would immediately ask about what he had recently taken to calling the holy trinity of crime. *Means, motive, opportunity.* On the face of it, whilst Harry or Lily could easily have the means to mount a campaign of harassment against Jolene, the opportunity bit posed more of a problem, with Kylie Winterburn patrolling the entrance to her office like a cold-war Soviet border guard.

But right now, that didn't matter because Maggie knew which of the trinity was always the most important. *Motive.* And both Lily Wu and Harry Newton had that in spades, but for different reasons.

The waitress had arrived to clear up their plates, reminding them that they had to vacate the table in less than five minutes. They got up to leave, Maggie making sure she kept a couple of arms-lengths away from him so that Redmond couldn't attempt a goodbye kiss.

'Been lovely Maggie,' he said. 'But you know, something quite interesting has just struck me when you confirmed that this matter concerned Jolene Cavendish. Yes, something very interesting indeed. Something I remember from a few years back.'

She gave him a surprised look. 'So do you know her then?'

He shook his head. 'Not *know* her, know *of* her. As I said, something from a few years' back.' Now he was smiling his trademark smug smile. 'Ah yes. *Interesting*.'

'What? What was it?' For a moment Maggie wondered if this was all an act simply designed to prolong their date. But it seemed not.

'Well there was some rumination at the time in her circles as to why she had left Fortnums in the first place. She was a partner and doing very well and it was all rather sudden and unexpected you see. Yes it *is* interesting, looking back at it now from today's perspective.'

'You're talking in riddles Nigel,' Maggie said crossly. 'Do you know something or don't you?'

'Let's just say it might be *productive* to re-open the case. That's how you would put it in your new profession isn't it? So just for you Maggie, I'm going to ask my friend to make some *special* enquiries and if he finds anything, then perhaps we could make a date for a little follow up? Maybe dinner this time, then we won't have to rush so much?'

It was the last thing she wanted but she couldn't deny that what he had said about Jolene had piqued her interest. But dinner? *God no*. Then suddenly her mood brightened.

'Yes, of course, brilliant, that would be great.' She took her phone from her pocket and scrolled to the calendar app. 'How about the twenty-fourth? That's a Wednesday.'

'Yes, great. Fantastic.' He looked surprised at how easily she had acquiesced to his request.

Not as surprised as he was going to be when she sent Jimmy along in her place.

Chapter 11

The voice at the other end of Frank's phone was bright and perky, her lengthening service with Police Scotland evidently still failing to knock the youthful enthusiasm out of her. *Not to worry* he thought, giving a cynical frown, *plenty of time yet.*

'New Gorbals Police Station, PC Lexy McDonald speaking. How can I help you?'

He had to shout to make himself heard above the busy hubbub of the railway station. 'You can help me by not being so bloody bouncy for a start. It's way too early for that, for god's sake.'

'Morning sir, and it's quarter past eleven by my watch. Would you call that early?' That was one of the many things he loved about Lexy, her sense of humour. And the fact that she had a very respectful way of being disrespectful.

'It is early if you got on a bloody train at six o'clock in the morning,' he said, laughing. 'Look, I've just got into the Central Station. I'm just going to grab a cab and I'll be with you in ten minutes.'

'It's only a mile and a half's walk sir.'

'Exactly. That's why I'm going to grab a cab. I'm calling you so you can get the coffees in.'

Much to his annoyance there was a queue at the taxi rank. He vaguely knew of course that his home city now had these Uber things kicking around, but he had no idea how they worked so a black cab was the only option. Half an hour later, he was sitting opposite her in the police station's little canteen, coffee in hand.

'So, how's things Lexy? All good?'

'Yes sir, thank you sir. I've got a new sergeant and she's very supportive of me becoming a DC.'

He smiled. 'So what happened to old Jim Muir then?' He already knew the answer. After the demise of Chief Constable Sir Brian Pollock following the Ardmore scandal, there had been a massive pruning of dead wood from top to bottom. Not before time too, in Frank's opinion.

'He took early retirement sir. At least, that's what we were told. It was all quite sudden.'

'Aye, I bet it was,' he said. 'Anyway, what time are we seeing our journalist friend?'

Her eyes lit up with undisguised excitement. 'What, you want me to come too sir? To meet Katherine McNally? To the BBC?'

'Well, if that's where she wants to meet us, then aye, to the BBC. And before you say it, I know their building's only a mile and half away. But we're not walking, just so you know.'

She smiled. 'She says she can meet us at half past one sir. She's hosting the lunchtime politics show and then she's got a half-hour window before the next editorial meeting.'

'Good to know,' he said, glancing at his watch. 'So just time for lunch then. Do they still do haggis and chips here?'

*****

He'd already worked out she was about his own age, although if anyone was asked based on their respective appearances, they would have knocked five years off hers and added at least five to his own. It was no surprise to him that she had made the leap from newsprint to television, where as well as being a frequent current affairs presenter on the national station down in London, she also was executive editor of BBC Scotland's entire news output. Brains as well as beauty was how they would have described her in a less enlightened age, before such sentiments became un-PC. Much to his surprise, he found himself entranced by her attractiveness and was worried he might betray his discomfort by gabbling incoherently. In a similar vein, it seemed Lexy McDonald had been rendered speechless simply by being in her presence.

'Miss McNally, it's really good of you to find the time for us,' he said, 'especially since it was a long time ago, the Petra Parrish business.'

'It's Katherine, please,' she said, smiling. 'And no, I was intrigued to hear from PC McDonald that there's renewed interest in the case. I got heavily involved in it at the time as you know.'

'Well it's not exactly that,' he said, 'interest in the case I mean.'

'Come come Inspector, I'm an investigative journalist, or at least I was once. I looked up your secretive little department on the Metropolitan Police website. Cold cases are what you specialise in, isn't that right?'

He gave her an uncertain smile, wondering if he should say *call me Frank*, but decided it wouldn't look right in front of the junior ranks.

'I didn't even know we had a website,' he said, quite truthfully. 'This isn't exactly a cold case in so much as we're not expecting to put anything in front of the official prosecutors. Let's just say we're looking into the professional and personal integrity of a certain party on behalf of other certain parties.' It sounded like a load of bollocks because it was a load of bollocks. Worse than that, it seemed that Katherine McNally was equipped with a built-in bullshit detector.

She gave him a sweet smile. 'Ok then, let me take a wild guess. A certain party, being Her Majesty's Government, has got itself into a terrible tizz because of the dizzying popularity of the *Chronicle's* James Parrish knighthood campaign and doesn't know what to do.'

He sighed. 'God, you're good. Got it in one. So as you said, the government, more precisely the PM, is anxious to ensure that nothing scandalous pops up five minutes after Parrish has done the old kneeling down and sword business in front of Her Majesty.'

'Something like murdering his wife you mean?'

'Aye, that would qualify. So you think he did it, do you?'

She nodded. 'I'm quite certain he did. But back then when I was doing my investigation I soon realised that it would be impossible to prove, especially after the Coroner had ruled it was Death by Misadventure.'

He frowned. 'So why were you so certain?'

'You know the old saying, which I think was from a Sherlock Holmes novel? Something like when you've ruled out the impossible then whatever is left, however improbable, must be the truth?'

'Aye, I use that one all the time but I didn't know it was from Sherlock Holmes. I thought it was Shakespeare.'

'The Casebook of Sherlock Holmes,' Lexy said, speaking for the first time. 'His ninth book I think, or was it his tenth?'

'Aye all right clever-clogs,' Frank said, suppressing a smile, 'so Katherine, maybe you can run through what you found out and what your thought processes were at the time.'

He'd already read through her old articles several times, easily accessed from the newspaper's web archive, so had a pretty good idea of the gist of her argument. But he wanted to hear it straight from the horse's mouth so to speak. Experience had taught him that talking through an investigation out loud with someone who wasn't close to the case often produced new insights or raised to prominence a particular point that had up until then seemed insignificant.

'Sure Frank,' she said, smiling. *Frank*. Hearing her say his name sent a little involuntary shiver down his spine.

'So the first point to make was that Petra Parrish was a very experienced sailor, much more experienced than her husband. Remember her family had owned their place on the loch for over thirty years and she had been messing about in boats almost since she could walk. So she knew all about the dangers of Loch More and its tidal race. There's no way she would have taken any chances with it. No way.'

He nodded. 'Aye I know a bit about that from my last case, about Loch More being a sea loch and its powerful currents and all that. So what's the significance in our case?'

'The wind and the tide. I don't know if you understand anything about sailing, and I mean boats with sails, and how they work?'

'I took a wee rowing boat out in Victoria Park once. Apart from that, nothing.'

She laughed. 'Right. Well I do, because I was in the Sea Scouts and before you say anything, they've always had girls, not just boys. That's really why I took an interest in the case, because they took us out on Loch More once and I was scared out of my wits. Because once that tidal race grabs hold of you, there's basically nothing you can do. You're getting dragged out to sea, and there's no way you can tack towards safety unless the wind is blowing strongly from the southeast. Which, I'm reliably informed, only happens about thirty or so days in an average year, the prevailing wind being a south-westerly.'

Frank gave her a perplexed look. 'I know I must be a bit thick, but I don't understand the significance of that.'

She laughed. 'Don't worry, it's not an easy concept for the layman. What it means is there are only a handful of days when it's safe to take a little sail-powered boat out on that water. That's when the wind is blowing straight up the loch towards Lochmorehead. From the southeast.'

'Ah, so is that what happened? James and his wife took their boat out on a day when it *wasn't* safe?'

She shook her head. 'On the contrary. The day she died was one of the safe days. I told you, there's no way she would have taken that boat out otherwise. I checked, and the wind was blowing a stiff south-easterly that day, nearly forty knots in fact. That's how I knew James Parrish's story was a lie.'

'Go on,' he said quietly.

'He said they were out in the middle of the loch when they were hit by a sudden violent current and a strong cross wind, which he said was threatening to capsize the boat. Petra, he said, immediately took control, being the more experienced of the pair, and got out on the trapeze to balance the weight. To stop the boat heeling any further.'

'I've seen them do that,' Frank said. 'Hanging nearly horizontally off the side with just their feet on the boat. Bloody scary.'

She laughed. 'No, it's brilliant, the best bit about sailing. You should try it sometime.'

'Thanks, but I get seasick in my bath. But sorry, I'm interrupting.'

'No problem. So then according to Parrish, Petra just disappeared into the water. One minute she was there, the next minute she wasn't, that's how he described it. He looked everywhere, so he says, but she had completely disappeared. In the end the Coroner concluded she must have been sucked under by the current and then out to sea.'

Frank nodded. 'Because her body has never been found, has it?'

'Correct,' she said, 'which is another reason why I know his story was a pile of crap.'

'How so?' he asked, enthralled.

'God, how long have you got? Well first of all, that boat was fin-keeled and it would take an Atlantic-sized storm to tip it up. Petra would have known that, so there's no way that she would have panicked just because things were getting a little hairy. Secondly, if she *had* gone out on the trapeze, she would have attached a safety line so that if she did end up in the water she could be quickly rescued. And thirdly, there is absolutely no way she would have got on that boat without wearing a life jacket. So even if she had been carried out to sea, there was every chance she would have been rescued by the coastguard, or at the very least her body would have been found floating somewhere.'

'So what's your theory?' Frank said. 'Tell me your Sherlock Holmes deduction.'

'Before I get to that, there's another thing. You see, they were seen setting off from the little jetty at Lochmorehead.'

'Aye, I know it, it's just in front of the hotel, isn't it?'

'Yes, that's right,' she said. 'So as I say, they were seen by an old guy, one of the locals, who was out tinkering with his boat at the time. He remembers it vividly because he was jealous they were getting out on one of these special days and just in time to catch the turning tide whilst he was stuck at the jetty.'

'So you mean the tide *wasn't* going out at the time the Parrishes were out there?'

Katherine nodded. 'Exactly. Parrish told the authorities they had set out at eight-thirty when in fact the old guy said it was sometime after ten. So you can see why I was so excited about the story.'

'I can see that,' Frank said. 'Understandable. So what do you think happened then?'

'Like I said, with all these impossible things ruled out, it could only be one thing. He must have overpowered poor Petra, removed her life-jacket, weighed her down with a bag of stones or something, then threw her overboard.'

'So she's still down there is she, at the bottom of Loch More?' Frank said, grimacing. 'That's bloody awful.'

She gave him a sad look. 'Yes, it is awful Frank, but I doubt if her body is still there. The undercurrents are so strong, she would have been dragged out to sea long ago, even if she had been weighed down.'

'So what about the police? Weren't they interested?'

She shook her head. 'No, not really. They sent a detective constable over from Helensburgh and he was polite enough but then they just seemed to drop it after a day or two.'

Frank sighed to himself. The fact that it was only a DC who was assigned to the investigation told you everything you needed to know about what the brass thought about it at the time. Without a body and the ability to subject it to thorough forensic examination, there was no evidence, and without evidence there was no case, no matter how guilty they thought James Parrish might be. He reflected he would have probably done the same himself if he had been in their shoes, and now more than ten years on, it wasn't looking any more promising. Not so much a cold case, this one was frozen like a woolly mammoth in a block of ice, and now equally prehistoric. It seemed that if James Parrish really had killed his wife, then he had got away with it.

'So what's going to happen now Frank?' Katherine asked. 'Will you be re-opening the case or whatever it is you do in these matters?'

He shrugged. 'I doubt it very much. I mean, I tend to agree with your analysis and all that, but the case is circumstantial at best. There is one thing though that struck me though. If, as you say, Parrish removed his wife's life jacket, where did it go? He could hardly have chucked it overboard because it still be floating there now, wouldn't it?'

'I could maybe track down that constable and see if they did an inventory or anything like that,' Lexy said. 'Of the stuff on the boat I mean.'

'Aye, do that,' Frank said. But he knew already she wouldn't find anything. Parrish could have just hung it up with all the other sailing paraphernalia, where it would have been hidden in plain sight. And as for the boat, it would probably have been sold long ago, might even have passed through several owners if indeed it was still in active service. Even if they tracked it down, that was going to be a dead end.

'I hope it's not been a wasted trip Frank,' Katherine said, 'but I told you all I know.'

'No no,' he said, smiling. 'That's police-work for you. This was the most promising lead we had so it had to be followed up. And it's been very helpful thank you.'

'So what are your plans? For the rest of the day I mean?'

The question took him by surprise. 'What? Well I was going to head back to the nick and have a wee debrief with Lexy here. I've got a hotel in the city centre for the night so I'm not rushing back down south. This evening I'll just grab something to eat, have a couple of beers and watch a bit of telly in my room.'

She smiled. 'Well, if you could stand some company, perhaps we could have dinner together? See if I can wheedle out of you what's going on with Parrish. Because I sense there might be a story in it for the wonderful BBC.'

He gave her a wry look. 'Oh aye, there's a story in it all right, but I'm afraid I'm sworn to secrecy.' Feeling uncomfortable, he was only too aware that he had not responded to her invitation. But she persisted.

'So what about dinner? I'll cook, maybe Italian if that's ok for you? And don't bother with wine, my rack is overflowing with the stuff at the moment.'

'Aye, that would be lovely,' he said, not sure what he had just agreed to.

And then suddenly he remembered what day it was. *Thursday.* The day of his regular pub date with Jimmy and Maggie when he was in town. The question was, could you be accused of two-timing when you had barely one-timed in the first place?

Chapter 12

It had come as a surprise to Maggie when Frank, by way of taciturn text, had suggested they should all meet up on Friday evening after work instead of their normal Thursday, which they had been forced to miss because of his visit to Glasgow on business apparently connected to the Parrish case. Luckily Marta had no plans for the evening and had volunteered to extend her working day indefinitely. What that meant was that her adored son Ollie would be in good hands, although she suspected he wouldn't make his designated seven-thirty bedtime under the care of their kindly but soft Polish nanny. Jimmy too was available, which made her realise that she had never given much thought as to how her colleague spent his weekends. She knew he sometimes went to the gym and that he had a racing bike which he often took out on marathon excursions with some old army pals. During the football season he would spend an occasional Saturday with his brother, supporting a local non-league club, Barnet or Bromley, she could never remember which one. What she did know however was that Jimmy's entire life was on hold, stuck in some weird limbo whilst he tried to figure out how to save his marriage to Flora. But now perhaps, there was light at the end of the tunnel, a shaft of illumination provided by the dazzling smile of Emily Smith.

And for the first time in a while, the three was to become four. Elsa Berger, the super-efficient and super-feisty Czech girl who administered Riverside House, the shared office facility that was the home of Maggie Bainbridge Associates, had somehow managed to invite herself along. Maggie thought she knew why. As well as being super-efficient, Elsa was super-nosey too, and she suspected that she had overheard her and Jimmy discussing his surprise liaison with Emily Smith. This was a development that would have displeased Elsa, who was very much in love with Jimmy, rather a lot.

Maggie arrived at the Old King's Head to find the pair of them already at the bar, Jimmy with pint in hand and Elsa clutching a large vodka in one hand and Jimmy's arm with the other. The two of them were always sharing some private joke or other and this evening was no exception. She often thought that her colleague rather indulged Elsa's puppy-like devotion to him, even although it was more than the ten-year age gap between them that made the likelihood of a relationship between them a fantasy that only the girl shared. But he wouldn't be unkind to her and he wouldn't lead her on either, Maggie knew that. It just wasn't in his nature.

'It's rammed tonight, isn't it?' he said in way of greeting. 'You can hardly hear yourself think.'

'Place has atmosphere I think,' Elsa said, her eyes shining. 'I like it.'

'Evening all.' Frank's booming voice effortlessly cut through the background hubbub as unseen, he glided up behind them. 'Everyone's got a drink except me I see. We'll need to change that forthwith.'

'I haven't,' Maggie said, 'but I'd like one very much.'

'Aye, nae bother. Large Chardonnay I'm presuming?'

Without waiting for her to answer, he raised an arm to attract the attention of one of the bar staff, ordering her wine and a pint of Doom Bar for himself.

'How'd it go in Glasgow?' she asked him as he handed her her drink, 'if it's not all too hush-hush to tell me.'

'Aye well it went ok, sort of. Pretty routine.' Was it her imagination or was there a hint of evasiveness in his voice? Whatever the case, he seemed keen to change the subject. 'And what about your Jolene case. Any developments on that front?'

'Yes, well there has been as a matter of fact, and me and Jimmy were hoping to pick your professional brain as to what we should do next.'

'Pick his brain?' Jimmy said, winking at Elsa. 'That shouldn't take long.'

Frank responded with an affectionate one-finger salute.

'Two of people in Jolene office have interesting back-story,' Elsa said. 'Making them suspects we think. And perhaps also Jolene leaved Fortnum Price under cloud. '

Maggie gave Jimmy a glance that said *how the hell did she know that?* But of course she knew how. The girl spent half her day with an ear pressed against their office door.

'Aye, that's right,' Jimmy said, 'but we don't know anything about Jolene's leaving circumstances at the moment. But yes, the other two worked at Fortnum Price too, and they also leaved place under cloud.'

'Yes, and one of suspects is football hooligan,' Elsa said, failing to detect Jimmy's gentle mickey-taking. 'He lost good job because of it.'

'Really?' Frank said, laughing. 'Well there's a lot of it about I'm afraid. But anyway, I won't bore you with the old means, motive and opportunity chestnut, because obviously you know all that stuff already. But there's one other thing I'm always interested in, even before all that.'

He stopped, a smug grin spreading across his face, then took a measured sip from his pint.

'What?' Jimmy said, a hint of exasperation in his tone. 'Aren't you going to tell us?'

'Connections and coincidences,' Elsa said before he could answer.

'How the bloody hell did you know that?' Frank said, surprised.

'I could be detective too,' she replied, without a hint of modesty. 'I read all Agatha Christie Czech editions when I was kid.'

He gave her an admiring look. 'Aye I think maybe you could wee Elsa. And as it happens you're right on this occasion. See, I don't believe in coincidences and so when you get a bunch of improbable connections, you're usually right to be suspicious.'

'Is that what you're thinking in your case?' Maggie asked him. 'I think you told us that two of James Parrish's wives died in suspicious circumstances didn't you? Are you thinking that must be more than a coincidence?'

'Or it might just be bad luck,' Jimmy said. 'Bad things happen, we all know that.'

'I don't believe in bad luck either,' Frank said darkly. 'At least, not the losing-two-wives-in-a-row kind of bad luck.'

'You met that TV woman when you were up there, didn't you?' Jimmy said. 'The one that investigated one of the deaths at the time. Any luck with her?' To Maggie's surprise the question seemed to make Frank blush.

'Nah, she was nice enough,' he said quickly, 'and she'd done a thorough job but there was really nothing that can be proved. So it was a bit of a dead end, unless I can beat a confession out of Parrish that is. That's my next plan.'

'I'm going to assume that's a joke,' Maggie said, raising an eyebrow.

'Aye well of course it is. But the thing is, guilt is a huge burden to bear, especially if you've murdered someone. So no matter how smart anyone thinks they are, there's never any harm in asking a suspect straight out if they did it. Especially if you try the old Colombo routine, you know, acting dumb. It works more times than you'd think, believe me.'

'And comes naturally to you bruv,' Jimmy said, smiling. 'Acting dumb I mean.'

'Aye, and it runs in the family pal,' Frank responded, evidently taking no offence, 'and with bloody bells on in your case.'

Maggie gave them a fond smile.

'Not something to claim bragging rights over I wouldn't have thought. But Frank, do you think we should try that with *our* suspects? Ask them straight out if it's them who've been harassing Jolene?'

'I think you today have not enough evidence,' Elsa said, butting in. 'You must have some credible evidence even if you do not have proof. That is important I think.'

Maggie caught Jimmy's wry expression and could see he was thinking the same thing she was. Since when did Elsa Berger become the bloody master detective? And to make things worse, it seemed that Frank, the only proper crime-fighting professional amongst them, was agreeing with her.

'Aye, she's right,' he said, his tone mildly apologetic. 'You see, in my investigation I've got some reasonable points of evidence about Petra Parrish's death, even if I don't have any proof. I know for example James Parrish lied about the time he set off from the wee jetty at Lochmorehead. I know his story about the tidal race and the wind direction doesn't stack up. I know his wife couldn't have been wearing her life jacket when she went overboard. So I've got more than enough stuff to confront him with, should I choose to do so. From what I hear, you guys don't have anything.'

Maggie couldn't help notice Elsa shooting her a triumphant look as she snuggled up closer to Jimmy. And the thing was, she knew the Czech minx was right. Bloody annoying, that.

'You're correct on that Frank,' she conceded, 'but at least it points us in the right direction as to what we should do next.'

'That's right,' Jimmy said, cottoning on. 'It's no use just assuming because Harry Newton is being bullied by Jolene and both him and Lily Wu used to work for the same firm as her in the past that we're in a position to accuse either of them. We need to dig up some specific evidence connecting the harassment incidents to one or both of our two suspects, although god knows how we're going to do that.'

'Can't help you with that,' Frank said, 'but aye, you need to think about all that stuff that ended up on Jolene's desk and how it might have got there.'

'I could help,' Elsa said. 'Examine scene of crime. Check for DNA. I get kit from Amazon, next day delivery.' From her expression, Maggie could see she was being quite serious.

'Aye thanks Elsa,' Jimmy said in a kindly but firm tone, 'but we've already got a cover story and it would look suspicious if anyone else turned up. But eh, thanks anyway.'

Elsa looked disappointed but evidently decided to say nothing for the moment, although Maggie wasn't expecting the silence to last long. But now she had something else on her mind and that was her annoying on-off relationship with

Frank, if you could call it a relationship. Because really, with all the pussy-footing about they had both done, it was hard to say it had ever been on in the first place. But this evening, she had a plan.

'So guys,' she said brightly, 'enough of this boring shop talk. How about we get something to eat, make a bit of a night of it? Don't you normally have a curry on Fridays Frank? I'm sure we could get a table at that Bombay Nights place, and it's no more than five minutes away.'

She could see the excitement in Elsa's eyes already, as the prospect of a whole evening with her beloved Jimmy began to unfold in her mind. Frank, however, seemed less enthralled by the idea. Frank, she couldn't help notice, was looking at his watch.

'You know what folks,' he said, not looking her in the eye. 'I've had a tough couple of days. I think I'll just call it a night now and slope off homewards if you don't mind.' He picked up his pint, still half-full, and downed it in one, before heading to the door without another word or even a backward glance.

'We can still go Jimmy if Maggie wants to go home,' Elsa said in an alarmed voice, evidently concerned that her perfect evening was crumbling in front of her eyes.

Jimmy ignored her, giving Maggie a stern look that verged on anger. 'You know what, you and Frankie-boy bloody well need to sort yourselves out. Even the TV soaps wouldn't string a storyline out for as long as this.'

'Sod him,' she found herself saying to no-one in particular. 'Sod bloody Frank Stewart.'

'Have nice weekend,' Elsa shouted after her as Maggie headed door-wards.

Chapter 13

Up until now, they'd all hoped that the Met's plan to shut down the Department and move them all out of Atlee House had been some kind of bad dream, but the morning was producing irrefutable evidence that the prospect was all too real.

'Who's that bird guvnor?' Ronnie French asked, pointing to a smartly dressed young woman who, wearing a frown, was at that moment chewing on a pencil and looking around the room. Today the detective was in uniform, he having had a change of mind and deciding to get his stint out of the way as quickly as possible. Short, fat and scruffy, he looked as if he was wearing fancy dress.

'I thought you were supposed to be a bloody detective?' Frank said, shaking his head. 'Laser measurement gizmo, wee clipboard, tight skirt and too much perfume. Plenty of clues there I would have thought, even for you mate.'

French shot back a sardonic smile then winked at Eleanor Campbell.

'Yeah I know, she's a bloody letting agent or whatever she calls herself. But we know it's not going to happen guv, not if we've got anything to do with it, letting agent or no letting agent. Ain't that right Eleanor?'

'Never going to happen,' she nodded, a solemn expression crossing her face. 'Like never ever.'

'Aye, well whatever you're both up to,' he said suspiciously, 'I don't think I want to know about it.'

'Nothing to worry about guv,' Ronnie French said, suddenly looking shifty.

'Nothing,' Eleanor said. 'Much.'

Frank gave a sigh, but secretly he was pleased. At his level, Detective Inspector, he was expected to toe the party line as laid down by the brass, so no matter how dumb or hare-brained an initiative was, he in public at least had to pay lip service to it. But Eleanor was a civil servant and Frenchie was of junior rank and also past redemption. They could more or less do what they liked without fear of the consequences. So yes, he was quite happy to let them run with whatever crazy schemes they had cooked up, so long as they didn't tell him about it. He knew that Eleanor Campbell, smart and tech-savvy, could always be relied on to pull something out of the hat, and he had lately come to realise that despite the shambolic demeanour, you underestimated Ronnie French at your peril. Something he hoped James Parrish would discover when they both paid him a wee visit later that day. But before that, Frank was anxious to find out how Eleanor had fared with the task he had set her.

'So wee Eleanor, I wondered if you've had time to take a look at that overdose thing I talked to you about? You know, Kelly Parrish, wife number two.'

That was the way you had to approach your dealings with the spiky forensic officer. With an overdose of deference, or arse-licking to put it another way. It was a pain in the neck but it was the only way to get results.

'Sure,' she said cagily. 'I can spare like ten minutes.'

'Great,' he said. 'Your place or mine?'

Glowering, she turned her back and strode across the office towards her desk. Leaving French to his own devices, he caught up with her, grabbed a chair from a neighbouring desk, pulled it up alongside hers and sat down.

'I guess it was quite a tough mission for you but I didn't think there was anyone else who could crack it.' He wondered if he'd overdone the gratuitous praise but she didn't seem to have noticed.

'Yeah it was,' she said, 'but Luke has access-all-areas to the NHS archive server farm. He gave me a one-time password.' She hammered a few instructions into the keyboard of her laptop, causing the screen to fill with the distinctive logo of Britain's revered National Health Service.

'Good to know,' Frank said, wondering for a moment whether he should ask who Luke was and what in hell's name was a server farm. But then he remembered she was only giving him ten minutes.

'So what are we looking at here?' he asked, peering at a collage of hand-written forms that had now papered the screen.

'Prescription records,' she said. 'Back then they were scanned and then uploaded to a server for archive.'

'What, every bloody prescription in the country?' he said, surprised.

'Like, *no*,' she said, as if he was the only person in the world who didn't know this. 'Only for controlled drugs.'

'Makes sense. So what's this telling us?' he said, peering at the screen again.

'I've no idea what it's telling us. I just crawled the servers and brought back all the prescriptions I could find for Kelly Parrish.'

'Aye, fair enough.' She was right of course. He was the detective, it was up to him to work out what if anything the evidence was telling them. The trouble was, the scans were all pretty low-resolution and being hand-written it was hard to make out what was on them.

'Can you make out what they're saying?' Frank asked her, screwing up his eyes.

'Yeah, just about,' Eleanor said, 'and I managed to sort them into date order.' She pointed to a group of images at the top of the screen. 'This first lot are for something called Prozac. I've heard of it.'

'Aye, me too. And what about the second lot?'

She moved her mouse to click one of the prescription images, causing it to expand.

'Amy- trip- something,' she said. 'I can't quite make it out. Wait a minute.'

After a few seconds of googling, she had the answer.

'Amytriptilene. I've not heard of that one,' she said, unconcerned.

But Frank had heard of it, having studied the Coroner's report just a few days earlier. *Cause of Death. Overdose of prescribed anti-depressant. Amytriptilene.*

And now there was only one final thing to be established, although Frank thought he already knew the answer. James Parrish was a doctor and he would be perfectly entitled to prescribe his own wife's medications, whether it was ethically dubious or not. What was unarguable though was, like all doctors, he had rubbish hand-writing.

'Can you make it out?' he asked Eleanor. 'The name of the doctor who was prescribing all this crap?'

Eleanor smiled. 'No need, the name of the prescribing doctor is held on the database.' With a few taps of the keyboard, she had a name for him. Dr Tanvi Patel, whoever the hell he was.

So there was another fine theory gone up in smoke.

*****

He'd obviously done pretty well for himself, thought Frank, as he surveyed the impressive frontage of James Parrish's riverside home. He wasn't a property buff, but he knew a place like this in Barnes would fetch well north of two million quid, but then again with two dead but rich wives behind him money probably wasn't a problem for the smooth surgeon.

'Nice gaff this,' Ronnie French said, 'bit different from my place in Bow.'

'Aye, but they're all toffee-nosed Chelsea fans around here,' Frank said. 'Wouldn't suit you at all.'

French laughed. 'You're probably right guv. But I wouldn't mind giving it a try.'

When Frank had phoned the previous day, he hadn't beaten about the bush. 'It's about your knighthood,' he had said, knowing it would pretty much guarantee him an audience, and so it had proved. Not only that, but Parrish had agreed to the mid-afternoon meeting time and at his home too, necessitating, Frank assumed, his surgical schedule being cleared. If nothing else, it showed how seriously James Parrish wanted that gong.

The door was opened by an attractive woman in her early thirties, slim and of medium height, a cropped pixie hairstyle accentuating finely-sculpted cheekbones. She gave Ronnie French, who was still in uniform, a look of mild disdain then extended a hand and said in a refined voice, 'Inspector Stewart I presume? Dawn Parrish. Please come in. My husband is in the study.'

The room was comfortably-furnished with a pair of large leather sofas against two walls and an old-fashioned mahogany desk facing the window, affording views across the Thames. A third wall was given over to bookshelves, filled almost exclusively with medical textbooks. Parrish stood up to greet them as they were ushered in. He was handsome although shorter than Frank expected, having only previously seen photographs of the man, barely five foot seven, but broad-shouldered with a squat stance that exuded power. In ancient times, he could see him as a Roman gladiator. Or in the present day, a mafia hit-man.

'Good of you to see us Dr Parrish, and this is my colleague DC French. As I said on the phone, it's just a routine visit, a wee tick in the box to do with this knighthood business. Shouldn't take long.'

It was quite deliberate, addressing Parrish as doctor when Frank knew very well that consultants were referred to by Mr or Mrs or whatever. How he reacted to the slight might give some indication as to how combative proceedings would turn out. But he either didn't notice or chose to ignore it.

'Sure, no problem,' the surgeon said, quite affably.

'I'll make some teas and coffees, shall I?' Dawn said. 'What will you have officers?'

'Actually Mrs Parrish, I'd like you to sit in on this if you don't mind.' He gave her what he hoped was an apologetic smile. 'All these wee boxes to be ticked. They like to know about the nearest and dearest too I'm afraid. As I said, it shouldn't take up much of your time.'

It was all part of the plan, to have the present Mrs P sit in on proceedings, for Frank very much doubted her husband had fully shared the circumstances surrounding her predecessors' premature deaths. Today he was going to revisit these events, keeping the atmosphere light and deferential but nonetheless hoping to scare the shit out of him. If Parrish did have something to hide, there was a faint chance he would let something slip, something that would turn suspicion into certainty.

'I'm not sure what your role in this is Inspector?' Parrish asked, taking his seat again. 'I would have thought vetting the honours list would be a matter for parliament or the Palace.'

'Aye, well you might ask,' Frank said, adopting a sympathetic tone. 'We're a right rag-tag bunch in my department and we get asked to look at all sorts of weird and wonderful stuff. That's right DC French, isn't it?'

French nodded. 'That's right sir. We're a sort of department without portfolio.'

Frank returned a look of amusement, it being the first time that he could recall the fat reprobate addressing him as sir rather than guv. Or indeed using a big word like portfolio in a sentence.

'But I think the actual reason it ended up with us cops is to do with the tragic events all those years ago.'

'What do you mean?' Parrish said, suddenly less affable. 'What events?'

Frank thought it was an odd thing to say, as if there could be any doubt what he was referring to.

'What I mean is that Mrs Kelly Parrish and Mrs Petra Parrish both died in very sad circumstances. An overdose and a drowning, if I'm not mistaken. Terrible accidents, both of them. It must have been very difficult for you, the fates dealing you such an awful hand.' Without waiting for a response, he reduced his voice to a conspiratorial whisper.

'The thing is Dr Parrish, people talk, don't they? I don't agree with it myself of course, but they do. And that's the wee problem we have here you see. Because certain people- I don't know exactly who these people are but let's just say they are prominent in your field - certain people have been whispering in the ear of the PM, saying maybe there's more to these deaths than meets the eye.'

'Outrageous,' Parrish spluttered. 'Nothing more than professional jealousy, that's what it is.'

'Aye, that might be right sir, especially with all that stuff you did for that wee acid girl and everything. But the thing is, I had a chat recently with a journalist up in Scotland who looked into the drowning at the time. Katherine McNally, you might remember her. She's on the telly now, on the BBC. Does that *News Tonight* show every now and then.'

'Oh yes I remember her all right,' Parrish said, suddenly calm again, 'with her so-called investigation which was nothing but vile insinuation. But she found nothing then, just as you won't find anything now Inspector.'

There was no hiding the arrogance in his tone, and as certain as Frank was that this unlikeable man had something to hide, he was equally certain that he would never be brought to justice. But that didn't mean Frank was going to give up on it. No way.

'There's another wee thing the honours folks seem to be getting their knickers in a twist about,' he said, changing the subject, 'and it's whether you were already conducting a relationship with Petra whilst you were still married to Kelly. I mean it all seems like moral bollocks to me in this day and age, and really, who cares about that kind of stuff, but there it is.'

He saw the look of disquiet that passed over the beautiful face of Dawn Parrish as he said it. Or was it a look of guilt, he wondered, driven by the fact they had been conducting an affair whilst he was still married to Petra? Or worse still, had she known in advance about his plans to murder Petra, perhaps even egging him on like some modern-day Lady Macbeth, until he had carried out the dreadful deed?

'Kelly had issues with her mental health throughout our marriage,' Parrish said smoothly. 'I did everything I could to help her, but in the end she was overcome by her illness. As you said, it was a great tragedy. But life must continue, that's the fact of the matter.'

Out of the blue Ronnie French said, 'You don't think she might have topped herself because she found out you were shagging that Petra bird?'

Parrish leapt to his feet and for a moment Frank thought he was going to swing a punch at French.

'How dare you,' he bellowed, his face turning crimson. 'How dare you make that vile accusation. I won't have it, and in my own home of all places.'

Frank gave him an apologetic look. 'Aye DC French, you should apologise to Dr Parrish right away. But to be fair sir, my DC's just saying out loud what a lot of the honours committee folks seem to be saying too. A load of nonsense of course, that's my opinion. I wouldn't say you have much to worry about in that regard sir.'

For a moment, Parrish seemed unsure how to react. Frank guessed his emotions would be urging him to throw them both out, but cold hard logic would be dictating otherwise. These two policemen for whatever reason had been given the job of vetting his suitability for the knighthood he coveted so much. It wouldn't pay to get on the wrong side of them, that's what he would be thinking.

'No need to apologise,' he said finally. 'I know you're only doing your job. And of course, I'll be happy to help you in any way I can.'

Frank nodded. 'Aye, well that's very good of you sir. And just to let you know, we'll be doing a wee review of all the paperwork, strictly routine as I said. Probably a waste of time but what the PM wants, the PM gets, isn't that right sir?'

He looked across at Dawn Parrish, who had been silent throughout, and looking more and more uncomfortable by the minute. He wondered if perhaps there was already a fifth Mrs Parrish on the horizon, evidenced by the unexplained bills on his credit card, the late nights, the unexpected stays away from home. And perhaps she was wondering if the same fate as Kelly and Petra might await her too.

But none of that was concerning Frank at that moment. Because he was thinking back to earlier in the meeting. *The tragic events all these years ago*. That's what he had said, and there could surely have been no doubt which events he had been referring to. And yet Parrish had seemed confused, unsure, momentarily losing his composure. *What do you mean?*

Frank allowed himself a quiet smile of satisfaction. So there was something else. Something from the past that Parrish had cause to worry about. With less than three weeks to go until the Sir Patrick-imposed deadline, he and Frenchie had better get their skates on if they were to find out what it was.

But they would, of that there was no doubt.

Chapter 14

'When's our appointment with Jolene then?' Jimmy shouted, 'and just to be clear, we're still going ahead with the original plan are we? I mean, to ask her outright what it might mean?'

They'd been back at Addison Redburn for more than two and a half hours, the vagaries of the hot-desking system placing them six desks away from each other in the big open-plan office. There was nothing much to do but spin the wheels until they met once more with the witch-bitch, but as Maggie had pointed out, they'd already spent enough time away during their short assignment to arouse suspicion amongst the other members of Jolene's team about their true role. So reluctantly he had conceded that they would have to put in a few eight o'clock starts like the rest of the drones, but that didn't mean he liked it. In the army, you got up when you were told and for nearly ten years he'd got used to being dragged out of bed at some ungodly hour. Now that he was in civvy street, he liked to take things at a more relaxed pace.

'Just five minutes now,' Maggie said, 'and yes, we're going to ask her what it might mean. Straight out.'

He frowned. '*I know what you did*. That's what the note said. That could cover a multitude of sins, couldn't it? Everything from murder to pinching somebody's lunch from the office fridge.'

'Of course,' Maggie replied, laughing, 'but I'm guessing it must be something more serious that nicking a tuna and sweetcorn sandwich. Anyway, we'll ask her and see what she says.'

Out the corner of his eye, he spotted Emily Smith approaching at pace, hair streaming behind her like a model in one of these shampoo adverts. As their eyes met, she shot him a smile.

'Sorry guys, can I just catch you for a moment,' she said, slightly breathless, 'I'm afraid I noticed you haven't taken our *Commitment to Respect* on-line training course yet. The thing is, it's mandatory for all staff and that includes contractors too. But don't worry, it only takes about twenty minutes. It's multiple choice, you just tick a few boxes.'

He laughed. 'Well I can assure you that me and Maggie are fully committed to respecting everyone, whether we've been on the course or not. But sure, we'll take a look at it as soon as we can. We wouldn't want to upset our HR department now, would we?'

There it was once again, that almost imperceptible flutter in his heart that he was beginning to feel every time he was with this lovely woman. He wasn't a fool and he knew that she could just as easily have sent an email reminding them to complete the stupid course. Instead she had delivered it in person, a convenient excuse to see him again, another chance to cast the spell she was slowly weaving, drawing him in like a helpless insect in a spider's web. And the truth was, he didn't care, in fact he was glad of it. Because the news that Flora was seeing someone else had hit him like a hammer blow, and for more than two months he had been barely able to function such was his pain. The fact that it was Hugo Blackman, so bloody smooth, so bloody handsome and so bloody accomplished didn't help matters either. He knew the guy had held a torch for her since they were all at university together, and Jimmy had always considered himself bloody lucky to have won that contest against all the odds. But Hugo had played the long game, keeping in touch, pretending to be a friend when he had only one objective in mind. He must have danced a jig of joy when he heard that Captain Jimmy Stewart had embarked on a crazy affair with the beautiful Swedish country music star Astrid Sorenson, an affair that he now regretted with every fibre of his being. And what hurt the most was that Flora now seemed to have drawn the curtain on that chapter of her life. The bitterness had evidently evaporated and she was now moving on, to use that terrible cliché. Rather than being angry with him, now it seemed she didn't care anymore, and it was that realisation that had extinguished all hope for him, leaving him crushed and defeated.

But now, to employ another terrible cliché, it seemed there was light at the end of the tunnel, if only the merest flicker, signifying that after all there could be life after Dr Flora Stewart. It was early days of course, but Emily Smith was sweet and beautiful and quite intoxicating.

'Oh by the way, I've booked us into a little French place for tomorrow evening, I hope you don't mind,' he heard her saying. 'It's unpretentious and not at all expensive and they can squeeze us in before the start of the event. I'm so excited to hear what Freja is going to say, aren't you?'

He caught the look that Maggie gave him, wondering if she was signifying disapproval or simply amusement.

'Aye, that will be great,' he said, 'and I think Maggie's going to come along too. That's right, isn't it boss?'

'Yes, I'll be there,' Maggie said, grinning, 'and before you ask, I'll give the dinner a miss.'

He saw her tap her watch. 'We're due in front of the witch-bitch in one minute. You know how much she hates lateness so we'd better get moving. No doubt I'll see you tomorrow evening Emily.'

He expected Maggie to say something as they traipsed up the stairs to Jolene's floor and he wasn't disappointed.

'*I've booked us in to a little French place. It's not at all expensive.* God, she's an operator, isn't she? You'd better watch yourself Jimmy Stewart, that's all I can say. Because I would say she's quite determined to get her claws into you.'

He laughed. 'Aye, maybe. But we're only going to a wee boring climate change event after all. It's not exactly the most romantic of settings. And anyway, you're going to be there to look after me. *Mum.*'

'Mum? You cheeky pig,' Maggie laughed. 'I'm not that bloody old, although I must admit I do feel it in *her* company.'

'There's ten years' age difference between you and me by my computation, so I suppose whilst it is just technically and biologically possible, it is highly improbable, I concede that. You being my mum I mean.'

'Well thanks very much for that,' she said, still laughing. 'Anyway, enough of this hilarity, are we all set for our Jolene meeting?'

'Roger that.'

As they approached her glass-fronted office, they could hear the raised voices.

'Oh-oh,' Jimmy said. 'Something's kicking off.'

Closer up, it wasn't difficult to make out what was being said. Or rather, being shouted.

'You made me look a complete imbecile in front of the client, both of you. It was nothing short of a frigging disaster.' Jolene was pacing around the office, her face wearing a scowl. Through the glass, he could see there were three other people in the room. Harry Newton, Lily Wu and Jolene's PA Kylie Winterburn.

'I don't know how this could have happened Jolene,' Harry said, looking perplexed and worried at the same time. 'We crossed-checked that contract, Lily and I, very thoroughly, I know we did. Something must have gone wrong with the collating machine, that's all I can think of.'

Jolene caught sight of them through the window and indicated that they should come in. Jimmy winked at Maggie as he pushed the door open. 'This should be interesting boss,' he whispered, 'and at least we can't be accused of being late.'

'Ah, Maggie and Jimmy, our intrepid investigators, welcome to the latest Newton and Wu screw-up,' Jolene said, her tone thick with sarcasm, 'and what good fortune you should join us at this point. So what shall we call this one? How about the case of the missing section? And not just any old section either, oh no. It was *only* the one that laid out the full terms of the financial settlement, and the only thing the client is really interested in. But of course these two *highly-skilled* lawyers decided it was so unimportant that it could quite simply be left out of the contract. Can you believe that?'

'It wasn't like that,' Lily said. 'When we uploaded the document on to the office server it was complete. So the pricing section must have got omitted when Kylie sent it to the document printer. Maybe she forgot to push it through the binder or something.'

'No way can you blame this on me,' the PA said haughtily. 'Jolene, it's a hands-off operation, you know that. I just forward what's on the server onto the printer. All I do is enter the number of copies then go and collect the bound copies from the collator. And that *never* goes wrong, it's automatic.'

'Yes, I know that dear,' Jolene said, 'and it is rather pathetic to try to blame a junior member of staff for your own foul-ups. I'm not surprised that you were involved with this Lily, because you've always been useless haven't you? And you Harry are worse, if in fact that is possible. I wouldn't have believed so myself, but you seem determined to prove me wrong.'

Jimmy heard Maggie give an audible gasp in response to the sheer malevolence of Jolene's words. And as he looked at

Harry Newton, he recognised something he'd seen plenty of times in the army. There, it was the caricature nasty sergeant-major picking on the most hopeless soldier in the platoon, his relentless attacks driving the man to breaking point. And he'd seen every reaction too, from the victim bursting into tears to him sticking a bayonet into the unfortunate RSM's gut. But in the army it was done for a reason, to toughen them up for the time when they would face a real enemy on a battleground. As for Jolene Cavendish, he guessed she did it simply because she could. But the fact was, if you chose to drive someone to breaking point, there was no predicting the consequences and so you'd better be ready for it. Something that she was about to find out, because now Harry Newton was on his feet, his hands shaking, his eyes blazing with venom. This was the moment when the worm turned.

He walked up to her and jabbed a finger in her chest, his face a mere few inches from hers.

'Screw you Jolene, screw you. Believe me, you're going to regret you ever said any of that. Trust me, I'm going to make bloody sure you do. And the meantime, you can take your stupid bloody contract and stick it right up your fat arse. *Witch-Bitch.*'

*****

Frank had spent the morning shuttling to and fro between his desk and Atlee House's hi-tech vending facility whilst he tried to figure out where the hell to go next on the Parrish case. Onto his fourth coffee with the wall-clock barely having reached eleven and three Twix bars down, the caffeine and sugar infusion had only seemed to increase the fuddle in his brain rather than clear it as he had hoped it would. The trouble was that looming bloody deadline, now only sixteen days away by his calculation, the date when the Prime Minister had to make up his mind about that bloody knighthood. The Petra Parrish drowning was a dead duck, even if more than ever he was quite certain the guy was guilty, and even if Parrish seemed to have something else to hide, god knows how he was going to dig that up in little more than a fortnight. All-in-all, it was looking a bit bleak.

Adding to his frustration was the fact that both Eleanor Campbell and Ronnie French had imposed radio silence with regard to their keep-Atlee-open scheming. Something was going on, he was sure of that, but whether they were working together or independently he did not know, and the lack of progress reports from either of them was doing his head in. Ruefully, he recognised that must be how his boss DCI Jill Smart felt most of the time, given his own reluctance to tell her what he got up to day-to-day.

The only chink of light on the horizon was that he'd received a text the previous evening from Katherine McNally of the BBC, informing him she was in London for her *News Tonight* duties and asking if they could meet for an early dinner when she would bring him up to speed on what she described as a couple of developments in the Parrish case. *The Parrish case.* For the first time he realised the case didn't even have a proper bloody name. He always liked to give his investigations a decent name, something evocative and catchy, because somehow a decent name served to lubricate the little grey cells. Sir Patrick *The Aphrodite Suicides,* now that was a good one from the past, somehow nailing the very essence of what turned out to be a very thorny investigation. *The Leonardo Murders,* that was a good one too. This one though was proving a bit trickier. The Knighthood Affair? Too clunky by a mile. So for the time being, it would just have to be the Parrish case. Dull admittedly, but it would get the job done for now until he came up with something better.

To be honest, he hadn't expected to hear from Katherine after the way they'd left things at their last encounter. Or to be more precise, the way *he'd* left things. Because to his astonishment or more accurately, his bewilderment, it seemed that she had been expecting that they would actually sleep together that evening. He was supposed to be the blooming detective, but it hadn't occurred to him for a moment how odd it had been that she had invited him to her place for dinner rather than opting for a restaurant. At the time, he'd assumed she was just being hospitable, and he had accepted her invitation on that basis. True, she was damned attractive, something he couldn't deny and wasn't trying to, but it hadn't occurred to him for a second that the attraction could possibly be mutual. All he could say looking back was that it had been a bloody awkward situation and no mistake. *Shall we go through to the bedroom?* He'd heard the words all right, but he hadn't been able to make sense of any of it. *What, do you mean to have sex?* Crass though it undoubtedly was, and rude to boot, that's exactly what he'd said, staring at her open-mouthed, rooted to the spot like a rabbit caught in the headlights. Then if that hadn't been bad enough, in his panic he'd come up with a second gem of dialogue, sounding for all the world like a bad actor in a badly-written play. *Actually, there's someone else.* It was the first semi-sensible thing that had come into his head, and he was glad he had thought of it, because it had had the effect he was hoping it would have, she apologizing but seemingly untroubled by the rebuff. The only thing was, he had thought of it before he had thought of Maggie. Shameful, that.

Now he found himself confused, because contrary to his expectations, he was looking forward to dinner with Katherine. Some of that was curiosity, interested to find out what she had uncovered about Parrish, but not all of it. Much of it he realised to his mild dismay, was good old-fashioned lust. To make matters worse, it was a Thursday of all nights, meaning he would have to give his normal King's Head drinking session with Maggie and Jimmy a miss again. The more he thought of it, the more he knew his brother was right. He and Maggie need to get themselves sorted out. If she was still talking to him, that was.

The restaurant was a stone's throw from the Portland Place headquarters of the BBC, selected he realised because Katherine was due on air later that evening. A waiter welcomed him then led him to their table, where she sat waiting, smiling as he approached. She was dressed in a plain but classy tailored dress in a subdued red hue, garnished by a simple pearl necklace. Her hair hung in ringlets on her shoulders, casual-looking but probably the expert work of the broadcaster's styling and make-up team.

'Hi Frank, good to see you,' she said, 'and sorry it was such short notice.'

He had been expecting the atmosphere to be mildly tricky, but to his relief she was showing no signs of it.

'No bother,' he said. 'You know us cops are always on duty, twenty-four-seven. Dedicated to public service.'

She laughed. 'Good to hear it.' She gave the menu a quick glance. 'It'll just have to be one course if that's ok by you. I've got to get back to W1A for the editorial review.'

'Sounds important,' he said. 'Not that I know what one of these is.'

'They're deadly boring generally. But not tonight, as it happens. Which is why I wanted to meet with you.'

'The Parrish case. These developments you mentioned?'

'Exactly. Look I'm just going to get a quick chicken salad from their set menu. What about you?'

'Same for me,' he said, without looking and forgetting momentarily how much he hated salads of any description.

A waitress glided up to their table, seemingly unfazed by the presence of the celebrity diner. Then again, Frank reflected, with the restaurant's proximity to the BBC, it was probably nonentities like himself that were the rarity in this place. She punched their order into a tablet computer and retreated, returning half a minute later with a jug of iced water. It looked like it was destined to be a dry evening, but he wasn't exactly surprised by that. Inebriation wasn't a good look for the presenter of the nation's most prestigious news analysis show, even though it would have been way more entertaining for the audience.

'So tonight we're running an interesting piece in our *Tomorrow's Newspapers* spot,' Katherine said. 'It's been given to us by *The Chronicle* in advance of publication and I think it's going to be a big scoop for them.'

'So why have they given it to you guys?' Frank said, looking puzzled. 'Because then it won't be a scoop surely?'

'Publicity of course. Think of it as free advertising. People will see our piece tonight and go out and buy the newspaper the next day. It's pretty common in the news game. A sort of you-scratch-my-back-and-I'll-scratch-yours.'

'Got it,' Frank said, unsure if he actually did.

'So Frank, do you remember that horrible tragedy in Syria a few months ago, when these little twin girls were blown up by a government land-mine?'

'It's wall-to-wall tragedy over there,' Frank said, nodding, 'but aye, I remember it. They suffered appalling injuries, and just because they were in the wrong place at the wrong time.'

'That's them. So tomorrow, the Chronicle is going to be breaking the story that James Parrish is planning to fly them to London and treat them, and all at his own expense. Guy's Hospital are putting an operating suite at his disposal and the newspaper are providing some funds for the transportation, but Parrish is going to be paying for all the staff costs and the aftercare too. There won't be much change from three hundred grand according to folks who know the cost of these things.'

'Christ, he *is* making a bid for sainthood, isn't he?'

'It seems like it. Of course the Chronicle are just loving all of this and you can bet your backside they'll be doubling down on their knighthood-for-Parrish campaign.'

Frank sighed. 'Brilliant, that's all I need.'

'Yes, I realise it's not good news for you,' she said, looking sympathetic, 'but I thought I ought to tell you anyway.'

He gave a rueful smile. 'Aye, and I'm grateful, honestly Katherine, and I'm happy for the wee girls too of course. But you know there's this bloody deadline before the PM has to go public on his decision and this isn't going to exactly help us.'

'I can see that. But actually, something else has come up, which might be rather interesting.'

'Really?' He shot out the word, as he focussed on what she had just said. Because he could tell by her tone that that was going to be more than just rather interesting.

'Yes, well I think so. You know of course that his second wife died of an overdose?'

'Aye Kelly, that was her name. And the Coroner passed an open verdict as to whether it was deliberate or accidental.'

'That's right.' She took a sip of her water and brushed her hair back from her face. 'So at the time I was investigating Petra's drowning, I did take a look at the Kelly death too. I didn't get too far with that one because my editor wanted me to move onto another story, but there were a couple of things I dug up that made me feel uneasy about it. And then when you brought the Parrish affair to my attention, it made me think about it again and I did some more investigating. Just in the last couple of days in fact.'

'Go on.' Now she had his full attention, his mind racing as he speculated on what she might be about to reveal.

'So the drug that she took, the one that killed her...'

'Amy-something-or other.'

She nodded. 'Yes, that's right. Amytriptilene. You see, it's quite a specialised drug and rather out of fashion because of its highly-addictive properties. Most doctors wouldn't prescribe it nowadays.'

'But Kelly Parrish's doctor did.' Frank said. 'This Dr Tanvi Patel guy.'

'So you know about that?' she said, sounding surprised. 'But actually, Dr Patel is a woman.'

'We just got the name,' he said, feeling faintly embarrassed. 'Nothing else. It was kind of on my to-do list to dig a wee bit deeper, but it seems you got there first.'

'So I guess there's quite a bit more you don't know about Dr Patel,' she said teasingly.

He laughed. 'Assume nothing and you'll be about right.'

'Well I'm the first to admit I had the benefit of a team of first-rate BBC newshounds helping me out. They were sitting around Broadcasting House with nothing much to get their teeth into, so I set them loose on it. That's the benefit of my exalted status in this great corporation. I get to order people around as and when I see fit.' She said it with a twinkle in her eye, but Frank had no doubt that it was true. Katherine McNally was BBC royalty.

'So first of all,' she continued, 'would you believe that Dr Patel was an exact contemporary of James Parrish? Yes that's right, they were at Glasgow Uni together and graduated at the same time.'

'So they might have been friends?' Frank said, thinking out loud. And knowing what he knew about Parrish's fondness for the opposite sex, maybe they had been friends with benefits too.

She nodded. 'Maybe they were, but it seems unlikely that we'll ever know that for certain. You see, Dr Tanvi Patel took her own life three years ago.'

'What?'

'Yes, that's right. It seems she was about to get struck off the medical register for bringing the profession into disrepute. And worse than that too, she was looking at spending the rest of her life in prison. For murder as it happens.'

He looked at her in astonishment. 'Murder? That's a serious charge.'

'You're right, it was *bloody* serious. She was selling assisted suicide services, for want of a better description. Euthanasia, to give it its scientific term.'

'What, do you mean she was *killing* people? Christ's sake.'

'Helping them to take their own lives,' Katherine said, 'but it amounts to the same thing.'

'So why didn't the story get into the media?' Frank said, frowning. 'Because I don't remember reading anything about it back then and I would have thought it would have been all over the front pages. You guys asleep at the wheel or what?'

'Yes it would have been quite a story,' she said, almost wistfully, 'but it turns out that Patel was shopped by one of her colleagues in her practice who was getting suspicious about her activities, and when the truth started to emerge then the British Medical Association dived into to hush the whole thing up. I guess it's a difficult ethical area for the profession, because the victims, if that's the correct description, are willing victims, aren't they? People whose life has become so intolerable through illness that they would rather die.'

'Aye, and I can imagine it sent the Crown Prosecutors into a right tizz. Because what would be gained from a prosecution when the victims dearly wanted it to happen? And yet the law is the law, and you can't really have doctors going around playing god. So she would have to have faced a murder rap, whether the authorities liked it or not. Otherwise there would have been a public outcry.'

Katherine nodded. 'Yes, it's a difficult one, the whole subject. But fortunately or unfortunately, I don't know which, Dr Patel saved everybody a whole lot of trouble by killing herself. It seems the CPS then decided it was best to sweep the whole thing under the carpet, and that's what happened, hence no press.'

'So I guess we'll never know what to make of this Doctor Patel,' Frank said. 'Was she a greedy money-grabbing leech with no morals or a courageous crusader trying to help desperate families end the suffering of their loved ones?'

'She was in it for the money, I'm pretty sure of that,' Katherine said firmly. 'One of my reporters managed to trace one of the families, and they told him she had been paid a hundred grand.'

'A tidy sum indeed,' he said, 'and maybe it gives us some insight into her morality, because as the old saying goes, a leopard seldom changes its spots.'

She frowned. 'So are you thinking that Dr Patel was in cahoots with Parrish to get rid of his second wife? A kind of medical killer for hire? That seems a big leap of logic to me.'

'Well why not Katherine?' he said, raising an eyebrow. 'It's all pure conjecture I know, but there must be at least an even chance, wouldn't you say?'

She was right of course, it was a big leap in logic, but this wasn't about logic, it was about gut feel, and in his gut he was sure he was right. Doctor Tanvi Patel had seemingly been exposed as a practitioner who was happy to play fast and loose with the ethical standards of her profession in return for financial reward, so who was to say she hadn't been doing this all the way through her career? A call from an old University pal, a bothersome wife prone to depression who was getting in the way of this old friend's wonderful new life. *Don't worry, I'll make it worth your while.* So the good doctor Patel prescribes a steady dose of Amytriptilene, perhaps an unconventional treatment but nothing illegal or even unethical about it, should anyone start to pry. All they had to do was ensure there was plenty of the stuff in Kelly Parrish's medicine cabinet and it would be well-nigh impossible to prove foul play if indeed that was what had happened.

'Sorry Frank, are you still with me?' Katherine said, laughing.

'What? No no, I was just thinking about this Patel thing. You know the problem is Katherine, it's a bit like the bloody drowning. There's plenty of circumstantial evidence but absolutely no way of proving it. And without proof, there's nothing much we can do about it.'

She shook her head. 'So James Parrish gets away with two murders then, does he? It's outrageous really, when you think about it.'

Frank shrugged. 'God knows. Maybe he's completely innocent and he's just been visited by terrible tragedy. It happens, and you see it in this job quite a lot. Tragedy I mean.'

But he knew that wasn't what had happened here. *One hundred percent.* It had been a tragedy for the two women but he was becoming more certain by the minute that these had been no accidents. And now, with Sir Patrick Hopkins' deadline looming he had to flesh out a half-decent plan of action. The more he thought about it, the more it seemed there was already a big enough pile of crap surrounding James Parrish to make anyone think twice about his character, and if he himself was the Prime Minister, he wouldn't touch the bloody knighthood with a bargepole. But then again, he wasn't launching a re-election campaign, a campaign which in reality was going to be a popularity contest between the incumbent and the charismatic leader of the opposition. He understood why the PM needed a big triumph, just like Department 12B needed to nail this case to knock all the closing-it-down nonsense on the head. No doubt about it, the stakes were sky-high for everyone.

So, to the plan. With what he now knew about Dr Tanvi Patel, there was plenty of ammunition to go back to James Parrish and open up the overdose case again. No proof of course, but contrary to what he had told Katherine, that didn't matter. The idea was to put pressure on Parrish. Ask him about the state of mind of his wife at the time of her death and about his questionable relationship with his university buddy. *See if he lets anything slip.* And this time, Frank was going to leave the task in the hands of Ronnie French, who had already demonstrated a talent for getting right up the pompous surgeon's nose. And as for himself, he now understood where he needed to focus his attention. *The tragic events all those years ago. A leopard never changes its spots.* He had to go back in time, dive deeper into Parrish's life story. Because it was highly probable that a man who had killed twice would have plenty more to hide.

To his horror, he realised he had drifted off into his own thoughts again and that Katherine was speaking. And as he listened to what she was saying, he felt his heart-rate creeping upwards, purely involuntarily.

'Look, I need to get back to the studios. I hope it's been worthwhile.' She raised a hand to signal to a passing waitress. As she handed the girl her credit card, she turned to him and said, quite casually, 'By the way, I'm staying at the Radisson tonight. It's just around the corner, I'm sure you know it. Just in case you fancy a little nightcap after I'm done with the programme. And they do a nice breakfast too.'

Bloody hell.

Chapter 15

As Maggie had expected, Freja Portman's return to the Park Lane Hilton had drawn out the world's media in their hoards. The hotel's management had allocated their largest public room to the teenager's climate-change symposium, but it was obvious that it was way too small to accommodate even half the number of hacks who had turned up to cover the story. As a result, the circus had spilled over into the entrance atrium, the air ripe with expletives as frazzled TV news producers yelled into their phones, struggling to make themselves heard whilst trying to explain to unsympathetic bosses why their crews had been excluded from the main hall. Making matters worse, a rumour had been circulating that the Prime Minister himself was to make a surprise appearance on the podium, hoping no doubt to benefit from the reflected glory of association with the environmental superstar. Maggie could understand the attraction in this election year. Freja had a social media following than ran to millions in the UK and fifty times that across the world. The prize for any politician who could demonstrate sincere-sounding support for her cause was huge, particularly because her following largely comprised a young and educated demographic that mainstream politics traditionally struggled to connect with. The trouble was, Maggie reflected, the PM wasn't very good at sounding sincere about anything.

Whether he was due to appear or not, this time the Metropolitan Police had not made the mistake they had made the first time round, a mistake that continued to haunt them with the failure to catch the perpetrator of the acid attack on the teenage activist. This time the place was wall-to-wall with uniformed officers in body armour, Koch semi-automatics held tight across their chests, every audience member pre-vetted and subject to a thorough and intrusive body-search before being allowed into the room. Additionally, it had emerged that Freja was to give her talk behind a sturdy transparent perspex screen, offering a layer of physical protection should some right-wing nutter with a grudge manage to evade the omnipresent security.

The original plan was to meet up with Jimmy and Emily Smith in reception so that they could be seated together. At least, that had been *her* idea. She suspected that the beautiful Miss Smith, fresh from her cosy little dinner with Jimmy, might have been thinking otherwise, keen to continue the process of wrapping her tentacles around his soul, unencumbered by the presence of a frumpy chaperone. In the event, the situation had been taken out of their hands by the hotel's hired-in stewards, who were not allowing any of the symposium attendees to linger in the reception atrium. As soon as Maggie had emerged from the revolving entrance door, she had been hustled through a security scanner and into the search area, then led to an allocated seat towards the rear of the conference room, her protests that she was meeting someone firmly and non-too-politely ignored. With more than half an hour before Freja was due on the platform, there was nothing to do but twiddle her thumbs and keep an eye out for the arrival of her colleague and his new friend. Giving her time too to reflect on why Jimmy's embryonic relationship with the lovely Emily should be bothering her so much. Not jealousy of course, because although Jimmy was as attractive a man as God had ever put on this planet, she knew she admired him more as a work of art rather than harbouring any feelings of *that* kind for him. It was just she couldn't help thinking that he was rushing into this new relationship without properly thinking it through. It was little more than three weeks ago since he had been hitting the bottle, as he tried to erase from his mind the devastating image of his adored wife Flora lying in the arms of another man. Maggie knew how much he loved her, yet now he seemed to be sweeping it all in to the dustbin of the past as if it had never existed. But really, what business was it of hers? When it came down to it, he was only her work colleague for goodness sake and she had no right to poke her nose into his affairs. But that didn't mean she didn't care about him deeply. He had been her saviour when her life had spiralled out of control and for that she was forever in his debt. Maybe this affair with Emily was the real thing or maybe it wasn't, only time would tell, but however it turned out, she was determined that she wouldn't let it hurt him.

'Hey Maggie!'

Snapped out of her reflections by Jimmy's shout, she looked up to see them shuffling along the row of seats directly in front of her, trailed by a protesting steward who evidently wished they should follow him to a row at the front of the room.

'You has to go to your allocated seats Miss,' she heard the steward say to Emily. 'It's for security, so the computer knows who's where, in case anything kicks off.'

'Aye, we understand,' Jimmy said, pointing at Maggie. 'But we just need to have a quick word with this lady here. She's my boss you see.' He gave the steward a knowing look, as if to *say bosses, we've all got them haven't we?*

'Yeah all right mate,' the steward said, with evident reluctance, 'but just two minutes and no more, got that? Then you goes to your own seats and no messing about.'

'Roger that,' Jimmy said, giving him a thumbs-up.

Maggie stood up to greet them, and as she did, she noticed it. *They were holding hands.* Now for the first time she recognised the speed at which this thing was moving, the act a certain indicator of the easy intimacy that was developing between them. There could be little doubt about it. Jimmy Stewart and Emily Smith were now an item.

'How was your dinner?' she said, forcing a smile.

'Lovely,' they said in unison, causing them to burst out laughing. God she thought, they're acting like a pair of giddy teenagers. More proof if she needed it of how things stood.

'Aye, it was really excellent,' Jimmy said, wearing a mischievous grin. 'Fabulous food and a great atmosphere. Sort of French but with a definite international slant I'd say.'

She laughed. 'So says Jimmy Stewart the world-renowned food critic.' As she said it, she noticed that Emily was looking at her with an expression that Maggie recognised. The same expression that her dead husband's lover had been wearing when she had caught them in post-coital dishevelment in

Maggie's own kitchen. She remembered it as if it was only yesterday, the sultry Mediterranean beauty Angelique Perez half-wearing one of Phillip's shirts, looking so young and so lovely but above all, so bloody triumphant. It was that look of triumph that she now saw on the face of Emily Smith, a look that said *he's mine now and you can't have him*. Which Maggie found rather odd, because it was not as if she could ever be considered a rival for Jimmy's affections. But then again, perhaps Emily hadn't worked that one out yet. It was just as well she hadn't yet met Elsa Berger, because then she would know what a love rival *really* looked like.

'They're saying the PM might turn up,' Jimmy said. 'I see there's two chairs on the platform.'

'Yes, I've heard that. I'd be surprised if he does, but you never know.'

'Aye, well I thought we'd better touch base,' he said, a little awkwardly. 'So anyway, I suppose Emily and I should mosey along down to our seats before we get chucked out. That steward guy looked as if he meant business.'

'Yes come on darling,' Emily said, squeezing his hand tighter. 'We wouldn't want to miss it, would we?'

Darling. Bloody hell, this thing *was* moving fast. Too fast for Maggie's liking but she recognised there was sod-all she could do about it. As they went off to claim their seats, her attention was drawn to the side of the room where she observed a uniformed policeman engaged in earnest conversation with another of the stewards. In his hand the policeman held a flip-topped notebook, and she smiled as she saw him take a pencil or pen from behind his ear and scribble something on the pad. She guessed he wasn't part of the security detachment because he wasn't wearing the body-armour and navy baseball cap that was part of their attire, and he wasn't young and fit-looking like the others either. He was hatless, and under his part-unbuttoned tunic he wore an open-necked white shirt, or at least it probably had been white when first taken out of its packaging several years in the past. Now it was more a dull grey, adding to the general air of sartorial disarray.

He seemed to sense her eyes on him, because suddenly he turned round to look at her, then frowned as if trying to work out whether he recognised her or not. She, on the other hand, had recognised him instantly. She watched as he excused himself from his interview and made his way over to her.

'DC French, isn't it?' she said, smiling. 'From Department 12B.'

'That's right. And you're that Maggie-whatsit woman, from the Alzahrani case and all that. And of course you're DI Stewart's missus, aren't you? He's my guv'nor of course. Sound bloke he is, even though he's a Jock.'

She gave him a wry smile. 'Is that what he told you Ronnie? That I was his *missus*?'

'No no,' he said hastily. 'Nothing like that, it's just me putting two and two together. You see, he talks about you a lot, all casual like, but it don't fool me one bit. I'm a detective, remember? It's what I do. Sniff out the truth.'

'Well I think in this case you're on the wrong track DC French, because if your guv'nor was the last man on earth I wouldn't be his missus, and you can tell him that from me when you see him.'

He gave her an uncertain look, evidently unsure whether she was being serious or not. Eventually he said, 'Sorry ma'am, but the Met don't do domestics. You'll have to tell him yourself.'

She laughed. 'No, I'm sure you don't, and yes I bloody will tell him, take it from me. Anyway, why are you here? Are you an environmentalist then Ronnie?'

He frowned. 'Nah, it's all bollocks ain't it? Eco-mentalists that's what I call them. The fuzzy-faces used to say it was global warming but then we had a few cold winters so suddenly it became climate change. I mean that *is* bollocks don't you think? It's just weather, that's my opinion for what it's worth. But don't get me wrong, she's a smart bird that Freja and I was disgusted with what happened to her. And let's face it, it's not exactly been our finest hour neither.'

'So still no breakthrough in the investigation then?' she asked him, although she already knew the answer.

'Nah, it's been totally hopeless. We've had our anti-terrorist boys rounding up everyone who's ever posted anything nasty about the girl online, plus all the usual right-wing suspects and the football hooligan crews have been hauled in for questioning, but absolutely nothing's turned up so far. Actually, that's why I toodled along here tonight. Just to take a look at the crime scene. Out of interest you know.'

She gave him a sharp look. 'So has your department been moved on to the case then?' If that was what had happened, then she was surprised that Frank hadn't mentioned it in one of their Thursday night sessions. But then she remembered that he had called off the last two get-togethers due to work commitments and so she hadn't seen him for nearly three weeks. And then she remembered she was supposed to be angry with him.

French gave her a look of alarm. 'Christ no, can you imagine the shit in the press if it came out that the force had already stopped looking for the acid guy and had bumped it off to some cold-case mob? No way is that going to happen, not in a month of Sundays.'

'But you're here Ronnie. So what is it, a bit of private enterprise?'

He frowned. 'Look, promise me you won't grass me up to my boss, he'll go mental if he finds out. As I said, it's just that I wanted to see for myself, ask a few questions, see if anything obvious had been missed. That was all. Nothing official-like.'

'And yet you're in uniform.'

He gave her a hang-dog look. 'Haven't you heard our top brass on the telly? Visible police presence on the streets ma'am. Makes the public feel safer. I'm just doing my bit.'

'Good to know,' she said, laughing. 'Anyway, it shouldn't be long before Miss Portman appears. I'm really looking forward to hearing what she has to say.'

'Yeah, me too,' he said, sounding anything but convincing. 'But actually, I wondered if you wouldn't mind hanging about for five minutes at the end? I think I might need to ask a little favour of you.'

*****

Freja Portman strode on to the platform to a tsunami of applause and not just from the paying audience but from the assembled media too, who rose to their feet as one in a show of spontaneous appreciation. She raised an acknowledging hand in a gesture that was almost presidential and then turned to welcome a second figure on to the stage, a smartly-groomed and attractive woman in her mid-forties who Maggie instantly recognised. Katherine McNally, one of the super-competent anchors of the BBC's *The News Tonight* current affairs show and by some ridiculous coincidence, the same Katherine McNally who over ten years ago had investigated the circumstances surrounding the suspicious drowning of surgeon James Parrish's third wife on beautiful Loch More. And who had met with bloody Frank Stewart on at least two occasions in the recent past to discuss the self-same subject. It occurred to her now that he'd not said much about their meetings, and she'd already noted that Ms. McNally was not wearing a ring of any description on her wedding finger. For a moment she wondered, and then smiled as she thought about it again. Frank and Katherine McNally of the BBC? *No chance.*

Freja and Katherine shook hands warmly as they posed for the cameras, the presence of the news anchor answering the question as to who was to occupy the second chair and thus ending speculation that the PM was to put in an appearance. Evidently this was to be a smoothly-scripted question-and-answer session, a professional operation designed to produce the slick media packages that would soon play out on a thousand news channels across the globe. In the auditorium, images of the two were being beamed onto a huge screen on the wall behind them, allowing Maggie to scrutinise at close quarters the amazing work of Freja's reconstructive surgeon, work that had been the subject of endless comment on social media. As normal, she was dressed in one of her sweet little flowery-print cotton dresses which suited her tall slim frame. Nature having blessed her with a body to die for, now James Parrish had created for her the most beautiful face to complete the package. Huge eyes, sculpted cheek-bones, a wide mouth and flawless skin, she had become a living Botticelli. In the front row of the room sat her parents Brian and Hermione, her father a left-leaning journalist who for thirty years or more had promulgated his controversial views on the future of the planet, her mother a doctor who spent much of Freja's childhood working for an international charity, prepared to leave her daughter in a heartbeat to rush to whichever of the world's human disaster zones was currently top of the news agenda. It was thus hardly surprising that young Freja had grown up with the same radical-progressive mindset. It was almost like a religion, Maggie suspected, the child brainwashed to adopt the world view of her parents without question. She wondered if one day the child might rebel, throwing off the beliefs of her elders in the same way that so many cast off religion when they were old enough to think for themselves. Now that *really* would be a story. But looking now at the poised young woman on the platform, she knew that was never going to happen. Brand Portman was already too big, and it was only going to get bigger.

In truth, the interview was turning out to be a rather a low-key affair covering familiar ground, Ms. McNally evidently having been directed to avoid asking any awkward questions, such as how the headlong rush to a zero-emission future was going to be paid for. But it was impossible not to be persuaded of the need for action by Freja's impassioned logic, even if the outcome seemed to Maggie like a retreat to a pre-industrial age when everyone lived off the fruits of the land and spent an entire lifetime within a few miles of their birthplace. It was a hard sell, but Portman had already succeeded in capturing the hearts and minds of the educated youth of the world and in twenty years' time it would be they who would be running things. It would be interesting to see if their idealism survived a bruising car-crash with harsh economic reality.

As well as being quite predictable, the talk went on a bit and soon she found her attention drifting. From where she sat, she could just about make out the backs of the heads of Jimmy and Emily. A few minutes into the session, she had seen Emily place her head casually on his shoulder, he raising his hand to tenderly stroke her hair. Not long after, she had planted a lingering kiss on his cheek, causing him to turn his head towards her. For a dreadful moment, Maggie thought they were going to have a full-on snog. Thankfully they desisted, but she then found it impossible to erase the image from her head. It seemed unlikely in such a short time, but every indicator was pointing the same way. Jimmy Stewart seemed to be falling in love with Emily Smith.

Thankfully the formal part of the evening was now drawing to a close, McNally thanking Freja for choosing her to conduct the interview and for being so inspiring, particularly after all she had been through. Now the young activist was to take questions from the media and Maggie wondered if they too had been pre-scripted. Looking around the room earlier, she had noted the presence of Yash Patel, a reporter from the Chronicle that she had occasion to work with in the past. Knowing him, there was no way that he would follow any script. His currency was sensation, and the more lurid the better, and she doubted he would be here unless he had something to stir up. But then she remembered that it was his own newspaper that was running the strident campaign to get James Parrish a knighthood. Surely he would have been placed on a three-line whip not to rock the boat? No doubt they would soon find out.

Glancing back to where he sat, she was surprised to see him in deep conversation with Ronnie French who had squeezed his corpulent frame into the chair next to the reporter. Evidently anxious to keep the subject of their talk secret, both were taking the trouble to obscure their mouths with their hands. It seemed to be French who was doing most of the talking, Patel responding from time to time with a vigorous nod of the head. Then they both stood up and shook hands, French giving a thumbs-up as he returned to the side of the room. Patel remained standing, waving an arm in the air in an attempt to catch the eye of McNally, but she was evidently working from a pre-prepared list and studiously ignored his presence.

'So first up we have Richard Frost from ITN,' she said, peering over her elegant reading glasses and scanning the room. 'Richard?'

The reporter raised a hand in acknowledgment then proceeded to ask a question of innocuous banality which Portman answered with polite enthusiasm.

'Penelope Cracknall, The Times. Brian White, The Sun......'

Methodically McNally worked down her list. *Do you acknowledge that not everyone will buy into the economic consequences of climate change? Are you saying we all have to become vegans? Do I need to stop driving my big comfortable SUV?* Portman answered each question with a steely conviction which Maggie found rather chilling. *We don't have any choice to pay whatever it takes if we want to save the world for our children. Livestock grazing is responsible for the production of fourteen-point-six percent of global greenhouse gases so yes we all have to stop eating meat. No-one needs to drive a big SUV when there are clean and efficient electric alternatives.* Chilling or not, there was no denying that the teenage activist was a highly effective figurehead for the cause.

'Yash Patel, the Chronicle!' The reporter's reedy voice carried across the room. 'I've a question. Miss Portman, please.'

Evidently McNally knew who he was, because she smiled and said, 'I'm sorry Yash, but I don't appear to have you on my list.' For some reason, her reply caused an outbreak of merriment amongst the media contingent. It seemed that his reputation went before him, and Maggie suspected he had spent his career forcing his way into events such as these, always with the intent of shaking up the cosy status quo. She thought also there was a hint of mischief in McNally's expression and that a question from the maverick Chronicle journalist might not be entirely unwelcome. However before the host had a chance to react, Freja took the matter out of her hands.

'I'm happy to answer your question Mr Patel,' she said in her trademark furrow-browed voice. 'Please, go ahead.'

'Ah great Freja, sound,' he replied. 'So my question is, as an avowed feminist, how are you going to feel if James Parrish is given a knighthood considering how badly he has treated all the women in his life?'

A gasp of astonishment reverberated around the room as Patel's words began to sink in, media colleagues no doubt speculating with some amusement how his editor was going to react when he found out about this very public slur against the man the paper had spent the last three months championing. Maggie knew that Yash wouldn't give a toss about any of that. All he cared about was his next big scoop, and now she wondered if he, like Katherine McNally before him, might be digging into Parrish's life story. That might explain why he had been talking so earnestly to Ronnie French just a few minutes ago. Were they sharing information, intent on the same goal, which was uncovering any dirty secrets that were buried in the hero surgeon's past?

Freja did not answer for a moment, and when she did speak, there was a definite icy edge to her tone.

'I don't recognise your description of me Mr Patel. I believe everyone has the right to be treated with respect, irrespective of how they self-identify.'

'Yep, I get all that identity stuff, although sometimes I wish that respect got extended to brown-skinned guys like me. But my question really was about the man who made it possible for you to be here today. Do you think he deserves to be honoured? A simple yes or no will do.'

For the first time, she looked unsure of herself, turning to Katherine McNally as if seeking her advice as to how she should answer. Sensing her discomfort, McNally gathered up her papers, placed a hand on Freja's arm and nodded towards the rear door through which they had earlier entered.

'I'm sure Freja is very grateful for everything Mr Parrish has done for her,' she said briskly. 'So if you don't mind ladies and gentlemen, I'd like to bring our evening to a close and it just remains for me to thank you all so much for coming.'

*****

They had arranged they should meet in the atrium, although Maggie doubted whether the threesome would be going for drinks afterwards given how possessive Emily Smith had already become with Jimmy. She estimated there had been close to two hundred people in the room and with her own seat having been right in the centre of the row it took more than five minutes for her to shuffle out into the reception area. Soon she expected to find out what it was that Ronnie French wanted her to do for him, although why he should be needing her services she could not at the moment fathom. The only thing she could be certain of was that knowing French, it would be something a bit suspect.

As she squeezed through the mass of earnest planet-savers emerging from the room, she spotted that French was already there, lounging against a little bar with Yash Patel, beers in hand. She was pretty sure there were rules against drinking whilst in uniform, but that wouldn't be concerning Ronnie one bit, particularly as she suspected that Patel's expense account would be picking up the tab. He had evidently been watching for her to emerge, because on seeing her he waved a hand in the air and yelled across.

'Miss Bainbridge, come over here and grab a drink!' She found it rather endearing that he should address her with professional formality, either using her surname or calling her *ma'am*. 'Don't worry, the boy Yash is paying.'

'Hello Yash,' she said as she arrived at the bar. 'It's been quite a while since our last meeting. What have you been up to?'

'Yeah, it was that Chief Constable business up in Scotland, wasn't it?' he said, smiling. 'I've been busy as you can imagine. Yourself?'

'Yes, all good, thank you.' It was the slightly awkward conversation you had with someone you didn't really know and she was pleased when they were interrupted by the arrival of Jimmy and Emily Smith. Who were still holding hands, Maggie noted with a mixture of amusement and annoyance.

'Wasn't she *wonderful*,' Emily gushed. 'A real inspiration to all of us.'

'Real smart woman,' Jimmy said. 'Like Emily said, Freja's a proper inspiration to us all.'

God, thought Maggie, they're even beginning to bloody *think* the same way, smiling to herself when she imagined how Frank would take the piss out of his brother had he chanced to overhear this sugary exchange.

'Maybe, but she lost my vote when she said we had to give up the Big Macs,' Ronnie said lugubriously. 'No way is that going to happen.' He shot a smile in Jimmy's direction. 'Anyway, I know you, don't I? You're my guv'nor's brother. And you work with Miss Bainbridge here.'

She laughed. 'Please call me Maggie, and you're right, Jimmy and I have the dubious pleasure of working together. What I mean is, it's a dubious pleasure for him.'

'And you're kind of detectives aren't you? Sort of private investigators?'

'Aye we are,' Jimmy said, 'but not so much of the *kind of* and *sort of* if you don't mind. Me and Maggie are professionals I'll have you know. And we've got the business cards to prove it.'

'No offence meant,' French said. 'But it's really handy that you're here too sir... actually, is it all right if I call you Jimmy?'

'Sure.'

'So Maggie and Jimmy.' He reduced his voice to a whisper and shot a furtive glance across the room. 'See that guy over there, standing in front of the reception desk?'

They looked over to where he was pointing. A man in his early twenties wearing a porter's uniform was leaning against the desk, flirting with a pretty receptionist.

'He should be knocking off his shift in five minutes or so. I want you to follow him when he goes. Just round the corner, it shouldn't take you too long, ten minutes at most. I'd do it myself of course but well, with these togs on...' He pointed to his tunic. '... not exactly inconspicuous, is it? Whereas you two, well you would just be a pair of lovers enjoying a night out on the town. He's not going to give you a second glance.'

'A pair of lovers eh?' Maggie said, giving Emily Smith a mischievous half-smile. 'I'm sure we could pull that off, don't you think so Jimmy?'

He laughed and then seemed to think better of it. 'Aye well...,' he said, rather unconvincingly, 'as long as it's only for ten minutes. You ok with that Emily?'

'Don't worry,' French said. 'We'll look after you miss. Yash will get you fixed up with a nice glass of wine and we can all relax until these two get back.'

Emily squeezed Jimmy's arm and planted a light kiss on his cheek. 'Just as long as you hurry back darling.'

Darling. There it was again, the word when taken together with the revolting hand-holding a sure indication of where this worrying relationship was now at.

He smiled. 'Of course I will.' At least he didn't say the damn word back to her, Maggie thought. That would just be too much.

'So what's our mission?' she asked. 'What is it you're trying to find out?'

'Simple job. There's an underground car park just round the corner. On Park Lane. I think that's where he'll be heading, at least according to the information I've been able to wheedle out of his work-mates.'

'What, a hotel porter who can afford to park in Park Lane?' Jimmy said, surprised. 'The tipping must be bloody good in this place.'

'Exactly mate,' French said. 'So that's your mission in a nutshell. Tail him and see if that's where he's heading.'

'And then hang about the entrance to see what sort of motor he's driving?'

'Got it in one Jimmy mate,' French said, giving a thumbs-up. 'Then toodle on back round here and let me know the outcome. And that'll be it, job done. Nice and simple. Five or ten minutes at most. We'll keep the bar warm for you and look after the little lady here.'

The little lady. Maggie laughed at that. Ronnie French, a twentieth-century man all at sea in the twenty-first.

'So what's this all about Ronnie?' she said, raising an eyebrow. 'You and Yash are up to something, I can tell. Has it got something to do with James Parrish?'

He shrugged. 'Maybe, maybe not. Early days.'

She smiled to herself as she recognised one of Frank's favourite sayings. According to him, every investigation was at the early-days stage until about two minutes before he cracked it. But one thing was for certain. Mr Yash Patel of the *Chronicle*, award-winning investigative journalist and general scourge of the Establishment, wouldn't be wasting his time on this if there wasn't a story in it. And not just any old story either, but something big and sensational too. She looked forward to finding out what it was.

'Looks like he's on the move,' Jimmy said, nodding in the porter's direction. He had slipped behind the reception desk and now emerged wearing a mid-length navy wool coat over his uniform. He raised a casual hand to say goodbye to the girl then sauntered towards the revolving doors. Maggie assumed a hotel this swish would have a sort of tradesmen's entrance to handle the comings and goings of their staff, but this guy had an arrogant swagger about him that suggested following rules might not be in his DNA.

'Come on, let's go,' Maggie said, grabbing Jimmy's arm. 'The chase is on.'

'Hardly a chase,' Jimmy said wryly, pointing to the door. 'He's stopped just outside to light a ciggie.'

They waited until he had set off again, then swung through the doors and followed him into Park Lane, being careful to maintain a distance of about thirty metres or so behind. In truth, they need hardly have worried about that because despite the late hour, the pavement was packed with Freja Portman's devoted followers making their way home, chatting excitedly about how they planned to save the world, starting tomorrow. The knee-jerk reaction of the Ronnie Frenchs of this world was cynicism, Maggie realised that, but surely everywhere you looked the evidence was overwhelming. Floods, wild-fires, melting ice-caps, dying coral reefs, you would need to be deaf, dumb and blind not to realise that something out of the ordinary was happening. If it took a teenage firebrand like Freja to make the world see sense, then she was all for it.

'Guy's in no rush,' Jimmy said, pointing ahead. The man had stopped again to re-light his cigarette, cupping it with his hand then discarding the match into the gutter with a deft flick. When he set off again, it was with a more purposeful gate. The crowd was beginning to thin out a bit and so instinctively they held back a little, although he hadn't looked round once since leaving the hotel. Now he was coming up to a swanky car dealership, the soft glow of the showroom lights reflecting off the sleek bodywork and spilling out onto its concourse. He paused for a moment as if deciding whether to take a closer look, but then continued on his way, Maggie guessing that since he passed the place a dozen times a week, the window-shopping could wait for another occasion.

Then just past the showroom, he veered off to the right, along one of the side-streets that presumably led to the underground car-park. This was embassy territory, the street lined with Mercedes, Range-Rovers and Bentleys carrying diplomatic plates which allowed them to ignore the parking tickets that piled up on their windscreens on a daily basis. Now it was just him, Maggie and Jimmy on the quiet street.

'We'd better hold back a bit,' Jimmy said, touching her on the elbow. 'Just in case he looks round.'

She smiled. 'If he does, you'll have to snog me. Then he won't be able to see our faces, and we'll just be a pair of star-crossed lovers out on the town, like Ronnie said.'

'Is that an order boss?' he said, grinning. 'Not that it will be any hardship of course.' Bless him, she thought, he managed to make that sound half-sincere.

'Absolutely, but hopefully it won't be necessary,' she said, thinking the exact opposite, and wondering if it did happen whether they might be able to grab a selfie for the benefit of Emily Smith. Cruel, that.

'Don't see a 'P' sign anywhere, do you?' Jimmy said, peering along the street.

'I doubt if there will be one. I assume the place will be packed full of Lamborghinis and Ferraris and such like. Not something you want to advertise.'

He laughed. 'I didn't take you for a car nerd.'

'I'm not, but Ollie is. He talks about it non-stop at home and his bedroom wall is plastered with pictures so you can't help absorbing some of it.'

Up ahead, they saw the man suddenly stop and fumble in a pocket of his coat.

'This will be it,' Jimmy said. 'He's looking for the swipe card I'm guessing.'

A second later, he disappeared from view as he skipped into a concealed doorway which presumably led down to the car park.

'Where's the vehicle entrance Jimmy?' Maggie asked. 'I don't see it.'

'Look, there's another street off to the right just down there,' he said, pointing ahead. 'It will be there I'm guessing. It must be a cul-de-sac, backing onto that BMW showroom we walked past.'

'So if we just stand across from where it joins this road, we should see him leave?' she asked.

'Bang on. And we should be able to get a photo no problem from there, because I expect DC French will want the registration number.'

'Sounds like a plan,' she said, 'and I like a man with a plan.'

They didn't have long to wait, the vehicle emerging up the steep exit ramp of the car-park and swinging on to the cul-de-sac with a squeal of its tyres. Big and imposing, the colour difficult to distinguish in the dark but she thought it might be some sort of subtle metallic grey.

'Range Rover,' she said to Jimmy. 'Range Rover Sport HSE to be exact. And with the big five-litre V8 from the sound of that exhaust. Quite a rare spec that is. Top of the range.' And she didn't need a consultation with her little son to know that this was a one-hundred-grand motorcar.

'There's just one thing,' Jimmy said as they made their way back to the hotel, 'we promised that Ronnie guy that we wouldn't tell Frank what he was up to.'

'*I* promised, *you* didn't,' Maggie replied. 'And your brother would want to know, don't you think?'

Chapter 16

The aftermath of the sensational office altercation between Jolene Cavendish and Harry Newton had been both swift and wide-ranging, which is why Jimmy was now sitting with Maggie, Asvina Rani and Emily Smith on the top floor of the Addison Redburn building, watching with mild amusement as Rupert Pattison, the firm's Managing Partner, paced around his palatial penthouse office having what could best be described as an emotional meltdown.

'Shit! I mean, for god's sake!'

It wasn't clear if he was expecting a response so no-one said anything.

'I mean, I can't imagine how things could be much worse for the firm. It's a five-star frigging disaster, isn't it? In fact it's ten times worse than that.'

Again, nobody said anything.

'Emily, give us a sit-rep,' he barked. Jimmy laughed to himself at that. The guy had obviously watched too many of these US political dramas, the ones where things were going tits-up on an hourly basis. Or maybe he thought he was in the military, in charge of some anti-insurgent operation. In Canary Wharf.

'Sorry Rupert?' Emily said, uncomprehending.

'A situation report,' Jimmy translated. 'You know, tell us where everything stands at the moment.'

'Right...yes, so not good I'm afraid Rupert. Firstly, both Harry Newton and Lily Wu have raised formal complaints to me as their HR manager about Jolene's bullying behaviour. They're both demanding that we do a proper investigation.'

'Oh really?' Pattison said sharply. 'Well we can kick that into the long grass for a start. No way are we going down that road. No way.'

Emily looked at him nervously. 'I'm not sure it's as easy as that Rupert. You see, if we don't conduct a proper investigation we could find ourselves liable if it goes to an employment tribunal. And that could turn out to be very expensive.'

'Stuff that. If they do dare take us to a tribunal, we'll take our chances. So what about the witch-bitch? I suppose she's got something to say about the situation?'

'She's decided that today will be her last day,' Asvina said.

'What do you mean, her last day?' Pattison said, his irritation obvious.

She patted her bump. 'Maternity leave. She's already worked well past the earliest date she could legally give up. So she's quite entitled to go anytime she wants now I'm afraid. She had intended to stay until the Hampton Defence deal was completed next week but now she's changed her mind.'

It must have crossed his mind that Asvina was in the self-same situation, and for a moment Jimmy thought he was going to bring it up with her. Instead he shook his head and said,

'Christ, so where does this leave us with the contract?'

Totally buggered was what Jimmy wanted to say but he wasn't sure how that would go down. As the thought crossed his mind, he saw Pattison looking at him, as if he had noticed his and Maggie's presence for the first time.

'So I thought you two were supposed to fix everything?' he said, his voice thick with sarcasm. 'That's not exactly gone brilliantly has it?'

It was a natural reaction, to lash out when your world was going pear-shaped, so Jimmy bore him no ill-will.

Calmly he said, 'Rupert, I think we're feeling pretty confident now that these harassment incidents are related to something she has done in the past. In fact, we were scheduled to tackle her on the subject when the punch-up distracted us.'

And now it occurred to Jimmy that if Jolene was set on walking out today, then they only had a few hours to get to her before it would be too late. But then Maggie put into words the same thought that had just flashed through his mind.

'I'm just wondering if there's any point to our investigation now if she's planning to quit today,' she said. 'Her mind is bound to be focussed on the arrival of her new baby. Maybe she might just decide to let everything go, forget about the whole thing.'

Asvina shook her head. 'I'm afraid that's not going to happen if I know Jolene. As Rupert says, yesterday's bust-up is just going to make the whole thing worse.'

'Asvina's right,' Emily said. 'In fact, I was just about to tell you all what she told me this morning, just before I came up here for the meeting. She said she's now made up her mind to quit permanently after her maternity leave and that she'll be launching a constructive dismissal claim against us.'

'Shit Emily, why didn't you tell me this earlier?' Pattison said.

'Well to be fair Rupert, you weren't really giving any of us a chance to speak,' Jimmy said. 'Perfectly understandable mind you, given the situation,' he added, in attempt to soften the message. He saw Maggie shoot him a wry smile and knew exactly what she would be thinking. *Gallant Jimmy, leaping to the defence of his new love.* And the fact was, she was not far wrong in her analysis of the developing relationship. Because improbable and unexpected as it might be, he was beginning to believe he might be falling in love with Emily Smith. He turned his head to look at her, seeing a hint of a smile cross her lips as their eyes met. God, she was bloody beautiful, and he wasn't afraid to admit to himself, bloody alluring too. They hadn't made love yet but when they did, he knew it would be special for both of them, and now he could feel his heart-rate rising involuntarily as he began to imagine her lying beside him. Not exactly the kind of thoughts you should be thinking when you were in the middle of an important business meeting. With no little effort, he turned his mind back to the situation in hand.

'Aye, I tend to agree with Asvina,' he said, addressing Rupert directly. 'This latest turmoil is just going to make matters worse.' He looked at Maggie. 'What I'm thinking boss is we have to get to Jolene today. I know that sounds obvious, but what I mean is we need to put that *I know what you did thing* in front of her ASAP.'

'Agreed,' Maggie said. 'And Rupert, where's your head at with regard to us brokering some sort of compromise agreement? Because I've been thinking that maybe we can take this opportunity to put together a mega compensation package that would make her think twice about quitting.'

'A dirty great big bribe, in other words,' Jimmy said. 'I know it'll probably stick in your throat Rupert, but think of the consequences of her walking out and screwing up the Hampton Defence deal. It'll be bad news for your bottom line, even before you factor in the reputational damage.'

From Pattison's expression, Jimmy could tell he wasn't liking any of this, as it slowly dawned on him he was trapped between the proverbial rock and the equally proverbial hard place. Every sinew of his being would be shouting *get stuffed Jolene, just sod off and do your worst and see if I care,* but the cool and rational lawyer in him would be saying that was exactly the most stupid thing he could do. Which of these inner voices was to be victorious? Jimmy suspected it might be too close to call.

Finally he spoke. 'How big is mega?' he asked Maggie. So, it seemed like calm and rational had won out. But there was no denying he looked worried.

She shrugged. 'Two, three times her annual salary. That would be at the upper end of one of these compensation packages, but I can't see her being swayed by much less.'

'Christ,' he said. 'And exactly how much is she on Emily do you know?'

Emily nodded. 'I looked it up just before the meeting. Last year with bonus Jolene earned just short of four hundred and sixty thousand pounds.'

'Christ,' he said again. 'So we're talking a million or more.'

Jimmy spread his arms in an open gesture and raised an eyebrow. 'And how much are you expecting to earn from the Hampton deal?'

Pattison didn't reply but his face told its own story.

'Exactly,' Jimmy said. 'Come on Maggie, let's do this thing.'

*****

After a bit of low-grade flirting with her PA Kylie Winterburn, he'd managed to secure them a fifteen-minute slot in Jolene's diary, a precious commodity on what could very well turn out to be her last day of employment with Addison Redburn.

'Twenty-past two, that's when we're in,' he told Maggie, 'but we've only got fifteen minutes I'm afraid.'

She shrugged. 'Then we'd better make it count.'

They'd manage to secure adjacent desks tucked away in the far corner, the least coveted location in the whole of the vast open-plan office due to its distance from any source of natural light. But at least it afforded a degree of privacy to allow them to conduct an ad-hoc review of how things stood. And the good news was, by the animation in her expression he suspected that Maggie Bainbridge might have a plan. He was right, she did.

'So I've been thinking it over and I'm now pretty clear what we need to do next,' she said, absent-mindedly chewing on a ballpoint, 'and much as I hate to mention his name in polite company, I've got to give Frank credit for some of it.'

He shook his head. 'I wish you two would sort out whatever it is that's going on. Because it's getting really boring.'

'Not going to happen,' she said briskly. 'Anyway, we'll get to that bit in a minute. First of all, here's what we're going to do with Jolene. No buggering about, we're just going to walk straight in there this afternoon and slap a million pounds on the table, figuratively speaking of course.'

She slammed her fist on the desk, startling Jimmy who was closest and causing a dozen colleagues to look up from their work in surprise.

'Bang! A million quid bonus on top of her salary if she stays on for three years. No messing about either. We'll give her twenty-four hours to accept otherwise the offer is withdrawn, in which case she can clear her desk and bugger off. And if she still wants to sue us, well that's fine. We'll take our chances with that.'

He gave her an admiring smile. 'God, you've turned into a right hard-nut haven't you? But aye, I think you're right on the money with this one. I mean, who's going to turn down the chance of an easy million?'

She laughed. 'And easy for us too when it's not our cash. But then as far as the harassment stuff is concerned, same approach. We slap that note on the table, bang, and ask her straight out. *I know what you did*. What does that mean Jolene? Are we talking about poor Lily Wu, doing a perfectly fine job at Fortnum Price despite not being qualified to their standard, but where you got her dismissed without even knowing who she was? Or was it something else? Come on Jolene, you need to tell us what it is if you want us to catch whoever is responsible.'

Listening to her, an uneasy thought came to him. 'There's a problem with this you realise? You see, Harry Newton doesn't fit, does he? Because I'm thinking his beef with Jolene is only since he started working here at Addisons. Even although he worked at Fortnum Price, he didn't have any connection with her back then.'

She sighed. 'Yeah, I'd thought of that too, I must admit. But maybe he knew about what happened to Lily, about her sacking?'

From the questioned inflection, he could recognise she was clutching at straws.

'I'm not so sure...,' he said, trying to avoid a critical tone. '...but look, as Frank said, the difference between his case and ours is that whilst he has no proof that Parrish drowned his wife, he has strong circumstantial evidence. That's what allowed him to confront Parrish. Whereas we've got nothing at all, and that's because we haven't really been looking, have we?'

It was half-question, half-statement and as the words left his lips, he realised it was the truth. Here they were embedded at the scene of crime and yet all they had focused on so far was the who and the why, not the how and the when. Because in every one of these incidents, a person or persons unknown had somehow managed to get into Jolene Cavendish's office and plant these vile objects and messages, completely undetected. Kylie Winterburn had insisted vehemently that no-one could possibly have got past her, situated as she always was like a sentry right next to Jolene's door, and he tended to believe her. So who had come in especially early on the days that the incidents had occurred? Or who perhaps had stayed unusually late the previous evening? *Someone would know*. Someone would have seen something. They just needed to start asking the right questions.

Detecting a distinct rumble in his stomach and knowing lunchtime must be approaching, he shot a quick glance at his smart phone which was lying face-up on the desk. *Twelve twenty-three.* Meaning that when the Met's serious-crime squad questioned him about everything afterwards, he was able to be pleasingly precise.

Suddenly a blood-curling scream pierced the air of the quiet office, a scream that was being repeated over and over again like the scene from a horror movie. In a second he was in her office, ignoring the protests of Kylie Winterburn who evidently had not yet taken in what had happened.

'Shit!' Quickly he appraised the scene, then turning back to Winterburn shouted, 'Call an ambulance and get the police here too. Right away.'

Jolene had collapsed onto the floor, convulsed by the agony of the burn that had turned both her hands black and was now seeping its way up her left arm. He dropped to one knee and lowered his head until it almost rested against hers. This close, he could hear her shallow breathing.

'Jolene, it's Jimmy Stewart, I'm here to help. You're in shock, but don't worry, everything's going to be ok.'

'My baby, my baby,' she said, her voice almost inaudible. 'Is my baby alright? Please, is my baby alright?'

Shit, he'd forgotten she was pregnant.

'The paramedics will be here any minute now. But I'm sure everything's going to be just fine. Trust me.'

'It was in the watering-can,' she whispered. 'I splashed it and then it burned and then I spilt some more...'

He'd already worked out what had happened and her words only served to confirm it. Acid, probably sulphuric, and a damned concentrated solution at that. As gently as he could, he moved her into the recovery position, removing his jacket and scrunching it into a makeshift pillow. Now he worried that the excruciating pain and shock would trigger something much worse, a heart attack or a stroke, and god knows what effect that would have on her unborn child.

'Stay back everyone, stay back.' He heard Maggie's voice immediately behind him and turned to see her blocking the door to prevent any of Jolene's co-workers entering the office.

'What's happened Jimmy?'

'Acid. In the little pink watering can. She's in a bad way.'

It seemed to take an age for the paramedics to arrive but in reality it was less than ten minutes. Five minutes later Jolene was in the ambulance and on her way to hospital. Not much later the first wave of police officers arrived, accompanied by their scene-of-crime and forensic support teams. The last time there had been an acid attack on their patch, it hadn't ended well for the Metropolitan Police. Evidently they didn't intend to make the same error again.

Chapter 17

Shaken in the aftermath of the terrible attack on Jolene Cavendish, there was only one thing that Maggie wanted to do and that was to get home and hold her little boy Ollie close to her. After making sure that Jimmy was ok, she had slipped through the door leading to an emergency stairwell and wound herself down to street level, emerging onto Canary Wharf through a tucked-away rear entrance. Outside there was chaos, a cacophony of sirens filling the air from the emergency services vehicles parked on the expansive concourse outside the front entrance.

For reasons she couldn't quite understand, the authorities had suspended the operation of the Docklands Light Railway in response to the incident. Perhaps after the chastening Freja Portman affair, they had decided that overkill was the better part of valour. Whatever the reason, there was no chance of getting an Uber or a taxi, so she had half-ran, half-walked all the way to Whitechapel. On Commercial Road she had managed to bag a black cab, the taciturn driver not bothering to hide his displeasure about being dragged through rush-hour traffic all the way up to Hampstead. At least she hadn't had to suffer the constant stream of inane chatter that was the stock-in trade of many in his profession. She'd got home just as Martha was bringing Ollie in from school, and she hugged him so tightly that he was forced to protest with an indignant '*ugh mummy*'. Then she had prepared tea and afterwards they had sat on the sofa and browsed one of his growing stock of car magazines, he declaring that when he grew up he would choose either a Ferrari or an Alfa-Romeo because Italian cars definitely gave the best driving experience, his earnestness making her laugh.

The plan had been an early night for both of them, but it had been disrupted first by a lovely phone call from Frank, his voice heavy with concern, she quite forgetting that she wasn't supposed to be talking to him. And then just after she'd hung up, there had been a second call, this one from Nigel Redmond of Drake Chambers. Nigel had been busy it seemed, or at least his Fortnum Price informant Des had been on his behalf, and as a result he would have something *extremely* interesting to reveal about Jolene Cavendish when they met for that little dinner on the twenty-fourth. Except that Maggie hadn't been prepared to wait that long, demanding to know what he had discovered right that minute. Canny Nigel had not been prepared to reveal his information without a guarantee that the dinner would happen and insisted on making a booking at some favoured Italian bistro of his whilst she hung on the line. And then, at last, he had told her.

'Bullying?' she asked him, although she was hardly surprised having seen how Jolene operated.

'That's right,' he had said. *'But she picked on the wrong girl. She was just a trainee, but it turned out the girl's father was a big-time employment lawyer at another firm, and he went after Jolene with all guns blazing. What Des hears is there was a six-figure settlement and your Miss Cavendish was quietly eased out the door.'*

Maggie knew how these things worked. 'And everybody would have signed a compromise agreement forcing them to keep schtum about everything for evermore.'

'Exactly, that's what happened,' he had agreed, *'so no-one would ever need to know.'*

Yes, no-one would ever know. But did that include Addison Redburn, Jolene's current employer, the firm that was paying her near on half-a-million a year for her expertise? Wouldn't they have wanted to know that their new partner was a cheap bully before taking her on on such an exorbitant salary? She had thanked Nigel for letting her know, telling him how much she looking forward to their dinner date with as much sincerity as she could muster. And then, just as she was about to hang up, he had gone on to reveal something more interesting still.

'There was something else too. You see, this girl had been in a relationship with Harry Newton. That's quite a coincidence, isn't it?'

Coincidence? There was no such thing. This was a connection, and a connection of such rock-solid nature that surely it had to mean something. Right now, she couldn't figure out what.

*****

The next day being Thursday and with everyone declaring the need for a drink or two after what Maggie and especially Jimmy had gone through, they had arranged a meet-up, but this time Jimmy and Frank would travel up to Hampstead to save Maggie the journey into town. There was a traditional old pub around the corner that she had been to on a couple of occasions, nothing special but generally quiet on weekdays, which would be good because she knew the threesome had plenty to talk about. When she got there, she found Jimmy and Frank already propping up the little bar.

'Been here long boys?' she said, nodding at their near-empty glasses.

'Five minutes,' Frank grinned, 'but it's thirsty work, battering our way up here on the tube. Anyway, how are you? Crazy situation isn't it?' He reached out a hand and squeezed her arm lightly, causing her to give a little shiver. In response, she placed her hand over his and held it there, longer than she should.

'I'm ok. I was a bit shook up after seeing what happened to Jolene but I'm ok now. How is she Jimmy by the way, have you heard anything?'

'Terrible burns on the hands and on her left arm,' he said, 'and they're having to sedate her at the moment. But the baby's ok thank goodness. I had a chat with one of the paramedics at the scene and he said he wouldn't be surprised if she was in hospital right up until her baby is born.'

'Understand,' Maggie said. 'She was going to be giving birth in a private clinic, the same one as Asvina in fact. Somewhere in Kensington. I guess that must be touch and go now?'

'Aye, I guess so,' Jimmy said, shrugging. 'Maybe she'll have to stay where she is.'

'Here, let me get you a drink Maggie,' Frank said, gesturing to the barman. 'Large Chardonnay please mate and two more Doom Bars.' He placed a twenty-pound note on the bar. 'And I want my change please, just so you know.'

Maggie forced a laugh. 'You're in leafy Hampstead. I'm not sure that'll even be enough for one drink.'

He responded with an exaggerated grimace. 'Anyway, you're bound to have seen on the London telly news who they've chosen to head up the case. None other than my old mate Detective Chief Superintendent Colin-bloody-Barker.'

'I wondered how long it would take you to bring that up,' she said, smirking. Barker was Frank Stewart's nemesis, the reason why he had ended up in Department 12B after he had punched the senior officer's lights out for a reason Maggie couldn't quite remember. 'I saw him do a media briefing last night. They're not treating it as related to the Portman attack but early enquiries suggest a connection to the Hampton Defence takeover deal. That was the gist of it.'

'Idiot,' Jimmy said. 'I've been with the police for hours today and of course I told them all about the previous incidents directed at Jolene, but the thicko DS who interviewed me didn't want to know. I even told him about that recent set-to she had with Harry and Lily but he still wasn't interested.'

'Something else has turned up that might interest them,' Maggie said. 'Nigel Redmond called me last night and it's very possible that Jolene Cavendish was actually sacked by Fortnums and that she didn't just resign.'

'Bloody hell, that's a turn up for the books,' Jimmy said, surprised. 'Why, what happened?'

Maggie smiled. 'Bullying. Bet you can't believe that. And there's something else too. The woman she was bullying had been in a relationship with Harry Newton.'

'Bloody hell,' Jimmy said again. 'This *is* a tangled web, isn't it?'

As he said it, a thought came to her.

'You know Jimmy, what if someone has found out about the sacking? *I know what you did*. What if that's what it's all about, her being sacked and not having told Addisons?'

'What? Jimmy said, frowning. 'You mean it's got nothing to do with Harry or Lily looking for revenge?'

As he said it, she began to get a sinking feeling, the one that seemed to appear every time an investigation was getting its knickers in a twist.

'Well yeah, maybe not,' she said, sighing, 'and worse than that, what if it's nothing to do with her sacking either and this *was* actually aimed at spooking her so as to disrupt the takeover? I hadn't thought of that before, but we shouldn't rule it out.'

'Well if it is that, it's certainly done the job,' Jimmy said. 'It's stopped the thing dead in its tracks. Jolene's out of action for months now and half her team are suffering from shock and have signed off sick. I doubt we'll see many of them back in the office for a while.'

Frank shook his head. 'This deal thing, it doesn't seem very likely to me. You see, if you wanted to put Addison's takeover team out of action, why piss about with all that earlier low-level stuff? I'm not as close to it as you guys, but I would still say this is definitely personal, directed at your witch-bitch woman. Just like you first thought. Oh aye, and I've got another observation to make, if you don't mind.'

'Go ahead bruv,' Jimmy said, smiling. 'You're the professional.'

'It's the old connections and coincidences thing again. You say that Jolene was sacked for bullying a young trainee and that this woman was in a relationship with your Newton guy? So what if the reason she was bullying this woman was *because* she was in a relationship with Newton. He's a powerful guy, the old green-eyed god, isn't he?'

'What *jealousy*?' Maggie said. 'Jolene was jealous of this woman's relationship with Harry Newton?'

'Why not?' Jimmy said. 'He's a good-looking guy. I can see a lot of woman falling for him, so why not Jolene?'

Maggie sighed. 'The fact is guys, we're floundering here. We've got a revenge motive with a couple of solid suspects, we've got the secret about Jolene's split with Fortnum Price, and what, now we're wondering if there was anything intimate between her and Harry Newton? It's a right mess, it really is. And the thing is, I still feel in my gut that we're missing something. And it must be something blooming obvious, surely?'

And that's when it struck her, something that *was* so blindingly obvious that she could kick herself for not seeing it before. It was when she remembered the first words Jolene Cavendish had said to them, right at the start of the investigation, when they were in her office, exchanging pleasantries about her pregnant state. *I'm thirty-three weeks so you're right, not long now. Almost exactly the same as Asvina, although of course this is my first.*

Although of course this is my first. No it bloody isn't, Maggie thought, not according to that twenty-five year old photograph of a pregnant you with slimy husband James Parrish and that mystery blonde.

So the question was, where was that child now?

Chapter 18

Frank allowed himself a half-smile as he wandered up the stairs of Atlee House, vending-machine-sourced coffee and Twix bar in hand, en-route to the desk of Ronnie French. It had been so nice to see Maggie the previous evening, and he couldn't help reflecting, unsavoury though the thought was, that the acid attacker had done him a huge favour. It was as if their little *estrangement*, if that's what it had been, had never happened and he was glad about that. Yes, that bloody estrangement, what had that been all about? The thing was, he hadn't been aware that he had done anything to trigger it, but there had been no mistaking how different she had been with him this past week or two. In fact, indifferent would be a better description. Cool to the point of freezing if he was being totally honest.

By brutal coincidence, he had begun to recognise that something inside him had changed in the last couple of weeks, and something big at that, a change that had both frightened and exhilarated him at the same time. It had been a combination of factors, seemingly disconnected but all conspiring to come together almost simultaneously to bring him up short. First of all, he had to blame -or was it thank- Eleanor Campbell for her role in the affair. In a moment of weakness, he'd made the mistake of letting slip what had happened with him and Mhari all these years ago, and in typical Eleanor fashion she would not let it rest. Bit by bit she had managed to wheedle more and more information from him. *What was her surname, where did she grow up, what was the name of the church where you should have got married but where instead you were left standing at the altar in utter humiliation like a prized pillock?* He hadn't wanted to reveal any of it but somehow it had all slipped out, and he knew exactly what she would do with it. Through the years he had hoped quite fervently that Mhari was having a shit life, but had never dared to actually discover if she was. Now Eleanor Campbell was going to find out for him.

And then there was the situation with Katherine McNally of the BBC. The clever and beautiful Katherine McNally, who much to his utter disbelief seemed intent on taking him into her bed. He'd never met a woman like her before, so self-assured, so certain of what she wanted and not afraid to ask for it. She had as good as asked him to sleep with her no more than two hours after they had met, and had then shown no anger or annoyance when he had tactfully declined the offer, and not just once but on two occasions. Contrast that with his own pathetic shilly-shallying, where he had known Maggie Bainbridge for over two years and still hadn't even asked her to dinner.

He arrived at French's desk without really knowing how he'd got there, such was his level of distraction. He was pleased to see the fat reprobate was in residence, but less pleased to see he wasn't alone.

'Well well, what have we here? Do I smell a conspiracy?'

Startled, Eleanor and French swivelled round with synchronised precision, but not before the young forensic officer had surreptitiously clicked on the *Close* button to shut down the website they had been studying. But not surreptitiously enough, because Frank had had enough time to recognise what they had been looking at. A website he, like every policeman in the country, had used a thousand times over the years.

'Now then you two, for why have you been surfing the DVLA site? That's the Driver and Vehicle Licensing Agency just in case you pretend not to know what I'm talking about.'

'We weren't,' French said.

'You bloody were,' Frank replied, stretching over to retrieve a scrap of paper that was lying on the desk.

'*TD19 URK. 2019 Range Rover HSE,*' he read. '*Registered to Thomas Patrick Holt, 21 Penrhyn Terrace, Walthamstow E17 5QH.* Interesting.'

'Yeah, one of me snouts gave me a tip-off about a bank job that's being planned,' French said smoothly. 'We think this might be the motor they're planning to use as the getaway wheels.'

Frank laughed. 'I've told you before Frenchie, you're watching way too many of these old cop shows. In case you haven't noticed, the bad guys don't do bank jobs any more. It's all internet scams and identity theft these days. Twice as profitable and half the chance of getting caught. And just so you know, on the odd occasion when they do a big break-in, they don't use pukka motors registered with the bloody DVLA.'

'Yeah, fair cop guv,' he said, without shame. 'It was actually in connection with this thing that me and El are working on.'

'It's *Eleanor*,' she said, giving a grimace.

French shrugged. 'Yeah, sorry, that me and *Eleanor* are working on.'

'And this Holt guy. Is he the guy you got Maggie Bainbridge and my brother to tail the other night?'

French's face dropped. 'How'd you get to know about that?'

Frank laughed. 'Blood's thicker than water mate. Should have thought about that when you extracted the promise.'

'Yeah well I suppose you can never trust a woman, can you?' French said, seemingly recovered from his brief disappointment. 'But it don't matter, they did a sound job for me. For us I mean.'

'And you're not going to tell me what it's all about?' Frank said.

'No guv, we're not,' he said, sounding defensive. 'And Maggie and your brother don't know either, if you were thinking of asking them. Let's just say I think I'm getting somewhere with this one...'

'We're getting somewhere with this one,' Eleanor interrupted, shooting daggers. *'We.'*

'Aye, well fair enough,' Frank said, anxious not to stir things up more than necessary. 'It certainly sounds like the *two* of you are doing a smashing job. And I've had your prior assurances that it's nothing illegal so that's good enough for me.' As he said it, Eleanor and French exchanged a look that made him question that last statement, but he decided to let it pass. *Out of sight out of mind.* Perhaps not the smartest management philosophy when dealing with Ronnie French, but it would have to do for now.

'So if you're done here Eleanor,' he said nodding in the direction of the stairwell. 'I'd like a wee word with Frenchie. Got a nice wee job for him. And then I'll nip down and see you afterwards, because I've got something for you too.'

As she stood up to leave, French gave her an enquiring look accompanied by a double thumbs-up. 'Quite happy with what you need to do now Eleanor?'

She scowled. 'Like *yeah*.'

Frank smiled to himself. The boy Ronnie had evidently quite a bit to learn when it came to dealing with the Maida Vale prima donna. But then again and as he himself knew only too well, learning to deal with Eleanor Campbell was a life's work.

'Bloody nightmare that woman,' French said when she was out of earshot. 'But smart as a carrot. Anyway guv, what is it you want me to do?'

Yes, what exactly was it he wanted Frenchie to do? The fact was, it had all been a bit cock-eyed in his mind, but with less than three weeks to go to the deadline, it was a relief that the plan was finally beginning to crystallize a bit more clearly. He had more or less settled that Ronnie French was going to play the Lieutenant Colombo part, it being Frank's opinion that if they were ever to re-make the famous detective show for British television, then Frenchie, scruffy and shambolic in equal measure, would be a shoo-in for the lead role. Ronnie's job was to haunt James Parrish's every waking hour, turning up unannounced at his home and his workplace, always unfailingly polite and always with just one more question to be asked. Anybody would be bloody annoyed by that and with French being effortlessly annoying right out of the box, the hope was that Parrish would crack and let something slip. Frank knew of course that the surgeon considered himself super-clever, no doubt thinking if the authorities were taking this vetting business seriously then they wouldn't have allocated just a lowly DC to the matter, and a useless superannuated one at that. Nothing to worry about would be his belief, nothing to do but go through the motions so they could tick all their stupid little boxes and then everything would be fine. But like many a suspect before him, he was likely to learn how much of a mistake it was to underestimate DC Ronnie French.

With Parrish taken care of, Frank himself could concentrate on what was a bit of a loose end, but one he thought might deliver the breakthrough that was so urgently required. In reality it was somewhat of a long-shot, but one that he hoped would be worth the investment of a bit of his time. He was going back in time, to a time long before the unfortunates Petra and Kelly had caught the eye of the womanising Parrish. To a time captured in a grainy newspaper photograph, where a heavily-pregnant Jolene Parrish had been forced to suffer the public indignity of watching her husband flirt with some unknown blonde. Except of course the blonde wouldn't have been unknown to either Parrish or his then wife. Which is why Frank had a minute earlier handed over a copy of the picture to French with an instruction that it should be the first question he asked, preferably in the presence of the present Mrs Parrish. *Who's the sexy blonde bird Dr Parrish? Looks a bit of a goer to me. And your wife pregnant as well. Tut-tut.* That's exactly what Ronnie would say or something along these lines, precision-calculated to get a reaction. The chances were Parrish would try to dismiss it as unimportant, maybe even claiming that it was just someone he had met at the do and he wasn't sure if he even remembered her name. But Jolene Cavendish wouldn't have forgotten, that was for sure, and in a day or two when she was feeling better he was going to ask Maggie or Jimmy to go and find out.

'Ok Ronnie get to it,' he said, getting to his feet, 'and maybe wear the uniform a couple of times and borrow a squad car? Our boy Parrish won't be a happy bunny if the neighbours get to see that parked outside his fancy place every evening.'

'Sure no problem guv,' French said, raising a hand in compliance. 'In fact maybe I'll wander down to his gaff this evening. Nothing on the telly that I fancy as far as I can remember. The missus said I could do with a bit of overtime.'

'You don't get overtime Frenchie, remember? You do it just for the love. Anyway, I'm away downstairs to see Eleanor.'

Unlike in French's case, it wasn't possible to sneak up unnoticed behind her desk, it being aligned such that it faced the stairwell. As a result, she was able to observe his approach, giving her time to suspend what she was doing and fold down the screen of her laptop. She tried to make it look natural but Frank wasn't fooled.

'Up to no good I suppose,' he said, smiling, 'or looking at engagement rings? Has he popped that bloody question yet, your Lloyd?'

She scowled at him but didn't say anything.

'Sorry, only joking,' he said, suddenly remembering what she knew about Mhari and what she might do with that information. 'What it was, I wanted you to do a bit more digging into these online register of marriages and deaths and whatnot, like you did when you were compiling that stuff on James Parrish's wives.'

'Ok,' she said, her tone noncommittal. 'I suppose I could do that.'

'But this time, we're looking for a birth. About twenty-five years ago, something like that.'

'Whereabouts?'

'Does that matter? he asked. 'Glasgow I think, but I'm not certain. But I was kind of assuming you might be using one of these web-bot thingies that could look anywhere in the universe.'

'Or I might just look it up on like a database,' she said, not bothering to disguise the sarcasm.

'Whatever.' It was Eleanor's favourite dismissive response, and he loved to play it back to her. This time, she didn't seem to notice the barb or if she did, she chose to ignore it.

'Do you have a name?' she asked. 'Of the parents. Actually, one will probably do for the search.'

'Parrish. James Parrish. Or Jolene Parrish. Either.'

'That surgeon guy you're investigating?' she said, sounding surprised. 'Why don't you just go and ask him?'

It was a good question, and he couldn't deny that course of action would have been perfectly simple and straightforward. But there was just something in his gut that had made him think twice about the matter. The thing was, nowhere in the pile of stuff Eleanor Campbell had dug up on Parrish was there a single mention of a son or a daughter. It was the same story in the millions of words written about him in the media since he shot to prominence through his transformation of Freja Portman. Of a child there was not a mention, not once. He wondered if in the past there had perhaps been some massive estrangement, the boy or girl involved in something so unspeakable that they had been wiped from the family history, his or her name destined never to be mentioned again. But Frank thought that unlikely. If a child existed, then the media, so interested in every minute aspect of Parrish's life, would surely have discovered it by now. But then Frank's other possible theory, that the couple had lost the child perhaps to a miscarriage, was not without its difficulties either. James Parrish was a self-promoter *par excellence*, and there was no way he would have omitted to weave this unfortunate but quite common event into the public narrative of his life. No, whatever the fate of the child Jolene Parrish had been carrying, her then husband seemed determined to keep it buried in the past. Now he wondered if he might get more joy if he approached Jolene directly. Or more exactly, if he got Maggie Bainbridge to do it for him. She hadn't mentioned anything about Jolene already having a child on the couple of occasions they'd all discussed the case, but Maggie was super-smart and he wouldn't be surprised if it was now top of her list too.

And at least it would give him a nice excuse to call her.

*****

Before accepting Frank's mission, Eleanor had made some half-hearted protests about how hard it was going to be to fit this thing into her busy schedule, how her boss kept piling more and more work on her, how under-appreciated she was and a thousand other things she wasn't happy about, but he wasn't bothered about any of that. He knew that if Eleanor was interested in an assignment, she would drop everything and give it her full attention. And as far as he could tell, she was interested in this one.

'So when do you think you could squeeze this in?' he asked, his tone hopeful.

'Give me a few hours,' she said, already punching away at her keyboard, 'and leave me to get on with it.'

'I'm gone,' he said, getting to his feet. 'Call me if you find anything.'

'Like *yeah*.' She shot out the response without looking up from her screen. He smiled to himself as he slipped away. Just like *whatever*, this was a catchphrase he could shoot back at her in the future. *Like yeah.*

At a bit of a loss, he wandered down the stairs to the vending area and dialled up another americano, then after losing a half-hearted argument with his conscience, fed a pound coin into the slot of the adjoining machine to summon another Twix bar. He guessed that Maggie and Jimmy would be a bit stuck too, unable to return to Addison Redburn's Canary Wharf office due to it now being a live crime scene, their investigation effectively in limbo whilst they waited to hear what the firm wanted them to do about it now.

She answered his call on the first ring. Evidently he was right about her being at a loss.

'*Frank, hi.*' She seemed pleased to hear from him, her voice bereft of the frostiness that he'd encountered in recent weeks. *Hallelujah for that.*

'I thought I'd just give you a call to see how you're doing. And cards on the table, to ask you a wee favour too.'

He heard her laugh. *'Doing fine thank you. We're back at our offices for the time being by the way, until your friend*

Chief Superintendent Barker decides to let everybody back in to Addisons.'

'Good to know,' Frank said. 'I'm mean that you're fine. So about that wee favour...'

'Don't tell me, it's to do with that photograph and that blonde woman. And particularly about Jolene's child and what happened to it? You know, I've no idea how we could have been so stupid as not to think of that one before.'

He laughed. 'Aye, that's it, are you a mind-reader or something? Tick-tick-tick for all three items on your list. And like you, it just suddenly struck me as being weird how we knew nothing about the child. Anyway, I've got Ronnie French chasing it up with James Parrish but I was wondering if you or Jimmy might put the question to Jolene, understanding of course how tricky that might be with what's just happened to her.'

'We're ahead of you there,' she said. He thought he detected a hint of smugness in her voice, prompting a fond smile and causing him to reflect if he had been talking to his brother, Jimmy wouldn't have just been smug, he would have been ramming it down his throat. *'So of course it would be difficult for us because we haven't known her very long, but obviously she and Asvina have been close colleagues for years and with Asvina just about to give birth too...'*

'And she's agreed to do all of that? That's amazing.'

'Yes it is, isn't it? Obviously I don't think we can get her to ask about the blonde woman, but certainly she can steer the

conversation around to previous pregnancies. Asvina suffered a miscarriage herself a few years ago before she had her boys so hopefully she can just bring it up quite naturally. In fact she's going up to visit Jolene tonight after work and she's also arranged for them to share a room at the private maternity hospital so that Jolene isn't alone. I thought that was so nice of her, don't you? Because mostly you have your own room in these fancy places.'

'That's brilliant Maggie, it really is.'

'So do you think it's important Frank?' she said. *'The fate of their child?'*

'Got to be.' But how important, he wasn't really sure, and as he thought about it again doubts began to surface. Jolene had probably just had a miscarriage and the event had now simply faded from the memory of both her and her ex-husband. 'But then again Maggie, I don't know. Let's just try and get the answer and then at least we can cross it from our list if it doesn't help us.'

'Yes, I guess you're right. And what about the other woman?'

He shrugged. 'Again I don't know. But Frenchie might manage to wheedle a name out of Parrish in which case we can go and ask her ourselves. We'll just have to wait and see.'

'That would be good,' she said. *'So I guess we see where it goes and then compare notes.'*

'Where, down the pub?'

He heard her laugh. *'Best place to do it Frank. Speak to you soon.'*

He hung up, pleased with the chance to speak with her but less pleased with where it had taken his thinking on the Parrish case. The fact was, he had to continually remind himself what it was he was trying to achieve and what was at stake if he failed. As far as the mission was concerned, he didn't have to find prosecutable-strength evidence that proved Parrish had committed some ghastly crime. All he needed was to dig up something dodgy from the surgeon's past that would seriously embarrass the government should it become known to the public at large. The suspicious deaths of two former wives, so promising on paper, had proved to be a dead-end, and if anything would generate sympathy for the man should the stories re-emerge in the media. *Such tragedy, how could anyone recover from such a terrible double loss? And yet here he is, rebuilding lives and giving hope where none existed.* Now Frank realised he was pinning his hopes on the flimsiest of hunches, centred around a dusty twenty-five-year-old photograph. He didn't like to think about it too much, but he could see this case ending in abject failure.

And the stakes? Nothing less than the survival of the Department, the department to which he had been dragged kicking and screaming but which he now loved with all his heart. Sure, Jill Smart had promised him a place somewhere in her organisation and he knew she had his back, but over at Paddington Green he would be just an insignificant cog in a big wheel, straight-jacketed by procedures and protocol, stripped of the freedom to run investigations in his own way.

The more he thought about it, the more the prospect horrified him.

But the fact was, there was something worse to worry about it. Something *much much* worse. It was Ronnie French's throwaway remark that had set him off. *Let's just say I think I'm getting somewhere with this one.* The trouble was, Frenchie was a chip off the old block as far as reporting progress on an investigation was concerned. Like Frank himself, he had a favourite phrase. *Early days.* And like himself, for Ronnie every case seemed to be in the early-days phase until about five minutes before he'd worked it all out. So if Ronnie said he was getting somewhere, it was time to get worried.

Because the last thing he wanted was bloody Eleanor Campbell and/or bloody Ronnie French stealing a march on him, no matter what half-cocked scheme they had rustled up. He'd never hear the end of it and that would be simply insufferable. It might easily take months or even years to recover from it, never mind whether it saved the Department or not. But no matter, it could be dealt with quite simply. He would give it a day or two and if the Parrish child-and-mystery-blonde investigation looked like heading up another cul-de-sac, he would just waltz in, pull rank and take the damn thing off them.

Shameless of course, no arguing with that. But necessary.

Chapter 19

He'd known from the start of course that the project was not without risk, but that had not worried him unduly because it was an absolute truth that nothing was worth doing in this world without it. Every time he walked into that operating theatre there was always a chance that the procedure would not be a success, and that the positive transformation every patient hoped for would not transpire. In his hands, the likelihood of that being the outcome was naturally rather small, which is why he had become pre-eminent in his field and why he deserved that damn knighthood. *Sir James Parrish*. On the subject of which he assumed he was now on the home run with regard to Downing Street's stupid vetting process. The smart-arsed Scottish DI originally assigned to the task now seemed to have given up on it and shunted it down the chain to the fat detective constable who had come with him on his first and only visit. That DC French guy might be seriously annoying with his stream of crude insinuations, but he was a long way from being the smartest sandwich in the picnic either. Clutching at straws of course, a last desperate throw of the dice. They had nothing on him, nothing at all. Give it a few more days and he expected all their little bureaucratic boxes would be ticked, they'd write their stupid report and that would be the end of the matter.

But coming back to the subject of risk. You see, there was no escaping the fact that in a surgical procedure, things could go wrong, all the way up to and including death, but that was part of the excitement of the job. He'd lost very few patients on the operating table thank god, but that didn't mean it wasn't a risk every time he picked up his scalpel and sliced into their soft yielding flesh. So you planned carefully, evaluated everything that might not go to plan, put in place a contingency to deal with every eventuality.

Just like he had done in respect of his delicious affair with little Ruby, his pleasingly sex-crazed personal assistant. Naturally at some point in the near future Dawn would have to be moved on. It was about time, and it was long past the point when he had any feelings left for his current wife. But the thought of Ruby as her replacement, of her becoming Lady Parrish of Barnes or whatever, was simply ludicrous, her being both under-educated and without money. But she filled a need and he had evaluated the risk of her wanting more than they already had as low to middling. If that was to change, then of course there was a Plan B. There was always a Plan B.

But coming back now to Thomas Holt, what was to be done with him? He been given the strictest of instructions never *ever* to contact him again unless he gave express permission, yet here he was in a blind funk just because he had been paid a little visit by a policeman. It was that stupid car of course, he knew it would cause trouble. He had told Holt to keep a low profile so as not to draw attention to his changed circumstances, but perhaps he hadn't fully factored in how both thick and vain the guy was. So instead he'd gone out and bought that ridiculous car, a car that a semi-professional footballer and part-time hotel porter could never afford in a month of Sundays. And now, by some ridiculous coincidence the cop he had received a visit from was the bumbling DC French. Naturally there was nothing to connect Holt back to himself but there still was no getting away from it. The risk of it all going pear-shaped had just escalated from low to high.

So wasn't it fortunate that he was able to schedule Holt to come in for another procedure, a little bit more reconstruction work on the handsome face that had been destroyed when its owner had been thrown through that car windscreen? To a surgeon of his skill and experience it was simply routine, the type of operation he had performed a thousand times before. *The type of operation that hardly ever went wrong.*

But then again, it would be nearly three weeks before Holt would lay on the operating table once more. Therefore the question had to be, why wait?

Chapter 20

It was Monday, mid-morning, and although Maggie and Jimmy's conference call with Rupert Pattison and Asvina Rani had been necessarily brief, the outcome had been more than satisfactory, at least from the fee-earning viewpoint of Maggie Bainbridge Associates. Given the tornado that had smashed through the eminent legal firm of Addison Redburn in recent days, it would have been understandable if their Managing Partner had more important things on his mind other than what to do with an investigation into a case of employee harassment, an investigation that had seemed to have been quite overtaken by events. But no, he appeared perfectly happy for it to carry on, although Maggie thought that agreeing to their request was simply to ensure the call was as short as possible, allowing him to concentrate on more pressing matters. Like how the hell his firm was going to cope with the loss of millions of pounds caused by the implosion of the Hampton Defence takeover deal.

So now the two of them had de-camped to their favourite Starbucks on Fleet Street in order to regroup and work out the plan of action for the next day or two. They had worked out that instead of just obsessing about motive, they had to gather some hard evidence, and as a first step it seemed sensible to try and gain access to Harry Newton and Lily Wu's work computers, although they had no real idea what they were looking for. Accordingly Maggie had just a few minutes earlier put in a call to one of Addison's IT management team, an austere-sounding woman called Mandy Fryer. The woman laboured under the title of *Head of Desktop, Web and Front Office Infrastructure for Europe and the Americas,* causing

Maggie to reflect it was just as well that business cards were going out of fashion. Her explanations were condescending, long-winded and laden with technical jargon, but the gist of it seemed to be that it was not necessary to have actual hands-on access to Newton and Wu's physical laptop computers. Apparently everything was done on the Cloud, whatever that was, and therefore could be accessed from any computer anywhere in the world so long as you had the necessary usercode and password. Which was good news, because Chief Superintendent Barker's crime-scene officers were still preventing any of the firm's staff going back into the office. The only problem was, Ms Fryer was resolute in her refusal to hand over the necessary codes, answering Maggie's request with a robust *I wouldn't even give them to the police without a court order, so I'm certainly not giving them to the likes of you.*

A setback, but one that Jimmy seemed to believe could be overcome.

'I'm pretty sure Emily would be able to get us access. She's boss of HR after all, so I wouldn't be surprised if she had a file with all that stuff in it. Shall I give her a call, see if she can help us?'

Maggie gave him a wry look. 'Talking of Emily, I should have asked you. How was your weekend?'

'Aye nice,' he said, a hint of evasiveness in his tone. 'It was a smart wee hotel and we did a couple of lovely walks along the Downs. It was a bit drizzly on Saturday afternoon but nothing too much to worry about. And we got great views across the Channel.'

No doubt followed by a lovely romantic dinner and then afterwards? They wouldn't have retired to single rooms, of that she was pretty certain. *Be careful you don't get hurt.* That was what she wanted to say to him, but really, what business was it of hers? Until very recently she had been sure that the only thing that would make Jimmy happy again was a reconciliation with Flora. Now she wasn't so sure, but she didn't know whether she should be pleased about that or not.

'I'm glad you enjoyed it,' she said, aware it was a half-truth at best, 'and yes, it would be great if you gave her a call.'

She watched as he swiped down to her number, watched the broad smile break across his face when she answered, watched him laugh as they shared some no doubt lascivious private joke.

'Aye, sure...yeah, Harry Newton and Lily Wu...you've got them, have you?...Aye, that would be great... Aye, just text them over. And the quicker the better please if you don't mind. Brilliant...bye darling.'

He gave her a thumbs up. 'She says she's got them on a spreadsheet somewhere. She's going to look them out and then text them over to us.'

Maggie was a little surprised when she heard a ping from Jimmy's phone not much more than a minute later. Emily

Smith had obviously not had to look too hard to find that spreadsheet. Not for her *darling* Jimmy.

'Fast work,' she said after he'd confirmed it was indeed the user-codes and passwords they'd asked for.

He grinned. 'I think she likes me. Anyway, do we know what to do with them?'

'They've got an employee portal. Asvina told me what it was. *AddisonStaff.com*. You just go to that website and log in.'

'Sounds easy,' Jimmy said uncertainly. 'I suppose we can get into it here on our phones? They've got pretty good internet and I quite fancy another coffee, what about you?'

'Definitely. And we can divide and conquer. I'll do Harry, you do Lily.'

He nodded. 'So where do we start? Any ideas?'

She laughed. 'Well I'm not exactly an IT guru so the only thing I know how to do is look at their browsing history. So that's where we'll begin.'

He gave her a sheepish look. 'I'm not sure I even know how to do that.'

'Here, give me.' She snatched his phone from him and clicked on the Safari browser. 'See...scroll across here...then select *that*...then scroll down to *this*...then tap *history*...'

She saw him looking at her with a mixture of amusement and bemusement. 'That's brilliant boss. But maybe you could just go through that again?'

'Cheeky boy,' she said fondly. 'Sod off and grab the coffees and then we can get started.'

It took him quite a while to get back with the order, on account of the pretty young barista quite shamelessly prolonging the preparation process to maximise the time she could spend gazing longingly at Jimmy.

'Quite a mission that was,' he said, grimacing as he slid her latte across the table. 'But I'm all set now.'

She punched Harry Newton's usercode and password into the Addison staff portal and was pleased that it responded instantly with a *Login Successful*. Looking up, she saw Jimmy furrow his brow in concentration as he tapped into his phone, then give a thumbs-up. Great, so they were both in, for once spared the brain-destroying frustration that in her experience seemed to accompany every IT-related activity she undertook. But it wasn't the technical challenge real or imagined that was causing her most concern. The fact was, she had no idea whether these investigations were likely to come up with anything worthwhile, and if they didn't, then she'd really no idea what to do next. The acid attack had moved the Jolene harassment campaign onto a whole new level, and she found herself wondering whether they had bitten off more than they could chew. Sure, Rupert Pattison was happy for them to continue alongside the police investigation, but really, what could her little firm do that the police, with a hundred times their experience and resources, couldn't? But then, she broke into a grin as she remembered some of their previous successes. The Alzahrani affair, the Leonardo murders, that business up in Loch More. There was plenty they could do, but not if she spent valuable investigation time wallowing in self-doubt.

Pushing the negative thoughts to one side, she continued with her browsing. At first glance, there was nothing in the least incriminating about Harry Newton's on-line activities. Most of his time it seemed was spent on the big legal library sites which the profession used to verify points of law, a facility she herself had taken advantage of plenty of times when she was a practising barrister. Every now and then he would check out a news site and there was an occasional visit to the home page of Arsenal Football Club, confirming his sporting allegiance. It was all pretty routine and a pattern of usage that to her surprise, showed Newton as a diligent worker.

Suddenly Jimmy gave a loud cackle.

'What?' Maggie said, smiling.

'Guess what?' he said. 'I think our Lily's obsessed with *Love Island*. Looks like she spends half her time looking at all these muscled guys with their shirts off. I don't think Jolene would be too pleased if she'd found out. Not when she's supposed to be working.'

'Probably not, although I can see the attraction myself.'

'If you say so boss,' he said, giving a smirk, 'although it doesn't do it for me. But wait a minute...what's this?'

She detected the change in tone.

'What is it?'

'I don't know,' he said, frowning. 'Something called Web-Guard. Web-Guard dot-com. I've found a few of them, they all seem to be saying the same thing. *Your search included prohibited keywords and was blocked by the server*.'

'Hang on,' she said. She punched the first few characters into Harry Newton's browser. *W-e-b-G-u.* 'Yeah, I've got some of them too. Let me count...yes, five of them.'

'Aye, Lily's the same,' Jimmy said. 'Five attempts as far as I can make out. Any idea what it means?'

She shrugged. 'Pretty much what it says I suppose. Some sort of software that stops you looking at things you're not meant to.'

'What, like good-looking young guys with their kit off? he laughed.

'Yeah, or girls in the same state,' she said. 'On-line porn in other words. But does it say when these searches happened?'

He nodded. 'Look at the bottom corner, there's a timestamp. About eight weeks ago in Lily's case. Tuesday the twelfth, eleven minutes past one.'

She screwed up her eyes and stared at her phone. 'Yes, I can see that now. That's funny... Harry's are on the same date. Here, look.' She held up the device in front of him. 'Tuesday the twelfth, two minutes past one.'

'What, at more or less the same time?' Jimmy said, sounding puzzled. 'That's a bit of a coincidence, isn't it?'

'I don't think so,' Maggie said. Suddenly she began to realise the significance of what they had just uncovered. 'Don't you see what's going on here?'

'No, sorry.'

'So Harry searches for something and it's blocked. He has a few unsuccessful attempts at whatever it is he's looking for and then asks Lily to do the same. Which probably rules out the porn angle I would think, unless they share some seriously weird hobbies.'

'That's an interesting thought, with them looking for the same thing.' Jimmy said. 'Because I don't think we ever considered them being anything other than colleagues, and not particularly close ones at that. So are you thinking it might be something more than that?'

'I don't know, it still might be nothing,' Maggie said, 'but it *is* interesting, that's for sure.'

Jimmy nodded. 'I'm wondering if that Mandy Fryer lady might be able to tell you what they were looking for? I'm no expert but I'm sort of guessing that this Web-Guard stuff reports these dodgy searches up to the IT management folks.'

'I'd imagine that's true,' Maggie said, but as she said it, she began to have her doubts. If Newton and Wu's blocked searches had been caught by Addison's IT security systems, surely they would have heard about it earlier in the investigation? The IT guys would have reported it up the management chain and being their line manager, the matter would have landed on Jolene Cavendish's desk. And yet she had said nothing, meaning either she didn't know or else she wanted to keep it to herself. Or what was more likely, the searches had been entirely innocent and it was just the Web-Guard software being over-zealous. Whatever the case, Maggie was pretty certain she and Jimmy wouldn't get any joy from asking the play-it-by-the-book Ms Fryer to look into it for them. Which meant that they would have to take the official route, going through the police to obtain the warrant or court order or whatever it was that would satisfy her. That didn't mean however they had to follow the *official* official route. She picked up her phone and scrolled to Frank's number.

'Hi Frank, how are you?'

She didn't wait for his reply. 'Listen, something's come up on the Jolene Cavendish investigation. I was hoping you might be able to help us. We think it might be important.'

She heard him laugh as she explained what she wanted him to do. She'd known of course that persuading him wouldn't be her toughest assignment, knowing how much he loved to put one over on Detective Chief Superintendent Colin Barker. And so it proved. *Aye, of course he would be delighted to help out and he might even go and see this Fryer woman himself so she understood how important it was. It might take a couple of days to sort because he'd need to get DCI Jill Smart to sign off the paperwork which meant there would have to be tedious explanations as to why he was tramping all over someone else's investigation, but that shouldn't be too difficult to overcome. After all, why had Department 12B been created if not to trample all over someone else's investigation?*

So they might have to wait a day or two to find out whether the blocked searches had any significance in the search for the harassers of Jolene Cavendish, and that would mean waiting a day or two before they could go and confront Newton and Wu about them. That wasn't the end of the world, and in her view they had already made significant progress. Because as Frank had told her, if you didn't believe in coincidences and you got a bunch of improbable connections, you were usually right to be suspicious. Two people each with their reasons to hate Jolene, two people who had both worked at Fortnum Price, and two people who had been searching online for the same thing at almost exactly the same time.

Pleased with the outcome, she was just about to hang up when he interrupted her.

'Actually, I'm glad you phoned Maggie..well you know it's always great to hear your voice but that's not it... what it is, something's come up on my side that I know you'll want to hear. It's something wee Eleanor Campbell's been working on and she just told me five minutes before you called.'

She reached over and nudged Jimmy on the shoulder, pointing at her phone.

'I'm just going to put you on speaker Frank, Jimmy's here with me.'

'Aye sure. So you know Jolene's first pregnancy? Eleanor's been crawling through the register of births with her magic wee web-bot thingy and we've finally traced what happened. She found the certificate you see. Turns out Jolene and James Parrish's baby was still-born.'

Chapter 21

It had been another early start for Frank but he wasn't too bothered about that. Earlier in the year the Met's travel team had done some deal with the train operator such that their police officers could travel first-class whilst on duty, meaning free coffee and biscuits on tap and maybe even the chance of a sneaky wee gin and tonic as they raced through the Cumbrian hills. The latter of course was not courtesy of the tax-payer, but he didn't mind shelling out a few quid of his own cash for the mixed-in-a-can refreshment. So he was off back to Glasgow, a trip he'd been looking forward to for a couple of days, ever since wee Eleanor's web-bot had done its work. He hadn't known there was a separate register and certificate for still-births but it turned out there was, and the clever forensic officer had found it, uncovering the Parrish's secret in the process.

Aye, secret. Because that's what it was, and the question had to be asked, why? Why keep secret an occurrence that though undoubtedly tragic, was not exactly rare? According to his Google search, something like one in every one hundred and sixty pregnancies ended that way. But more than that, his own lovely mother had suffered a stillbirth too, along with several miscarriages, which accounted for the nearly ten-year age gap between him and Jimmy. *You should have had a sister.* It was something his mum often said, the sense of loss still present after more than thirty years. She didn't dwell on it and with her two boys to be grateful for it hadn't affected her happiness, but she hadn't kept it a secret either. Now Frank's gut instinct was telling him that there was something connected to the Parrish's personal tragedy that might be the key to unlocking his investigation. Something that James Parrish in particular was keen to keep firmly buried in the past. And something that wasn't going to be quite so easy to hide now that Frank knew the address of the place where the still-birth had occurred and the name of the doctor who had signed the certificate.

But that wasn't the primary purpose of his visit to his home city. First of all, he was meeting up with his wee mate PC Lexy MacDonald and then they would be off up to Gilmorehill and to the records office of the University of Glasgow. Less pleasingly, he expected that Katherine McNally of the BBC would be there too, she having independently sniffed out that perhaps there was a story to be had by going further back in James Parrish's timeline. Why the prospect of meeting her again filled him with such trepidation he couldn't quite say, as he knew that most men would swim the length of the Clyde in their underpants for a date with her. Perhaps it was because her unsettling directness was forcing him to confront the sort of life decisions he didn't want or like to make. The truth was that after fifteen years of kicking that particular can down the road, the need now to do something about it one way or another frightened him. But what the hell, he could easily put it off for a few more years if he wanted to. Despite how he felt inside, no-one was actually *forcing* him.

Feeling better, he glanced out of the window, vaguely conscious they had just left a station but unsure which one it was. He remembered pulling into Preston about twenty minutes earlier so this must have been Lancaster, last stop before the climb up to Shap Summit and the prettiest stretch of the route.

'Tea, coffee, drinks, snacks, complimentary newspaper?'

The trolley attendant announced his menu in a cheery sing-song tone reminiscent of the newspaper boys Frank had heard in the old movies. He raised a hand to catch the youth's attention.

'Yes please, I'll have a G & T and I'll take a Chronicle off your hands if you've got one left.' The first-class passengers had been offered newspapers when they'd taken their seats at Euston, but two hours ago Frank had too much on his mind to be able to do one justice so declined. Now with the way ahead clearer, he could afford a few minutes of relaxation, mainly to catch up on what was happening in the football world. The attendant handed him the small can and a plastic glass containing a single ice-cube and a thin slice of dried-up lemon, together with his newspaper.

'Cheers mate,' Frank said, handing him a crumpled fiver. 'Keep the change.'

'That'll be four pounds ninety-five pence,' the attendant replied, sounding distinctly less cheery.

The front page was dominated by a photograph of Freja Portman, speaking at another of her climate events, this time in Berlin to which she had travelled by train in a show of what the paper called environmental virtue-signalling. The Chronicle had produced an elaborate analysis supported by a barrage of graphs and bar-charts that seemed to show it was no more eco-friendly to travel by rail than to take a short-haul flight when you took into account the energy that had been expended to manufacture the train in the first place. It was all too complicated for Frank to follow even if he had been interested in understanding it, which he wasn't. It wasn't that he denied there was a need to take action, far from it. It was just that it seemed impossible to get to the truth of the matter because each side of the argument seemed to be able to bend the facts to suit their own particular narrative.

But then he noticed a smaller headline tucked away in a bottom corner of the page. *Footballer Murdered.* The story was accompanied by a grainy photograph of what was obviously a London street, the entrance to a terraced house blocked off by a line of fluorescent crime-scene tape. Quickly he scanned down the story. The victim, whose name was being withheld until the family was informed, was a non-league footballer and according to neighbours also worked shifts at a Park Lane hotel. Then he noticed something that brought him up short. *Police say the Penrhyn Terrace murder was committed in the early hours of yesterday morning.*

Penrhyn Terrace. He recognised it as the address on that scrap of paper he'd caught Ronnie French with back at Atlee House, when he and Eleanor had been surfing the DVLA website. He fumbled in his pocket, pulled out his phone and found French's number. After a few rings it went through to the DC's voicemail. *This is Ronnie. I can't take your call right now. Please leave a message after the tone and I might get back to you.*

'I'll leave you a bloody message alright.' He couldn't help raising his voice in exasperation, causing the handful of passengers in the coach to look up from their newspapers and laptops. 'So ok Ronnie, I don't know what the *hell's* going on here, but you'd better phone me right back now. And I mean *now*. *Pronto*.'

Next he tried Eleanor and wasn't surprised to get the same result, but this time he didn't bother to leave a message. He knew a conspiracy when he saw one, could visualize the two of them taking the swift glance down at the caller ID and then as agreed, ignoring all his calls. When he got back to London he was going to bloody well string them up, but right now he was worried about what the hell they'd got themselves into. A guy had been murdered, and he'd bet his pension it was the same guy who for some reason had been on Frenchie's radar. The problem was, if Ronnie had known the guy's life was in danger and had done nothing about it, then it would be another nail in the coffin of Department 12B.

But he realised there was nothing he could do about it right now, and he also realised that another gin and tonic would go a long way to soothing his fraying nerves. Twenty minutes later and suitably fortified, he closed his eyes just as the train crossed the border, drifting off into a dream-free sleep that lasted until they eased their way into Glasgow Central Station exactly on schedule. As arranged, Lexy was waiting for him on the platform, waving to him in a manner he considered a tad undignified for a uniformed police officer.

'Great to see you again sir,' she said brightly as he approached her. 'Good journey?'

He gave her a thumbs-up. 'Aye, fine Lexy, brilliant. Now before you say anything, I've checked and it's too far to walk to the Uni.'

'One-point-seven miles and thirty-five minutes sir, well within walking distance. But don't worry, I've got a car outside. Round in Hope Street. Nae bother.'

She had left the marked patrol car on the no-parking double-yellow lines, the blue light on the roof flashing in an insouciant tempo, as if unconcerned about the traffic chaos it was causing. This being Glasgow, he was surprised one of the frustrated locals hadn't already nicked the wheels off the brand-new Astra, but the little car seemed intact.

'We're meeting that BBC woman again sir, aren't we?' she said, as he settled into the passenger seat. 'She's nice-looking isn't she? My dad really fancies her you know. He says she's the only woman he would swap my mum for.'

Frank laughed. 'Oh aye? And what does your mum say to that?'

'She says she's got a list of fifty men she would swap *him* for, and that's without even trying too hard.'

He laughed again. 'Good for her. And aye, Katherine is nice-looking, I'll give you that.' And it was true, there was no denying it, but that wasn't the reason they had invited her along for their meeting with the matriculation secretary of the University. Instead it was a sort of payment in kind for her having identified the location where that seminal photograph of the Parrishes and the mystery blonde had been taken. Not in some civic offices of the City Council as he had first thought, but in the University's Bute Hall, a grand gothic edifice and the scene of examination terror for generations of undergraduates but considerable joy too, because it was where the graduation ceremonies took place, if you were lucky and diligent enough to make it to the end of your studies. In between these duties, according to his Wikipedia search, it was also used for public lectures, conferences, weddings and other functions, with seating for over a thousand. That was where the photograph was taken, with the likelihood that it had been some sort of alumni do, meaning all the participants would be graduates of the University. Including, he hoped, the mystery blonde.

'Let's park with a bit more consideration for the good citizens of this city shall we?' he said as they made their way up University Avenue. 'We could be in here for a few hours.'

Lexy laughed. 'Of course sir. But it should all be pretty straightforward though, don't you think? Good old-fashioned police work and all that.'

'Aye, exactly.'

They pulled into the visitors' car-park, found a spot, then made their way to the Matriculation office. He expected that Katherine would already be there and he was proved correct. She was standing with her back to them in the vaulted reception area talking to a plump grey-haired woman in her late fifties who Frank took to be the Mrs Sandra Good with whom they had an appointment. It was an imposing room in spite of its modest function, the elaborate painted ceiling supported by a circle of pointed arches which was the defining characteristic of the Gothic Revival architectural style in which it was constructed. This was all the fashion when the fourteenth-century University was relocated to Gilmorehill in the late Victorian era, and it bestowed a classical elegance to the buildings which they still possessed in the twenty-first century. When he thought about it, it was a description that could equally be applied to Katherine McNally. Classic elegance just about summed her up, her slim and willowy frame always dressed with subdued but expensive good taste. Today she was wearing a silk navy dress with a swishy pleated skirt, one he was pretty sure he had seen her wearing on television before, and in which she looked simply stunning.

Mrs Good had seen their arrival and broke off her conversation to come and greet them.

'Inspector Stewart I presume?' she said with a warm smile. 'Sandra Good, Chief Matriculation Officer. Welcome to the University. Miss McNally has given me a brief summary of what it is you hope we can help you with.'

'Oh has she now?' he said, grinning. 'Hi Katherine, good to see you. So you've already sorted it all out for us then? That's brilliant.'

She smiled. 'Hardly Frank, I've only been here five minutes, but Sandra is fairly confident that we'll be successful. And thank you for telling me about the Parrish's still-birth by the way. It's quite an interesting development isn't it?'

'Yes it is, and it would be good if it didn't make it into the media for a wee while yet.' He said it in a light tone, but he hoped she would detect that he meant it.

'Of course not,' she said, 'but promise me I'll get the inside track if it turns into a story.'

'Sure, I can do that. Just so long as you're willing to put in the hard yards today. No gain without pain, isn't that what they say?'

'I've cleared my diary today and so I'm all yours.' There was something in the way she looked into his eyes as she said it that made his heart skip a beat. *I'm all yours*. It was a bloody tempting prospect and he wasn't sure if he could or even wanted to resist.

'Right then,' he said, trying to sound brisk and businesslike. 'So Sandra, how does this work?'

She smiled. 'Ok, follow me folks and I'll show you.'

She led them through to a large light-filled room which reminded Frank of a particularly grand school hall. A dozen or more desks were laid out in classroom fashion to further accentuate the effect. On each desk was a bulky contraption that looked rather like an old-style TV set.

'This is our microfiche room,' she explained with a hint of apology. 'Rather old-school I'm afraid if you will forgive the phrase, but we only started digitising our records about twenty years ago. Everything before then was recorded on microfiche. Essentially that means it was photographed and miniaturised by the microfiche process.'

'Including the student records?' Lexy asked.

'I'm afraid so. And there's around six thousand students in each year group. Obviously it would help if you knew which year the woman you are looking for graduated.'

Frank gave a sigh. 'We don't really know. She looks as if she's in her late twenties or so and the picture was taken in ninety-six I think. So she probably graduated in nineteen eighty-eight or eighty-nine, but it could easily be two years either way.'

'So that's about thirty-six thousand records we've got to look through,' Lexy said, screwing up her nose. 'Twelve thousand each.'

'That's a lot,' Sandra Good said, failing to lift the rapidly-crashing mood.

'So much for your good old-fashioned police work Lexy,' he said, giving a wry smile. 'What do you think about that now?'

'I've done the maths,' she said, evidently unaffected by his gloom. 'We can probably get through about ten a minute and at least half will be men so we don't need to give them a second glance. So that's six hundred an hour, which works out at about five thousand a day.'

'That's each,' Katherine said. 'So we won't be far from doing half in one day.'

'Exactly,' Lexy said. 'Probably no more than three days' work at the most, and statistics say she won't be the last person we look at. It wouldn't surprise me if it takes way less than that.'

Frank looked at Katherine and smiled. 'But I'm guessing you've not got three days to give to this?'

She shook her head. 'Sorry Frank, I've only got today and that's it. I don't mind working late though.'

'I hope you don't mind if I make a suggestion?' Sandra Good said. 'You see, these sort of events are often faculty-organised, so you may be able to narrow down the search by looking at their own graduates first. I think you said the gentleman in the photograph was a doctor and his wife a lawyer?'

'Can you do that?' Frank said, his mood lifting.

'Easily. That's how they're organised in the records, by faculty.'

'And if we did that how many would it reduce it by?' he asked.

'Just let me think about that.' She paused for a moment, evidently performing the mental calculation. 'Yes, I would say we graduate around four hundred medics each year and probably about the same from the law school. So eight or nine hundred in total. I'm sure that number is there or thereabouts.'

'Let's assume eight hundred multiplied by six years which makes four-thousand-eight-hundred,' Lexy said. 'That means if we take sixteen hundred each it's only about three hours work to get through them all.'

Frank laughed. 'Well thank you very much young Einstein, that sounds a lot more like it. So there's just one question before we get stuck in. Can we get a wee coffee and a fruit scone anywhere around here?'

*****

As it turned out, neither he nor Katherine needed to get hands-on in the search for the mystery woman. With the number of records to be eye-balled cut to manageable proportions, Sandra Good stepped in and offered the services of a couple of her administrative staff on the grounds that their expertise would speed up the search even further, an offer that Frank was grateful to accept. He doubted whether they would get a conclusive result that day, even with the super-diligent PC Lexy McDonald directing operations. The combination of the low-resolution photo-booth pictures used in the nineteen-eighties matriculation cards and the low quality of the original newspaper photograph led him to believe they might end up with a couple of dozen possibilities which would then need some leg-work to follow up and eliminate the mismatches. But they would get there in the end, of that he had little doubt. As ever, patience was a virtue in any investigation. Instead, he was heading for a late lunch with Katherine at the Refectory, where he was hopeful that Scotch pie, baked beans and chips would still be on the menu even although it was nearing two o'clock, a culinary treat denied to him since he'd moved down south. But before that he had some business with DCI Jill Smart.

She answered his call on the first ring, which immediately made him wary.

'Oh hi ma'am, how's it going?'

From her tone, he surmised that Smart was not in the mood for pleasantries.

'I was just about to call you Frank. Have you heard about that murder over in Walthamstow? Some footballer I've never heard of?'

Frank doubted if Jill had even heard of David Beckham but decided it would not be prudent to mention the fact right now.

'Well yes and no ma'am. I read about it in the paper coming up on the train but that's all.'

'And do we know anything about the victim?'

He had to hand it to her, she was a cunning operator. By *we*, she didn't mean himself and herself, she meant the Department. As a matter of routine, the Met's database analysts would have run a database sweep to see if they had any other activity recorded against the victim's address, and that would have shown up the fact that Ronnie French had been looking at the dead guy's Vehicle Licensing record not more than ten days earlier. Now that fact would be in the hands of DCI Smart. He saw that this thing could get difficult, but worse than that, there was no way he was going to be able to prevent himself looking completely useless. Quickly thinking it through, he decided there was nothing for it but a full confession.

'I think DC French might have been running some line of enquiry on him ma'am but I don't know what it was.' There was silence on the end of the line, which he didn't like. But finally she spoke.

'Should we have known what he was doing?' Her emphasis on the *should* meant there was only one answer.

'Aye ma'am, we should have. I mean, *I* should have. I'm sorry.'

His apology didn't seem to improve her mood. *'You know these bloody data sweeps get widely distributed, right up to the top brass. I don't need to tell you if an AC gets wind of this then we're all going to look like fools.'*

Of course she was right, they would look like fools and there was no escaping the fact it was his fault. It wasn't exactly a secret that if you let Ronnie French go off-piste it was likely to end in disaster, and yet that was exactly what he had done. Now all he could hope for was to rustle up some damage-limitation scheme, but to do that, he'd first need to track down the incorrigible waster and find out what the hell he'd been up to.

'Look, leave it with me ma'am, I'll sort it out, I promise. And I'm sorry again.'

'Well that's all right Frank.' He heard her voice soften and wondered if now was the time to bring up what he'd called her for in the first place. But she resolved his dilemma by bringing it up herself.

'So, different subject. This warrant you've asked me to get for you. Isn't that under Chief Superintendent Barker's jurisdiction? His acid attack case at Addison Redburn?'

For the second time in five minutes he decided honesty was the best policy.

'Aye ma'am it is, but let's just say the case might benefit from a more open-minded approach. Did you know Maggie Bainbridge's firm were working on the harassment investigation before that attack was carried out?'

'I didn't. But she's a very clever woman so I expect she has got some theories as to what's behind it all?'

'Aye she is and she has. But look, I'm not trying to get one up on Barker.' *For once*, he could have added. 'It's just that he's convinced the motive is connected to that big takeover Jolene Cavendish was working on but Maggie and my brother Jimmy have uncovered something that brings that theory seriously into question. If anything comes out of the angle they're working, we'll hand it straight over to the Chief Super's team. Honest ma'am, you can trust me on that.'

He heard her laugh. *'Well that's just as well, because I had the warrant signed off this morning. It should be in your inbox already.'*

He heaved a sigh of relief, partly because he'd got the result he'd been hoping for and partly because something like normal relations seemed to have been restored with Jill.

'Fantastic ma'am, I'm really grateful. And believe me, when I get a hold of Frenchie I'm going to wring his flipping neck and I'll give it an extra squeeze for you.'

Now his grumbling stomach was telling him it was time for pie, beans and chips. And for that little speech he had prepared for the beautiful Katherine McNally.

Chapter 22

Maggie had tried to drop the question casually into conversation during a visit to their favourite Fleet Street Starbucks, a routine visit to prepare for the upcoming meeting with Addison's IT harridan Mandy Fryer. A meeting that she hoped would prove productive now that a warrant had been granted to reveal the contents of Harry Newton and Lily Wu's blocked internet searches.

How are you and Emily getting along? It sounded innocuous enough, but she knew he'd spent at least a couple of weekends in her company and she guessed that meant staying with her at Emily's Wimbledon flat. In Maggie's eyes, that raised the seriousness of the relationship up by several notches, but Jimmy evidently did not agree. *Fine, nothing serious, we're just having a bit of fun.* His reply wasn't entirely convincing but she elected against making any further comment, and besides it was really none of her business. It was just that she feared that it was all moving too fast and he hadn't really thought it through, the liaison being nothing more than a screw-you reaction to the news that Flora was in a relationship with her old flame Dr Hugo Blackman. She didn't have any direct experience of it herself, but the received wisdom was that love-on-the-rebound affairs seldom ended well. But then she remembered that Flora Stewart's relationship with the opportunist Blackman could very well be placed in the same category and immediately felt a bit better. That one was bound to fall apart surely, because hadn't the then Flora McLeod rejected Hugo in favour of Jimmy ten years earlier? So there was hope that

Jimmy's marriage wasn't quite dead yet and she decided to leave it at that.

'They've moved their IT team to a temporary office just round the corner so we don't have far to go,' Maggie told him as they sipped their coffees.

'So the forensic guys have still got their Canary Wharf place in lockdown?' Jimmy asked.

'For just one more day I think. I expect Rupert Pattison will be mighty relieved at that.'

'I bet he will,' he said, 'and what about Asvina? How's she doing?'

Maggie smiled. 'She's at home now but the baby's due any day now. I spoke to her earlier in fact. Her bag's all packed and ready to go. And she's very excited of course.'

'Naturally. And Jolene's due too, isn't she?'

'Yes, on exactly the same day by coincidence. I do hope it goes well for her, after all she's been through.'

'Aye, me too,' Jimmy said.

It took them little more than five minutes to walk to Addison's temporary office accommodation, the anonymous entrance located in a narrow alleyway half-way up Farringdon Street. Dull and gloomy and decorated in a dirty beige, it reminded Maggie of Frank's Atlee House before it got its recent makeover. Alerted to their arrival by a phone call, Mandy Fryer was waiting for them at the top of the entrance stairway and seemed in a much better mood than in their last meeting. But then again, she hadn't met Jimmy Stewart before. His presence usually had that effect on any woman with a pulse.

'Sorry about the mess of boxes and cables everywhere,' Fryer said as she led them to her desk. 'We had to up sticks and get everything set up at very short notice as you can imagine. Just grab a couple of these chairs and drag them over, and watch you don't trip over something.'

Jimmy smiled at her. 'You'll be glad to be getting back tomorrow then.'

She returned his smile, the kind of smile that Maggie had seen a hundred times before when any woman was within fifty yards of her handsome colleague. 'Actually it's not too bad here. And it's a bit of an easier commute for me as well. But anyway, I've been authorised by my manager to help you in any way I can.'

'That's really nice of you,' Maggie said pleasantly, although with the warrant being in place Miss Fryer really had no other choice but to cooperate. 'So it's about Harry Newton and Lucy Wu and these blocked searches from a few weeks ago.'

Fryer nodded. 'Yes, I've got one of the team to print them out for you. She should be over with them in a minute or two.'

'So how does this work?' Jimmy asked. 'This Web-Guard stuff?'

'It's pretty standard for all organisations. It just checks for inappropriate phrases, blocks the search and then records who, what and when. Ninety percent of it is porn-related or to do with on-line gambling. We get a few dozen a month, pretty average I think for a firm our size.'

'Even though the staff know they are being monitored?' he asked, surprised.

She gave a half-smile. 'Not all of them know about it, not until they get caught that is. We don't publicise that we're doing it, obviously.'

'And what do you do when you see things you don't like?' Maggie said.

She shrugged. 'IT don't look at it. It ends up on the line manager's desk and it's up to them what they do about it. Generally the staff member will get a verbal warning and that will be the end of it. Unless it's something really serious.'

A young girl approached holding a sheet of paper. 'Here you go Mandy,' she said, slipping it on to the desk.

'Thanks Lucy.'

Fryer slid the paper towards her and began to read. And then suddenly, she let out a startled cry.

'God's sake.' There was no hiding the shock in her voice. 'Christ.'

'What? What is it?'

Maggie grabbed the paper and rotated it round so that she and Jimmy could read it.

'Flipping heck,' he said, alarmed. 'This is bloody mental.'

The brief report had been laid out in table format, with ten rows, one for each of the five searches that Newton and Wu had tried to conduct, with columns showing who had performed the search and the time it was done. But Maggie and Jimmy only needed to read the first of these rows to make the pair's intentions all too clear.

'*How to construct a simple bomb*?' Maggie read the words out loud, her voice dripping with incredulity. 'And look at these others. *Making explosive from fertilizer. How to make a remote timer. Putting together a petrol bomb.* This is absolutely mental.'

'Aye it is,' Jimmy said, nodding, 'and it looks like Newton and Wu have each made the exact-same searches too, just a few minutes apart. So what do you think this means Maggie?'

She gave him a grave look. 'I think it means Jolene got lucky. And everybody in that office too, if this was their Plan A.'

'What, do you think maybe they found building a bomb was too difficult and decided on the acid attack instead?'

She nodded. 'Looks that way doesn't it? And it also looks like they're in this together. But you know, this is way above our pay-grade Jimmy. We're going to have to report this to the police right away. So Mandy, just to be clear, are you saying this stuff would have *definitely* ended up with Jolene Cavendish?'

She nodded. 'If she was their line manager, yes it would. Absolutely.'

So if this incredibly serious matter had reached the desk of Jolene as it seemed almost certain it would have, why had she not done anything about it or even mentioned it to them at the start of their investigation? The more Maggie thought about it, the more certain she was that the answer to that question was going to hold the key to everything that had been going on. The trouble was, with Miss Cavendish still suffering from her injuries and no more than a day or two away from giving birth, how in hell's name were they going to ask a question like that?

*****

Frank hadn't expected to get an instant result from the face-matching exercise up in Glasgow and he hadn't been wrong. Still, there were many reasons to be cheerful because the combination of Sandra Good's expert administrators and the off-the-scale enthusiasm of PC Lexy McDonald meant they battered through the near one-thousand possibles in just two hours flat. The shortlist turned out not to be that short, running to twenty-eight young women, a figure which was disappointing but understandable, especially after he'd taken a look at the pictures for himself. He'd wandered back over to the records office after his two-hour lunch with Katherine to find that Lexy had laid out the matriculation cards of the candidates in a mosaic pattern and was studying them intently with of all things a magnifying glass, apparently standard issue to members of Mrs Good's admin team. He had a go with it himself, but it didn't really help, simply serving to accentuate the poor quality of both the newspaper photograph and the microfiched student records. Now it would need a big dollop of that highly over-rated old-fashioned police work to track down and eliminate each of these women from their enquiries. Until, he hoped, they would be left with just one. But with twenty-five years having passed since the majority of them had graduated, the task seemed unfeasibly daunting. That was until the quietly-efficient Mrs Good casually remarked that almost all the medics and a goodly proportion of the lawyers were likely to be signed-up members of the University's Alumni Association and that she would therefore have their most recent addresses, e-mails and phone numbers on file. A grovelling call to Lexy's sergeant at New Gorbals nick confirmed that it was ok for the young PC to spend a few more days on the case and that was it sorted.

A day and a half later he was back in London, striding purposefully through the double glass doors of Maida Vale Labs where he fully expected to find Eleanor Campbell tucked away in a dark corner of the vast open-plan office. It was nearly forty-eight hours since his difficult conversation with DCI Smart, forty-eight hours in which he had still failed to find the elusive DC Ronnie French. The problem was, it wasn't unusual for a detective working a sensitive investigation to go days without coming back to the station, so technically the fat turd had not broken any rules. Short of filing a missing persons report, there wasn't much he could do about it for now, other than putting the word around Atlee that if he was to turn up, whoever spotted him should call Frank immediately. Besides he knew that sooner or later Ronnie would have to break radio silence and Frank would be ready to pounce when that happened. For forensic officers though, it was a different story. They were expected to be at their desks when they weren't at a crime scene or in a laboratory. Eleanor's situation was more complicated only in so much that she maintained desks at both Atlee House and Maida Vale. Given that he'd just come from the former and drawn a blank, you didn't need to be Sherlock Holmes to conclude she would be at the latter. She was, and this time she had selected a desk facing away from the stairs. *Schoolgirl error.*

He crept up behind her and tapped her lightly on the shoulder, bending down to whisper in her ear.

'Well well,' he said, 'it's the female Scarlet Pimpernel. Long time no-hear-from.'

Startled, she spun round on her chair.

'I've been like busy,' she said, studiously avoiding eye-contact.

'Good to know. Doing what?'

'Forensic stuff. It's what I do.'

He gave her a stern look. 'Stuff for Ronnie French when you're only supposed to do stuff for me?'

Still she didn't look at him. 'Maybe.'

Normally he would have been happy to prolong the banter, but with DCI Smart reading the riot act, this wasn't the time.

'Look Eleanor, this is bloody serious. A guy's been murdered for god's sake. So I need you to tell me right now what you two have been up to. Right now ok? And no pissing about.'

He could see she was shocked by the change in tone but it seemed to have the desired effect.

'I don't know exactly, but Ronnie thinks there's a connection between the murdered guy...'

'Thomas Holt...'

'...yeah, him, and that he's somehow connected to that Parrish dude you're investigating. That's what Ronnie's been working on.'

'Connected? How?'

'Ronnie's found out that Holt had a bad car accident and it was Parrish who treated him afterwards. Apparently he went through the windscreen and his face was a mess. He had to have like a ton of reconstructive surgery and it was Parrish who did it.'

'Ok...' He spoke slowly, his brain trying to process what it all meant. Then suddenly he remembered about Jimmy and Maggie tailing Holt to the car park and Eleanor and Ronnie's Vehicle Licensing search.

'The shiny motor. How does that fit in?'

She shrugged. 'That's how it all began. Ronnie started mooching around the hotel talking to the staff and lots of them mentioned that Holt had recently got a big Land Ranger or whatever it is.'

'Range Rover.'

'And he's just like a bellhop or whatever,' she added.

'Aye he is.'

'And so they were wondering how he could afford one. He told them he'd got compensation for his accident but that was a lie, because everyone knew it was his own fault.'

And now a scenario was beginning to form in his head, a scenario so despicable and outrageous that he could scarcely believe it to be true. Yet the more he thought about it, the more it all fitted. Perfectly.

'And what's your role in Ronnie's wee scheme?' he asked her, although he already knew the answer.

She spun round and nodded at her screen. Looking at it, he immediately recognised the distinctive logo of the software they'd used in the Aphrodite case twelve months earlier, the fancy *Fraudbreaker* stuff that Eleanor or was it Ronnie had got from their mate Jayden, late of MI6, that allowed you to track dodgy bank accounts anywhere in the world.

'I'm following the money,' she said simply.

Chapter 23

Maggie and Jimmy had no choice of course but to report what they'd found to the police, and barely twenty-four hours later Chief Superintendent Colin Barker was again in front of the media hailing his latest triumph. Two suspects, a man and a woman, had been detained in the small hours at separate addresses and were helping the police with their enquiries, and yes, he was confident they would be filing serious assault charges in the very near future, following the normal consultations with the Crown Prosecution Service. The fact that his Hampton Defence takeover theory had now been abruptly abandoned was not mentioned and attempts by the press to question him on the subject were briskly dismissed.

So now it was Thursday morning and they were back in their little Fleet Street office, mulling over what it all meant to their Jolene Cavendish investigation, whilst looking forward to their regular evening catch-up at the Old King's Head. Unusually Frank was not going to be present, which Maggie thought was a great shame, and not just because they had a lot of important stuff to talk about. The fact was, she had been missing him.

'It's going to be bloody chaos round Hyde Park tonight,' Jimmy said, pausing to take a sip from the coffee that Elsa had brought him a minute earlier. 'I've read they're expecting more than fifty thousand to turn up. No wonder the police are going to be out in force.'

She laughed. 'I expect he'll be a bit grumpy, especially since he's not exactly a Freja Portman fan. And a midnight vigil of all things? Can't see him being pleased that she's depriving him of his beauty sleep.'

'I don't think it's that,' he said. 'Frank's actually a big believer in climate change, I mean that it's really happening and all that. He just doesn't like the circus surrounding the wee teenager. He says it's all become a bit of a cult.'

'I'd second that. But she's a genius communicator isn't she? The Vigil in Hyde Park and One Thousand Days to Save the World. They're powerful slogans.'

'Aye, it's total bollocks but it is totally brilliant too, I have to give her that. But anyway, back to the million-dollar question.'

'Which is?'

'Which is, do you really think that Harry Newton and Lily Wu did it?'

It was the same question that had been dominating her thoughts ever since they had uncovered the incriminating Internet searches. The trouble was although cold logic said yes, her gut was saying otherwise.

She frowned. 'You know Jimmy, I'm really struggling with all of this. I think it's all way too neat and tidy.'

His replied surprised her. 'Aye, you and me both Maggie, you and me both.'

'What, you're having your doubts too?' she said, giving him a quizzical look.

He nodded. 'Like you say, it's all too neat and tidy. And funnily enough it's that connection thing between Harry and Lily that's really doing it for me. Or not doing it, to be more accurate. In fact it's doing my head in.'

'What do you mean?'

'So two folks who used to work for Fortnum Price turn up at Addison Redburn and suddenly bad things start to happen, although inconveniently, only one of them has any bad history with Jolene Cavendish. Then a couple of months in, there's a bloody huge escalation when someone fills her wee watering can with sulphuric acid.'

'But surely even Barker will see how flimsy the whole thing is?' Maggie said, frowning. 'Ok, so there's means, motive and opportunity but there isn't a shred of credible evidence linking Harry or Lily to the earlier harassments, let alone the acid attack.'

'Do you think that will worry him?' Jimmy said. 'He just wants a result, he doesn't care about little details like truth and justice. We should know that by now from our previous dealings with him.'

He was silent for a moment, as if deciding whether what had obviously just come into his mind was worth saying.

'But you know, I've been thinking...'

She laughed. 'Yes, I could hear the cogs grinding.'

'Seriously, I know it's not exactly original, but it's that old Sherlock Holmes thing that put me on to it. The one I heard Frank going on about the other day.'

She nodded. 'Once you have eliminated the impossible whatever remains, no matter how improbable, must be the truth.'

'Exactly. And it was that which made me realise what's been bothering me.'

'What?'

He smiled. 'Actually not what but who. Specifically, Miss Kylie Winterburn.'

She gave him a surprised look. 'You mean Jolene's PA?'

'Aye her. You see, she's the gate keeper to Jolene's office and she's always maintained that it would be impossible for anyone to get past her if she was sat at her desk. Remember how adamant she was that the witch's hat and all these notes must have been planted out of hours, when she wasn't there?'

'I remember.'

'But that baby doll was planted during office hours, and so was the filling of the watering can with acid. But there was something else too. You see, when I ran to help Jolene when I heard her scream, Kylie was just sitting there, at her desk. Still sitting there, despite all the commotion. It was as if she didn't know how to act. Because she already knew what had happened.'

Now Maggie began to understand where he was going with his line of reasoning.

'She's involved, isn't she?'

He nodded. 'Must be. Improbable I know, but it's impossible that anyone could have gone into that office at that time without her knowing.'

'But the police would have questioned her just like they questioned everybody else.'

And as she said it she realised the potential flaw in his theory.

'What if she *did* see someone going into the office and that someone was Harry Newton or Lily Wu?'

He gave her a wry look. 'Or more to the point, what if she *told* Barker she saw someone. Doesn't mean she actually did.'

'Bloody hell,' Maggie said. 'We need to find out more about this woman, don't we?'

'Aye we do,' Jimmy said, nodding sagely. 'We need to call Frank.'

*****

He was delighted to get Maggie's call and not just because it was always lovely to hear from her. That morning he'd been stuck in a stuffy briefing room over at Paddington Green police station, forced to listen to a fast-track Assistant Commissioner droning on about policing with the consent of the people and the need to maintain a light-touch footprint, whatever the hell that was. And taking an hour and half over something that could easily have been accomplished in five minutes, boring them all half to death in the process. The thing was, the brass were absolutely besides themselves over the possibility that Freja Portman's big rally would go pear-shaped and so they were taking no chances. Every officer in the force would be on duty, every officer was getting a high-level briefing as to what was expected of them, and in what to Frank seemed to be the diametrical opposite of light touch policing, five snatch squads had been set up to wade into the crowd at the first sign of trouble and arrest any ring-leaders. The Met's failure to arrest the person responsible for the acid attack on the teenager still stung and it was evident they didn't intend to make the same mistake twice.

Forced to keep the conversation brief but grateful for the interruption, two minutes later he was surreptitiously punching *Kylie Winterburn* into the criminal records app on his phone, glancing up occasionally, like half the coppers in the room who were also surfing their devices, to pretend to listen to the AC. In the twenty seconds their call had lasted Maggie could only give him the sketchiest background so he had no idea what he would find, if anything. However it turned out that her and Jimmy's instincts had been sound. The girl had a criminal record if not quite as long as her arm, then which pointed to a habitual dishonesty stretching back to her early teens. With half a dozen convictions for offences ranging from minor assault to petty theft, she had been lucky to have escaped a custodial sentence.

Maggie had asked one specific question though. Was there any connection between Winterburn and the eminent law firm of Fortnum Price? Scanning down the list of offences, he saw that there was. Three years ago the firm's Christmas party fund had gone missing, a sum touching twenty thousand pounds. The administrator of the fund was one Katie Winterburn, the money transferred from the firm's account to one in her own name. Not the smartest crime on the face of it but she'd managed to burn through nearly sixteen grand before being found out. It was a cast-iron certainty it would have spelt the end of her career at Fortnums although that information was outside the scope of the criminal records system.

The AC was still in full flow and looked like he had at least another twenty minutes in him, so Frank composed a quick WhatsApp back to Maggie.

Winterburn ex-Fortnums like you thought. Nicked the Xmas party fund 3yrs ago! Got 300hrs community service. Hope this helps.

And then, quite automatically and for the first time in any of their communications, he added it.

x.

Then like an angst-ridden schoolboy, he pressed *send* before he had a chance to change his mind.

Now he was desperate to turn his attention back to the Parrish investigation and specifically, the tracking down of Ronnie-bloody-French, but to do either, he had to get out of this room. After a moment of silent contemplation, he took a glance around then got to his feet.

'Eh sorry sir, but do you mind if I ask how much longer you're going to be?'

A gale of laughter swept across the room. The AC, who had been explaining some turgid point of operational detail on a large-scale map of Hyde Park which had been projected onto the screen, spun round sharply.

'Who said that?'

Frank gave a wave. 'Me sir. Inspector Frank Stewart, Department 12B. It's just that I'm due in court in the next hour.' It wasn't quite the truth, in fact it wasn't any sort of truth at all, but it was plausible and given that the Parrish investigation had been commissioned from the very top of government, Frank considered it a just-about-acceptable little white lie.

'Very well,' the AC said, with obvious reluctance. 'What's the trial?'

Frank had been worried he might ask that but he was ready for it.

'Apologies, but I'm not sure I'm allowed to say sir, not with so many folks in the room. It's one of these closed-door affairs you see, with video evidence and all that sort of stuff. They're the kind of things that often come to our wee department all the time. State secrets and all that.'

The AC gave him an uncertain look but evidently had elected against taking it any further.

'Very well,' he said again. 'You'd better go. Just make sure you're back here at eighteen hundred hours for the pre-op briefing, ok?'

Frank suppressed a grimace. 'Wouldn't dream of missing it sir, see you then.'

Five minutes later he was in his car and heading back to Atlee House, alerted by an email from one of his informers that Ronnie French had been spotted entering the building an hour earlier. So the fat reprobate had come in from the cold, had he? That could only mean that he was ready to spill the beans on whatever it was he and Eleanor Campbell had been working on. That was a conversation he was very much looking forward to.

As he drove, he allowed himself a smile of satisfaction. There was no doubt about it, everything was coming together rather beautifully and Ronnie's wee bit of private enterprise looked like it was going to be the icing on the cake. If his theory was right, and he was growing more sure by the minute that it was, then James Parrish could say bye-bye to any thoughts of his knighthood.

First thing on the list was to get an update from Lexy on how she was getting on with the mystery blonde trace. He'd never bothered to master that complicated Bluetooth stuff so hands-free wasn't an option. Instead he took his phone from his pocket, chucked it onto the passenger seat, scrolled distractedly to her number and jabbed the speakerphone icon.

As he expected, she answered immediately.

'Morning sir. How are you?'

'Aye good,' he said, 'but more to the point, how are you getting on with calling up all these women?'

He thought he heard her laugh. *'Calling? Didn't need to do that sir, not for most of them at least. Mrs Good had their emails from her alumni records, so I sent off a mail-shot yesterday containing the photograph and asking them if they recognised themselves or if they knew who the other woman was. I've already had six replies out of the twenty-three I sent out. No luck yet but it looks like we might get a fast response, because somebody is bound to know who she is even if we don't track down the woman herself.'*

'That's brilliant,' he said. 'Great work. So if my maths is right, you've got four or five where we haven't got an email. I'm guessing they won't take too long to track down manually, if that's the right way to put it.'

'That's right sir. And we've got social media these days so I expect they'll be on Facebook or LinkedIn or something like that.'

He laughed. 'Hey, less of the *these days* stuff PC McDonald if you don't mind. I'm not a total technology dinosaur you know.'

'Of course you're not sir,' she said with a mischievous lilt. *'By the way, are you hands free? It's regulation you know.'*

'Naturally,' he lied. 'But listen, I won't keep you any longer. Just make sure you let me know immediately you find anything.'

'Of course sir. Have a good day.'

Not for the first time he applauded his good fortune in having PC McDonald on his side. When he considered it, he felt much the same way about Eleanor Campbell, notwithstanding the fact that the feisty forensic officer came with a bit of a high-maintenance downside. He pulled into the Atlee car park, jumped out and slammed the door behind him, not bothering to lock it. With no need to hide from him anymore, he guessed Eleanor would have moved back into her first-floor den, where he fully expected she had already had a visit from French. With any luck he would still be there, presenting a two-birds-with-one-stone opportunity. But he wasn't.

Spotting his approach, she gave him a wary look but didn't say anything.

'Morning wee Eleanor,' he said brightly. 'Good to see you.' He had deliberately decided to dial back the banter, experience telling him this was the best approach when you needed her to do something for you. He'd also elected not to mention Ronnie either, because that was bound to raise her hackles, and once Eleanor's hackles were raised, it wasn't easy to get them back down again.

'Morning,' she mumbled, sounding suspicious.

'And how's Lloyd? Doing alright?'

'Like *yeah*,' she replied, sounding even more suspicious.

'Good to know. So anyway Eleanor, you remember that prescription records search you did for Kelly Parrish? I was wondering if there's any way the same sort of thing can be done for someone's medical records.'

'That stuff's like confidential,' she said primly. 'But yeah, it's on-line. Most of it.'

He thought he understood what she was implying. 'So does that mean it can be...' He was going to say *hacked* then changed his mind. Eleanor didn't like to be called a hacker even although that's exactly what she was. 'So does that mean it can be *accessed*?'

'If you've got a court order or something, then I guess it could be.'

He nodded. 'Ok, so let's assume we have one of them. What else would we need?'

She thought for a moment. 'A name, obviously. And a date of birth and maybe a National Health Service number too. But with a name and some idea of when the person was born, that would probably be enough. Oh and whether it's Scotland or England. I think there's two separate databases.'

He nodded. 'Right, I think I get all that.' Now came the difficult bit. 'And let's just say we didn't *quite* have the court order or whatever in place yet?'

Her reply came as a surprise. 'Has this got anything to do with that Parrish guy?'

'Well as a matter a fact it does. So does that make a difference?'

'Absolutely. Give me the details and I'll get onto it right away.'

He gave her a look of astonishment. 'Well sure, right away. So it's Jolene Parrish and I think she would have been born around nineteen-seventy. This will be in the Scottish database and I'm interested in her pregnancy. That would be around nineteen-ninety-seven or ninety-eight.'

'She's the woman who had the still-birth, right?'

'Aye, that's right.' For a while he hadn't been able to put his finger on exactly why he thought that fact was so significant, other than it not being something you generally kept a secret. But now he had a hunch or a theory, call it what you will. Crazy as it was, if it proved true it would explain everything.

As he stood up to leave he said, 'So tell me Eleanor, why does the fact that it's to do with James Parrish make a difference to you?'

She smiled. 'Ronnie will tell you.'

'What, you've seen him? So where is he now?'

'He was going out to get an all-day breakfast last time I spoke to him,' she said, giving a shrug. 'But he said he was going to leave a note on your desk.'

Showing an atypical turn of speed, Frank headed up the stairs to his desk, taking the steps two at a time, which he couldn't remember ever having done before. The note was centre stage, hand-written and as scruffy as its author, and was as short as it was unfathomable.

'Hi guv, just to let you know. ~~I've~~ We've saved the department. Explain later.'

Frustrated and angry, he picked up his phone and scrolled to French's number, fully expecting to reach his voicemail. But to his surprise it was answered by the fat reprobate himself.

'Sorry guv, got a mouthful of sausage. Let me just take a slurp of my coffee and I'll be with you.'

And then Ronnie went on to explain everything, about his astonishing coup that was surely destined to go down in the annuls of Metropolitan Police history and, Frank realised, a coup that would make it quite impossible for the brass to close down the department. Not only that, and with a slight pang of jealousy, he realised that French's triumph probably rendered his own current line of investigation irrelevant. But sod his own feelings, it was a massive success for the department, and the more he thought about it, the more pleased he became. But the thing was, what happened all these years ago in Glasgow was still a crime and a serious one at that so he had a duty to see it through.

Now chuckling to himself at Ronnie's news and whistling *that* tune, he wandered down to the vending area to grab a coffee and a chocolate bar then headed back to his desk. With a couple of hours to kill before he was due on duty for the Freja Portman rally, he could relax a bit, idly speculating that if both Lexy and Eleanor came up with the goods before he had to head out to Paddington Green, then this would truly be a day to remember.

It was Lexy who was first to call, almost breathless with excitement.

'Sir, sir, I've found her. I know who she is. And it's a terrible tragedy sir, it really is. That's why so many of her class-mates remember her.'

'Brilliant work Lexy, but what do you mean, a tragedy?'

'She killed herself sir, just a year later. Walked in a front of a train on the Edinburgh line. Can you believe it sir? Such a beautiful woman and a doctor too.'

'So she *was* a doctor then?'

'Yes sir, and not just any doctor sir.'

He could feel his heart start to race as her words sunk in. Instinctively, he knew what her answer would be but he still had to ask the question.

'What do you mean Lexy, not just any doctor?'

'She was the one that signed that still-born certificate sir. The same one. That can't be a coincidence sir, can it?'

For a moment he was speechless as he tried to process what it meant. The beautiful mystery blonde, the woman who in the photograph seemed rather too close to James Parrish, had signed that certificate. What it meant was that his crazy theory might not be so crazy after all.

'Are you still there sir?'

'Aye, I'm still here. This is bloody good work Lexy, very well done.'

'Thank you sir. By the way, Miss McNally was on the phone asking me if I'd had any success with the search. I thought I'd better speak to you first before I told her anything.'

Damn, he'd forgotten about Katherine and his promise to give her first refusal on the story. Not that she was exactly easy to forget, although he'd wondered how she would react after he'd made it plain, tactfully he hoped although he was far from sure, that he didn't intend to take up her generous offer of carnal relations. *There's someone else, I'd forgotten.* That's what she had said. *Sort of*, he had replied. Really, what kind of answer was that?

'Leave it to me Lexy, I'll give her a call. I'll tell her what we've found but ask her to hold off for a bit. I'm sure she'll understand.'

'Ok sir. Speak to you soon.'

And then just as he thought the day couldn't get any better, Eleanor Campbell turned up at his desk carrying her laptop under her arm with that pleased-with-herself expression on her face.

'I've like found something,' she said as she set up the device on his desk. 'I don't know what it means but I expect you will.'

He laughed. 'Are you feeling ok Eleanor? Because that must be the first time in living memory you've ever said anything nice to me.'

'Whatever.' She continued with her set up, Frank watching with heightened anticipation as she opened up her browser and navigated to a website.

'This is the NHS Scotland Patient Records system,' she said, her explanation unnecessary since the site's name was splashed all over the screen. 'It's confidential naturally but my mate Zak gave me an admin usercode and password and a two-factor authentication hack.'

'Nice one,' he said, finding himself ready to praise the callow secret-service geek for the second time in not many more days. 'He's a useful guy to know your Zak. Especially with these two-factor authentication hacks of his. Always liked them.'

She gave him a withering look before continuing. 'So we just key in the name...*Jolene Parrish*....and the date of birth....*25-12-70*...'

'What, she was a Christmas Day baby?' Frank said as he recognised the date.

Eleanor shook her head. 'No, that's another Zak hack. If you just know the year but not the actual date, you put in Christmas and it does a search. I had to use her maiden name for that but we know that.'

He was about to launch into another eulogy for Zak the hack guy when he thought better of it. The thing was, Eleanor didn't like rivals and so it was wise to go easy in that department lest she threw a strop and walked off the job. Instead he simply said,

'Aye Johnson, isn't it. So is that all we need?'

She nodded. 'Nearly. Just need to put in the date range we're interested in ...*Jan 1997 -Dec 1998*...' She keyed in the dates, then clicked on a button labelled *Submit.*

'So what's this we're looking at?' Frank said, squinting to focus on the small type.

'It's all her appointments during her pregnancy,' Eleanor said. 'Mainly to the hospital.'

The hospital in question was the Glasgow Royal Infirmary, the grand Edwardian edifice built alongside the city's ancient Cathedral and extended many times since. He knew the place well, but professionally, not as a patient. On a typical weekend, its Accident & Emergency department hosted a constant stream of drunks and ne'er-do-wells and during his

Gorbals cop-shop service he was often called up there to sort out trouble. *Happy days*.

'She seemed to be there a lot,' he said. 'For scans, if I'm reading this right.'

'Yeah, I guess,' she said, sounding impatient, 'but that's not why I said I'd found something. It was *this*.' She pointed to the bottom row. '*Performed amniocentesis.* I don't know what it means but I thought it was important.'

'I knew it! I bloody knew it!' His reaction was as explosive as it was involuntary. 'I knew there was something that didn't add up. Bloody hell. I *knew* I was right.'

What was it they called it, a red-letter day or something like that? Aye, if that was it, then there was no doubt about it, this was the red-letter day to end all red-letter days. But perhaps not for James Parrish FRCS.

Chapter 24

It was Thursday, the evening of their regular Old King's Head meet-up when they could relax, enjoy a drink and a few laughs whilst chewing the fat about their various investigations. But this evening the atmosphere was subdued, Maggie's head in a spin as she struggled to make sense of everything that had hit her that afternoon. Tonight it was just her and Jimmy, Frank being on duty at the big Freja Portman rally, and god what she would have given to have him here. Because she sensed that if the mad but plausible theory that was slowly taking shape proved to be correct, then the evening was going to be *very* difficult indeed, and she could really do with his support. However, at least there was some good news to be celebrated and Jimmy, quite unaware of what was going on in his boss's head, was evidently intending to do so. They were standing at the bar, he somewhat detached as he tried to catch the attention of the barmaid.

'We really should get a glass of fizz or something to celebrate the arrival of two brand-new wee human beings into this world. Asvina's girl's a right wee beauty, I saw your photo. And Jolene's too, a lovely wee boy.'

'Yes it is wonderful,' Maggie agreed, 'and both mothers and their babies are doing well by all accounts. Although they're being kept in for a day or two, being older mums.'

'Aye, I suppose that's pretty normal,' he said. 'At least it shouldn't be too much of a hardship in that fancy place they're in. It's like a bijou hotel. It was good that Jolene was well enough to be moved.'

Jimmy had finally succeeded in ordering, handing her a large glass of prosecco and chinking his own glass against it.

'Cheers Maggie. Here's to the miracle of new life.'

She smiled. 'That's a lovely thing to say. Are you religious then Jimmy? Because if you are, you've kept it well-hidden up to now.'

'You joking?' he said, almost spitting the words out. 'It's only that I've seen way too much death not to appreciate how special life is. But how we got here in the first place, I haven't a clue. Maybe there is a creator, who knows? But I'll tell you one thing, if he was going to do it all over again, I bet he wouldn't make us so dumb this time round.'

She laughed. 'What makes you so sure it's a *he*?'

'Well it must be a *he*,' he said, 'because he made a total arse of it first time round, didn't he? I mean, we've been here what, a million years and we're still killing each other. That wouldn't have happened if he was a she. We'd all be baking cakes and arranging flowers and going to the Women's Institute, and that wouldn't be such a bad thing.'

'Maybe *she* wouldn't bother with men at all next time round,' Maggie said. 'I think we women could have a perfectly nice time without them,' her face flushing a little as she realised what she had just said.

He raised an eyebrow but thankfully didn't make any comment, although he was obviously amused by her embarrassment.

'So what about the Kylie Winterburn news?' he said brightly. 'That's interesting isn't it? Sort of backs up my theory I think, that she's involved in some way.'

She was glad that he had brought up the subject himself because since getting the news from Frank earlier, she had scarcely being able to think of anything else. Finding out that Winterburn had worked at Fortnum Price, the same place as Harry Newton and Lily Wu, and just like that pair had what could best be described as a chequered history had set Maggie down a path which as far as the investigation was concerned was as promising as it was disturbing. A path that had led to a phone call with slimy Nigel Redmond of Drake Chambers, who after consulting with his Fortnums inside man Des, had confirmed her suspicions. This was indeed going to be difficult. *Bloody difficult.*

'Yes you're right, I think she was,' she said, looking serious. 'Look, I need to run something past you. A theory, a crazy theory perhaps. Just to see what you think.'

He gave her a thumbs-up. 'Aye, of course boss. Shoot.'

She took a fortifying gulp from her glass before beginning.

'So we've always kind of assumed that the harassment of Jolene started when Harry Newton and Lily Wu joined the team, bringing with them their grudge against her because of what happened when they were all working together at Fortnum Price. That's right isn't it?'

He gave her a searching look. 'Aye, that's what we've always thought. Because it seemed to make sense.'

She nodded. 'Yes it did, which I think caused us to overlook the most obvious thing of all.'

'Which is?'

'That this all actually started when Jolene became pregnant. And not only that, it started *because* she became pregnant.'

'I'm not sure I get it,' he said, looking puzzled. 'Where you're going with this I mean.'

'So what if someone at Addison Redburn has a reason to hate Jolene Cavendish and that person has been quietly lying low, biding their time for perhaps years until the right moment comes along so they can exact their revenge? And then quite unexpectedly, Jolene gets pregnant and they see their chance.'

'But what is the person trying to achieve?' Jimmy said. 'When you say revenge.'

Maggie shrugged. 'I don't know exactly, but I think maybe they want to scare her enough so she leaves or has a nervous breakdown or something.'

And it was true, there must have been some initiating incident in the past, perhaps a career slight or maybe it was just pure jealousy for how well Jolene had done for herself, with all the money and status that went with it, and now as the icing on the cake, she was having a baby. A superabundance of success and achievement that the perpetrator felt had been unfairly denied to her. Yes, and that was right. *Her*. There was no point in trying to conceal it from him any longer. She reached over and squeezed his arm, fearful for how he might to react to what she was about to say.

'Look Jimmy...I'm sorry, but I think it might be Emily.'

'What, are you bloody crazy? No way!'

It was what she had expected, a quite understandable eruption of shock and anger, but as she momentarily caught his eye, she saw there was something else too. It was almost imperceptible, but nonetheless it was present through his rage. *Fear*. She knew him so well, well enough to know that he would surely have had the same suspicions, but blinded by his love for her, he would have pushed them to the back of his mind, unwilling to contemplate even for a moment that they could be true.

'I'm sorry,' she said again, 'but it's just...' There was no way of escaping it, she had to tell him what she believed had happened.

'Look, Harry Newton and Lily Wu were basically both unemployable after what happened at Fortnums, and yet they were both somehow able to secure positions at Addison Redburn, one of the most prestigious law firms in London. You remember what Jolene told us Jimmy, don't you?'

'No I don't,' he said. His tone edged on the petulant but his eyes betrayed sadness.

She gave a heavy sigh. 'She said that in the mad panic to get bums on seats to handle the escalating Hampton Defence workload Jolene had delegated all recruitment decisions to HR, or more specifically to Emily Smith.'

'But there was nothing wrong with that,' he said defensively. 'They were both well-qualified lawyers, it made perfect sense.'

'No no Jimmy, it didn't make sense, not with their track-record and certainly not for a firm like Addisons. And who do you think recruited Kylie Winterburn? And she had a criminal record for Pete's sake.'

'Everybody deserves a second chance, don't they?' he said, but she suspected from his subdued tone that his doubts were beginning to grow.

'Emily lied to us Jimmy. To me *and* to you. Because when you asked her for a list of staff who had worked with Jolene at Fortnum Price, she left Winterburn off the list.'

'Perhaps she forgot.'

'She didn't forget. And she left herself off the list too. Oh yes, she worked there too, didn't you know that? My old clerk at Drake Chambers has got contacts in there and he told me today. Now why would Emily have done that Jimmy? Why?'

She let the question hang in the air, sliding her hand down his arm and placing it in his.

He hesitated. 'Look...there was something in her life, something awful. Years and years ago. She often hinted at it but she would never tell me what it was.'

And as Maggie heard his words, it hit her, like an express train crashing out of a tunnel into the blinding daylight. *The mystery blonde in that photograph. Now it all made perfect sense.* There was just one more piece in the jigsaw to be slotted into place and for that she had to speak to Frank. *Right now.*

It rang for what seemed like minutes and she was worried that it might flip over to his voicemail, but then he answered, sounding flustered.

'Not a good time Maggie, we've got a wee bit of a situation here. You'll need to make it a quick one.'

She could barely make him out above the roar of a crowd in the background, but she could clearly make out the stream of non-complimentary explicatives directed at the police.

'Get that bastard,' she heard him shout. *'Look, there, that skinny guy with the black bomber jacket. Not him, the other guy! Sorry Maggie, what was it you wanted?'*

'Sorry Frank I won't keep you long.' She hoped he would see the funny side of that. 'But did you get a name? For that woman in the picture? I know you were working on it.'

And then he told her. *Everything*. That the beautiful young woman had been a doctor, and she had been the doctor who had signed the certificate for Jolene's tragically still-born baby, and that she had taken her own life less than one year later. And then he told Maggie her name.

Dr Helen Smith.

'Shit! Jimmy, where's Emily? The words spilled out, urgent, imploring. 'What was she doing tonight?'

'Christ,' he said, his voice betraying raw fear. 'She was going to visit Jolene. To see the baby, to take the wee lad a present.'

'We've got to get there now,' she shouted. 'We really do. Come on.'

Squeezing his hand tighter, she dragged him towards the door.

'A cab,' she said as they tumbled out onto the pavement. 'We need to get a cab. And we need to call the police, get them round there right away.'

He gave her an incredulous look. 'Are you crazy? Tonight? We'll never get a taxi to take us up to Kensington, not with that Freja Portman rally in full flight. The streets will be rammed. And I don't think we'll get much of a police response either.'

'Then it's up to us,' she said. 'Look, there's a taxi coming. Flag him down.'

The cab driver spotted Jimmy's wave and pulled up alongside them.

'Where to mate?' he shouted through the open window.

Jimmy stuck his head through. 'South Kensington. Brompton Park Maternity Hospital. Just off Lexham Road.'

The cabbie shook his head dismissively. 'I know it and let me tell you there's no way mate, not with all that climate shit kicking off up there. Sorry pal, but I'd never get back, never mind getting there in the first place.'

It seemed as if he was about to drive off until Maggie squeezed her head in alongside Jimmy's and gave the taxi driver a plaintive look, her words spilling out in a torrent. 'But it's an emergency. My waters just broke and I'm going into labour and I think our baby could be born any minute. Please, please will you help us? We've tried to call an ambulance but I think the emergency services are overwhelmed because of the Freja thing and I'm frantic with worry.' She hoped he wouldn't look down in the direction of her non-existent bump. 'And my baby's eight weeks premature,' she added, just in case. She gave Jimmy a sharp look, worried that he might inadvertently say something to give the game away, but evidently he had cottoned on. 'It's our first you see,' he said, with convincing concern, 'and we're worried because the wee mite is *so* premature.'

'Shit,' the driver said, 'if you'll pardon my French. Look, I'm not promising nothing but maybe we can get there if we heads over the river and then comes in from the south-west. Yeah, we'd need to do that cos everything north of the river is going to be like a car-park. So if we beetle over Tower Bridge and then make for Stamford Street and the South Bank then maybe try and sneak back north over Vauxhall Bridge, that might just do it.'

He was silent for a moment, Maggie unsure whether he was contemplating alternative routings or whether to accept the mission at all. Then finally he said, 'Right, get in. And I don't want no bitching about the fare neither. The meter will be running and it's going to be a long way round. Sixty quid at least.'

'No worries mate, price no object,' Jimmy said, opening the rear door and pushing Maggie in. 'And it goes without saying, you need to get the hammer down.'

Nearing eight o'clock, light was fading on the murky early October evening, the drizzle of rain that had been falling now looking as if it might turn into something more substantial. But progress was swift, the driver taking full advantage of the designated taxi and bus lanes and gunning traffic lights to ensure their progress wasn't halted too much. In keeping with the stereotype of the London cabbie, he kept up a constant prattle the entire length of the journey. *'Me name's Terry by the way... nah, I've never had a lady give birth in me cab before...'course I've a few close-run things in me time... and you'll never guess what but I had that reality bird once from that Essex telly programme... she must have been at least eight months gone and the kid weren't her husband's as it turned out...'*

Peering through the rain-splattered window, Maggie could just about make out the distinctive silhouette of the Houses of Parliament on the other side of the river. Ten minutes into the journey, she guessed they were still only half-way there. It was unbearable, the tension gnawing away at her insides but she knew there was nothing they could do but rely on Terry to get them there as quickly as he could.

'Change of plan,' the cabbie said as if reading her thoughts. 'I think Battersea's going to be the best place to cross. Then up past Earls Court. Keeps us as far away from the Park as possible. Should save us a few minutes.'

'We're in your hands,' Jimmy said, 'but aye, fast as you can mate.'

Soon they had reached Battersea Bridge and were ready to turn north again, the traffic perceptibly busier and a string of pedestrians in regulation gaudy cagoules streaming towards the Portman vigil, already too late to bag a place near the front of the stage.

Their speed had reduced to a crawl and Terry spun his head round to speak to them. 'Look guys, I'm not sure how close we're going to be able to get. The sat-nav's telling me Warwick and Earls Court Roads are both going nowhere. We might just about make it to the Cromwell Road if we're lucky but I wouldn't even bet on that.'

Maggie was vaguely familiar with the geography of the area and reckoned that would get them within half a mile of the hospital. Close enough, but it might take five minutes or more to get to the Cromwell Road, and as the sense of utter helplessness threatening to overwhelm her, she knew she couldn't sit in this cab a minute longer.

'Pay the man Jimmy,' she said, reaching for the door handle. 'Pay Terry and let's get out now.'

'Are you sure?' Terry said, sounding concerned. 'In your condition?'

'I'll be fine and thank you so much for helping us.' Now she felt bad about deceiving him and wondered if she should come clean. But there wasn't time.

'Pleasure love.' He rummaged around in a pocket and emerged with a business card which he thrust into Jimmy's hand. 'Don't bother with all that payment palaver now mate. You two get on your way and you can settle up with me later. And good luck. Send me a photo of your baby.'

They were already on the pavement and breaking into a run before he'd finished speaking.

'It's about a mile or so I think,' Jimmy said. 'Not far.'

Maggie knew that his idea of *not far* was very different from her own and that in any case she couldn't hope to match his pace. And they didn't have a moment to lose.

'Don't wait for me,' she said, already breathless. 'You've got to get there as fast as you can. I think Jolene and Asvina are in terrible danger. And their little babies too.'

Now she could only prey they weren't already too late.

*****

As Terry the cabbie had forecast, Earls Court Road was beginning to jam up, and not just with vehicular traffic. The pavements too were now crammed shoulder-to-shoulder with the citizens of the great city making their way to Hyde Park, anxious to make a public show of their environmental credentials and demonstrate their love for the high priestess Freja Portman. As a result, it was impossible to make any kind of rapid progress, even by threading his way through the maze of now-stationary cars, vans and buses. He had to get off the main drag and hope that not too many folks had the same idea. He took the first side road he came to, heading east, already panting heavily as he pushed the pace up. And then north, along Laverton Place, which if his navigation was correct, would lead very nearly to the door of the maternity hospital. The pavements were still busy, but with the residential street having restricted-access for vehicles he was able to make good use of the roadway. In his army days he'd been a useful middle-distance runner, clocking respectable times in both 800 and 1500 metres but now he rued allowing himself to get so out of condition. But then again, half of distance running was in the mind, and you never lost *that*. As he gritted his teeth, he could hear the ethereal voice of his sadistic army PE instructor ringing in his ear. *Dig deep Stewart you lazy bastard, dig deep.* Even in this condition, he knew he should be able to clock under six minutes for the mile, better if he really pushed it. *He needed to push it.*

Ahead he could make out the glow of lights from the stationary traffic on the Brompton Road perhaps two or three hundred yards ahead. In a minute he'd be there, then it would be a matter of threading his way across the road and making the final sprint to the hospital.

And then of course he would be faced with his next problem. *How to get past security*. Because this place wasn't a common-or-garden maternity hospital. Their clientele were millionaires and film stars and royalty, and they weren't going to let any Tom, Dick or Harry just wander in off the street, especially after visiting hours.

As he reached the wide entrance porch, he sneaked a glance at his watch. Six minutes eight seconds for what he estimated was a mile plus a couple of hundred yards, which all-in-all wasn't too bad. So now to the security guy, if it was a guy, and to Plan A. *Persuasion*.

It was a guy, and as Jimmy sprinted into the reception area the uniformed man got to his feet and gave him an enquiring look.

'Visiting time's closed now sir, I'm afraid, if that's why you're here. All our little babies will be tucked up in their cots by now.'

He had the look of ex-military about him, powerfully-built and straight-backed with greying cropped hair. Which Jimmy realised might prove a bit of a problem if he was forced to move to Plan B. *Direct action.*

He shot the words out, struggling to catch his breath. 'Mate, I'm a private detective and I need your help. It's Mrs Cavendish and Mrs Rani, the two ladies who're sharing a room. They're in terrible danger. The woman who is visiting them, she means to do them harm. We need to get to them right away.'

The guard shook his head. 'All the visitors have gone nearly an hour ago. We do an announcement over the tannoy at seven-ten sharp and everyone has to be out by seven-fifteen. Nobody here now.'

'But do you actually check? Count them in and count them out?'

'What? Course we don't, but no-one overstays their welcome. The rules are quite strict.'

'I don't care about that.' Jimmy was shouting now, his face only a few inches from the guard's. 'This woman has already tried to harm one of the mothers and I believe she means to do it again. You need to let me through. Right now. Please.'

It was becoming evident to Jimmy that his Plan A was rapidly running out of steam. 'What? No way mate,' the guard said. 'I can't leave my post, and you're not going anywhere neither.' With a conspicuous lack of urgency, he wandered back to his desk. 'But if you like, we'll take a quick gander at the CCTV, see what's what. I know them two ladies, they're in room eighteen I think.'

Time for Plan B. Jimmy reached the desk in one stride, simultaneously launching a powerful right hook that caught the guard completely by surprise, knocking him off his swivel chair and leaving him sprawling on the floor. Running round behind the desk, he searched and swiftly discovered what he was looking for, the button that released the remote lock on the entrance door to the corridors. He heard the buzz and then a click, sprinting over and pushing them open before the time switch locked them again. He guessed he had no more than thirty seconds or so before the guard recovered and set off in pursuit. Thirty seconds to locate and get to room eighteen. Fortunately that part of the mission wasn't going to be too complicated, as a large sign on the facing wall helpfully pointed the way. *Rooms 1-10, to the left. Rooms 11-20, to the right.* He took the right-hand corridor, half-running, reading the room numbers as he went. Then he saw two nurses walking along the corridor towards him, cutting short their conversation when they saw his approach. The older of the two give him a searching look, he assuming she had noticed that he was not wearing a security pass.

'Can I help you sir?' she said, sounding suspicious.

'Yes you can,' he said, his tone urgent. 'The mums in room eighteen, they're in danger. When did you last check on them?'

She looked at her colleague. 'What was it Rose? About thirty minutes ago I suppose. But what's this all about? And who are you?'

There was no time to explain. 'Take me there, please. They're in danger, really they are, deadly danger. And call the police. They should already know about it but we need to be sure.'

She paused for a moment, as if weighing up whether to believe him or not before evidently being convinced. 'It's just round this corner. Second door on the left.'

'Ok. And I don't want to alarm you, but the assailant might have a bomb. So get everyone out of their rooms to a place of safety. Right away. Please, don't argue, just do it.'

Reaching the door to maternity room eighteen, he pushed down on the handle. *Locked.* Banging the door with his fist he yelled at the top of his voice. 'Emily. Emily darling. It's Jimmy. Let me in. I want to talk to you. Please.' *No answer.*

Turning round, he saw that the security guard had recovered and was heading straight for him, red-faced and seething with anger.

'Wait wait pal,' Jimmy said holding his hands out in front of him. 'The room's locked, look you can try it for yourself. That's not normal is it? Look, try it.'

'We never lock the doors Brian,' the younger nurse said to the guard. 'Something's not right here.'

And then unexpectedly they heard the click of a key turning in the lock.

'Please, leave this to me,' Jimmy said. 'And get these other rooms evacuated. And Brian, my colleague should be arriving any minute now. Maggie Bainbridge her name is. Whatever you do, don't let her in, ok?'

Gingerly Jimmy pushed at the door, letting it swing open but remaining in the corridor. He'd done dozens of these sweeps during his Afghanistan service, and every time you had to shove to the back of your mind the ever-present threat of booby-traps. But this time it wasn't insurgents he had to worry about. This time it was the woman he had fallen in love with.

He could see Asvina sitting on her bed, clutching her little baby daughter tight to her chest. Directly opposite sat Jolene, sobbing quietly, her arm still heavily bandaged from the acid attack. She wasn't holding her baby. And then he caught Asvina's eye, saw her signal with an almost imperceptible movement of her head.

'I'm coming in Emily,' he said in a quiet voice. 'I know you're behind the door. I just want to talk to you and we can get this all sorted out.' He walked slowly into the room, automatically closing the door behind him. That was one of the basic rules he remembered from his simulated training in that mock village on Salisbury Plain. Do everything you can to contain the blast should the worst come to the worst. Hopefully it wouldn't come to that.

She had her back to the corner, standing stock-still, her hair tousled, dark mascara tracing a line down her cheek from where she had been crying, cradling a new-born in her arms. And she was wearing a backpack.

'Hello Jimmy, this is baby Sam,' she said, her head unnaturally motionless. 'Please kiss me.'

'Christ, not now Emily,' he said, pulling his head away. 'Look, whatever this is all about, it's not worth all of this.'

'She killed my sister,' she said, nodding at Jolene. 'Her and her *famous* husband. And now it's time for payback.'

'Please give me my baby,' Jolene said, her voice trembling. 'He's done nothing to you. You can kill me but spare my little boy.'

'Nobody's going to die here,' Jimmy said, sounding more confident than he felt. 'I don't know what happened all these years ago but this isn't going to solve anything. Come on Emily, give me the baby please.'

Now his professional head began to kick in. She didn't seem to be holding a remote switch or anything of that nature but he'd already worked out how the bomb was to be detonated anyway. Somewhere in that backpack she had wired up some sort of motion sensor, which accounted for her standing there like a statue. *Shit.* The slightest movement and bang, they would all be dead. *Double shit.* It was a favourite tactic of the Helmand suicide bombers or at least of the evil men who manipulated the minds of the young people they exploited. Which meant there was only one possible way to mitigate the inevitable carnage that would ensue and that was to slam the bomber tight against a wall so that their body absorbed the lion's share of the blast. Unfortunately, the person doing the slamming was odds-on certain to die too. No matter how you looked at it, there were no good outcomes. So really, there was only one practical option here. Back to Plan A. *Persuasion.* Except that didn't exactly work out well the last time he'd tried it.

His train of thought was broken by a commotion going on behind him out in the corridor.

'Let me through. Look, I'm her best friend, she needs me. And *he* needs me too. Let me *through.*'

It seemed that she had done a better job in persuading Brian the guard than he had, not that it was any surprise knowing how she operated. But now he had to make sure she didn't do anything stupid. As Maggie slipped into the room, he nodded his head in Emily's direction.

'Boss, we've got a wee bit of a situation here so we need to keep everything nice and calm.'

But it seemed she already understood.

'Hello Emily,' she said, smiling, her voice warm and soothing. 'I wanted to talk to you because I've got some good news. You see, the police have found out what James Parrish did all these years ago. What both of them did, James and Jolene. He's going to be arrested in the morning so you will have your justice. You don't need to do any of this. Come on, give me the baby and we can get all of this sorted out.'

'Do you think I want justice?' Emily said, spitting out the words. 'I gave up on that years ago. What I want is *revenge*.'

'It won't make you feel better,' Jimmy said. 'I've tried it and it doesn't work. But getting justice will. You might not see that now, but believe me in time you will. Stop all of this now and you'll still be able to have a great life. The justice system will be sympathetic, I'm sure of it. But only if you stop now. Please darling, give me the wee baby. He's so innocent, he doesn't deserve to be mixed up in this.'

She gave him an uncertain look. 'But they need to pay, don't they? For everything they've done.'

'And they will,' Maggie said. 'James Parrish is going to prison and after all he's done, he's going to die there.' She turned to Jolene Cavendish. 'And I'm afraid you're going to prison too. You're not going to see your little boy growing up. You see, *I know what you did*.'

Jolene gave a harrowing cry as tears beginning to trickle down her cheek. 'He made me do it. He was cold and manipulative and he said he would leave me for *her* sister if I didn't go along with it. I'd no choice and I was so young.'

Jimmy looked at Maggie and could see what she was thinking. Everybody has choices, and the choices that Jolene and her husband had made had led, directly and indirectly, to the loss of two innocent lives. But that was an issue for another day. Right now, there were slightly more important matters to be dealt with. He took a half-step towards Emily, then as softly as he could, stretched out his arm and stroked her cheek with the back of his hand.

'So you see, they *are* going to pay a heavy price and it's no more than they deserve. But you don't have to. You're young, you're clever, you're beautiful. So please, don't do this. Give me the baby Emily. Please give me the baby.'

She gave him a sad look, but he could see her resistance was starting to fade.

'Come on Emily. This wee guy doesn't deserve any of this.' He held out his hands in front of him. 'No more deaths, please. Come on wee baby, come to me. Nice and easy.'

With a whimper, she placed the baby in Jimmy's arms, her face convulsed with pain.

'Thank you Emily,' he said. 'You did the right thing. You did the right thing.'

He turned and handed the baby to Maggie, nodding towards Asvina and Jolene, his voice urgent.

'Get them the hell out of here. And you too. And I don't want to see you in here again until this is over, understand?'

Maggie looked as if she was about to protest until Asvina intervened.

'I'll make sure she doesn't Jimmy. And thank you, thank you so much. Come on Maggie, do as Jimmy says. Quickly.'

*****

With the room safely evacuated, he could turn his attention to Emily Smith, the woman who he once thought he might be in love with, and who was now in imminent danger of blowing them both to pieces.

'Emily, please listen to me. What have you used for the trigger? Something you found on the web I'm assuming?'

She looked to be in shock and for a moment he thought it had robbed her of the power of speech. But finally she said, 'A vibration sensor.'

'Right.' Now he had to think fast. He'd seen the type of device before, the trigger mechanism crude but effective, but the good news was, admittedly only relatively-speaking, that they needed a pretty definitive motion to set them off. Jumping up and down, yes. A gentle sway, probably not. Thank goodness for small mercies.

'Ok Emily,' he said. 'So we're going to have to get that backpack off you. I'm not sure how yet, but we will.'

She was crying again. 'I don't want to die Jimmy. I don't want to die.'

'No, me neither,' he said, attempting a smile. 'So just keep really still whilst I think about this.'

His thoughts were interrupted by a light rap on the door. It was Brian the security guard.

'I've just been outside talking to the police, giving them an update. The upshot is, they're surrounding the place but they won't come in. They say it's a hostage situation and the procedure is to send in a specialist negotiator. They only problem is she's in Chelmsford and won't be here for at least forty minutes.'

Jimmy shook his head in disgust. 'Bloody hell, that's a great help.' But as he spoke, an idea suddenly came into his head.

'Listen Brian, I'm getting a feeling you might be ex-forces, am I right?'

'Corporal Brian Ford, Royal Engineers,' the guard said, the pride obvious in his voice. 'Retired.'

'Captain Jimmy Stewart, 11 EOD&S Regiment Bomb Squad. Now then Corporal Ford, how do you fancy signing up for one more very short tour of duty?'

His reply was instant. 'Love to sir,' he said, giving a grin. 'Await your orders. But just don't make the tour of duty too short sir, if you get my drift.'

Jimmy laughed. 'I'll try not to mate. So we'll need a sharp knife, can you get one?'

'Yep, they'll have them in the delivery suites. Two seconds, I'll be back.'

It was more like ten, but it was still bloody quick. He could tell that he and Ford were going to get on just fine.

'So Emily,' Jimmy said, 'I need you to be very brave and don't move a muscle. What's going to happen is that Corporal Ford here is going to cut the shoulder straps of your backpack and then I'm going to take its weight. Then when I say ready, I need you to step forward as slowly as you can. Just give a gentle nod if you understand. But don't move until I tell you. Corporal Ford, are you ready?'

Ford nodded. 'Ready sir.'

'Ok,' Jimmy said. 'So I'll kneel down behind her and support the backpack from below, so that you've got room to work. Make sure you let me know before you make the final cut on each strap so that I can confirm I'm taking the weight.'

'Ok sir.' Ford slipped round behind them and began to cut. 'It's going through very easily sir. Couple of seconds and the first one will be done...yeah, there we go... ready to take the weight sir?'

'Ready.'

'Done. Right sir moving onto the second one now...cutting...cutting. Right sir, I'm ready for the final cut.'

'Ok,' Jimmy said, speaking slowly. 'So Emily, we're just about there. When Corporal Ford makes that final cut, I'll be holding the backpack and everything will be quite safe. I will say ready, and I want you to walk away as gently as you can, one step at a time. And I repeat, don't move until I say ready.'

He looked up at Ford.

'Ready Corporal?

'Ready to cut sir,' Ford said, 'when you give the order.'

'Ok, let's just take a quick breath before we do this.' His arms were beginning to hurt with the effort of holding up the heavy backpack and he wasn't sure how much longer he could keep it in a stable position. So it was now or never.

'Ok Corporal. Cut!'

Now he felt the full weight of the device as the final supporting strands of the strap gave way.

'Ready Emily,' he barked. 'Go.'

For what seemed like an age she did not move, but then at last she stepped forward, moving tentatively, freeing herself from her murderous burden.

'Get her out of here Corporal. Now.'

As Ford led Emily Smith from the room, Jimmy began to lower the backpack to the floor, sweat streaming down his face, his heart banging in his chest. One false move and that would be the end of everything for him, a situation he had faced before but had never expected to face again.

But finally, it was done.

Chapter 25

The Holly Tree in Belgravia was the sort of place you had to triple your credit card limit before you booked it, its reputation for fine food only matched by its stratospheric prices. But Maggie wasn't worried about that because today Sir Patrick Hopkins was picking up the lunch tab, or more accurately she suspected, Her Majesty's Government was, or more accurate still, the British tax-payer. They'd hired a private room, necessary to accommodate the extensive guest list, and the efficient waiting staff had just cleared away the desserts and were about to serve the cheese and port.

Positioned as she was at one end of the long table, she was able to effortlessly survey the noisy scene where conversation was in full flow, lubricated by an excellent and extensive wine list chosen personally by Sir Patrick. He sat immediately to her left, accompanied by his researcher, a stick insect of a girl lacking in humour whom Maggie suspected provided rather more than research services to the amiable cabinet minister. Next to them and wearing an expression that suggested she would rather be anywhere on earth than here was Dame Amanda Compton, Commissioner of the Metropolitan Police, forced to attend by order of the Home Secretary as a cruel form of punishment for her many failures in the role. Next to her, Detective Constable Ronnie French, hero of the hour and the man likely to be responsible for Dame Amanda losing her job. He was accompanied by his wife, an attractive and well-groomed woman who looked about ten years younger than her husband and about five levels above his social class. Which just went to prove what

Frank had always said about Ronnie. You underestimated him at your peril.

Next to them and laughing their heads off at some unspecified joke were PC Lexy Macdonald and Eleanor Campbell, an unlikely pairing but who had seemed to hit it off from the start. It was Frank who had insisted on their attendance as a reward for their hard work on the case. She knew he respected them greatly although they were as different as chalk and cheese.

And then of course there was Jimmy, on the opposite side of the table and looking amazing in the new suit he had bought for the Addison Redburn assignment, flanked by what she now thought of as his harem, although she would never describe them as such in his presence. To his right, the puppy-like Elsa Berger who somehow had managed to wangle herself an invitation, wearing her devotion to him on her sleeve. To his left, the rather more subtle DCI Jill Smart whom Maggie suspected was no less ardent in her feelings for him, playing the long game with skill and cunning.

Katherine McNally was there too, somehow looking several years younger in person than she did on television. She was lovely, causing Maggie to reflect that so much of life's success was due to the cards that fate dealt you, or that God provided you with if you believed in that sort of thing. Katherine was beautiful and she was clever and had used these gifts to build an enviable career. On top of that, she could probably have any man she wanted too. But not Frank, or so it seemed. He sat next to her and they were talking and smiling and evidently were very comfortable in each other's company. But it was no more than that, Maggie was sure from reading their body chemistry, and she was pleased about that.

There was a ring from a cheese knife clinking against a wineglass and Sir Patrick stood up, evidently intending to address the gathering. He waited for a few seconds until the room quietened before speaking.

'So ladies and gentlemen, what a splendid lunch we've been treated to don't you think? And I've heard they keep the best cheese board in London so it's not over yet, not to mention the port of course.'

Everybody laughed, and there was a ripple of applause too.

'Thank you, thank you,' he said, grinning. 'We are here of course today to celebrate success. It's something my civil service colleagues - or should I call them minders - are very keen that we should do. So here we are, doing just that. And goodness, haven't we got a lot to celebrate?'

That prompted polite murmurs of acknowledgement.

'So, where do we start? DCI Smart, why don't you tell us all about the splendid work of your Department in exposing that bounder Parrish and what he did to that young girl?'

Maggie gave a quiet smile. Sir Patrick was delightfully old fashioned, occupying a world where you addressed people as ladies and gentlemen and not guys, where the bad guys were bounders and where no lunch could possibly be complete without cheese and port.

'Thank you Sir Patrick,' Jill Smart said, 'but Department 12B is in the safe hands of Inspector Stewart so I'll let Frank take the stage if you don't mind.'

Frank shook his head.

'Aye, I'd love to,' he said, smiling, 'but you see I really had sod-all to do with it although I am naturally prepared to take the glory, and the knighthood too if there's one going.'

He raised a hand to acknowledge the laughter.

'No, this was all down to my splendid colleagues Detective Constable French and forensic officer Eleanor Campbell. So Ronnie, I believe it's you who's going to be doing the talking?'

French gave a laconic smile. 'That's right guv. I do all the talking and Eleanor does all the work. The fact is it all started when we heard the brass were planning to close down Department 12B just to save a few quid. I mean, what sort of plonker would want to do that given all the successes we've had?'

Maggie looked at Commissioner Compton, who was wearing a face like thunder. Then she looked at Sir Patrick, who was obviously trying to suppress a laugh. It seemed this was going to be an uncomfortable few minutes for the sanctimonious and self-regarding Dame.

'So me and Eleanor started thinking that what we needed was a big success for the department, so that there was no way we could be closed down. And then by luck I was talking to my mate Barry at the snooker club, and that's when I got the idea. You see Barry's a good lad but he's one of them eco-mentalists and he was there at that terrible acid attack at that hotel. But anyways, he tells me that the vetting to get into Freja's do was really stringent, if that's the right word. You needed to send your passport and send two utility bills, and they did a check for a criminal record and all sorts of stuff. So the upshot was, it was pretty impossible to get in if you weren't pukka.'

'Interesting,' Sir Patrick said.

'Yeah it was sir,' French continued. 'And that's when I knew that the investigations we were doing were a heap of bollocks. We were scouring the city rounding up every right-wing nutter with a shaved head and bomber jacket and talking crap to the media about imminent breakthroughs when the truth was right under our noses.'

It looked to Maggie as if Compton was going to say something and then changed her mind. Maybe she had realised you couldn't defend the indefensible.

'So I decided to do some digging for myself,' French said. He looked at Frank and gave a rueful smile. 'I'm sorry I didn't tell you guv, but I didn't want you getting into trouble for stamping all over somebody else's investigation. Anyway, my hunch was it had to be an inside job. Obvious really, when you think of it, given the vetting of the audience. So I start asking the hotel staff a few questions about who was on duty that night and whatnot and bang, up pops this guy Thomas Holt. He's obviously a bit of a boy racer because he's got a string of convictions for motoring offences, speeding, dangerous driving, the whole works. And then one day his luck runs out and he goes flying through a windscreen. And that's when he meets James Parrish.'

'Interesting,' Sir Patrick said again, an analysis evidently not shared by Dame Amanda if her scowl was anything to go by.

French nodded. 'Parrish had got this mad obsession about getting a knighthood and the whole Freja Portman circus gave him the idea. So he paid the toe-rag Hunt a hundred grand to spray her with that sulphuric acid, so that he could play the big hero by rebuilding her.'

'And it nearly worked didn't it?' said Maggie, 'if hadn't been for Holt blowing the money on that Range Rover.'

'Yeah, that's right,' French agreed. 'As soon as Holt started drawing attention to himself it was only going to end one way. With him lying on a slab in a mortuary somewhere.'

'So what about evidence?' Sir Patrick asked.

'Looking good sir,' Frank said. 'Because young Eleanor here was able to trace the money back to an offshore account in the Cayman Isles in the name of one James Parrish.'

'It wasn't like *easy*,' Eleanor interjected, drawing a vigorous nod of agreement from Lexy, 'there was a whole mountain of fake companies and accounts all tangled up like spaghetti. It took tons of work from me and my mate Zak.'

'Zak?' Sir Patrick asked.

'You don't want to know sir,' Frank said, giving him a knowing look.

'Jolly good,' he said, nodding. 'Understand. But absolutely excellent work Eleanor. Top-notch.'

Maggie smiled as Frank winked at her from the other end of the table, a gesture she hoped the blushing Eleanor hadn't spotted. The girl liked to be praised for her work whilst trying to pretend that she didn't, but this time she couldn't hide her pride.

'But what about the murder?' Sir Patrick continued. 'How are we looking on that?'

'You'd be better asking Dame Amanda about that,' Frank said, giving a seraphic smile, 'because it's been handled by the murder squad, but I understand they've found some very strong circumstantial evidence. The victim was incapacitated by an injection of a general anaesthetic, and then his wrists were cut in what the pathologists described as an expert manner, whatever the hell that is. No DNA or fingerprints, but then you wouldn't expect a guy like Parrish to make that sort of mistake. But it all points to someone with detailed medical knowledge.'

'Amanda, would you like to comment?' Sir Patrick said, knowing exactly what he was doing. It seemed to Maggie that the Establishment had fallen out of love with their Commissioner of Police and they wanted her to know it.

'Inspector Stewart is correct,' Compton replied stiffly. 'The evidence is mainly circumstantial but we believe we have enough for the CPS, given the overwhelming motive and the strong evidence of him orchestrating Miss Portman's attack.'

'Jolly good,' he said, smiling, 'and you must be very pleased that Inspector Stewart's department has dug you out of the hole you were in?'

'Yes,' she said through gritted teeth. 'Very pleased.'

'Jolly good,' he said for the third or fourth time, 'but Inspector Stewart, I believe those two terrible crimes are not everything on Mr Parrish's charge-sheet?'

Frank nodded. 'Aye, you're right Sir Patrick, he's one bad guy our famous surgeon. But I can't claim the credit for uncovering the other one either. You'd be better hearing the story from Maggie, definitely.'

'Yes, I'd heard all about the excellent work of Miss Bainbridge's firm,' Sir Patrick said. 'So, over to you as they say.'

She smiled at him. 'Thank you Sir Patrick, but it was most definitely a great team effort. But yes, I'm happy to be the spokesman. So I guess everybody knows it started when Jimmy and I were asked to look into a case of harassment at

Addison Redburn, the big law firm where in fact I began my own career. Jolene Cavendish, one of the senior partners had been having some rather nasty notes and objects left on her desk. At first it was all rather low level stuff which you could even dismiss as nothing more than pranks, but then it began to escalate until finally it culminated with the acid attack. That of course took the affair to a whole new level.'

'Attempted murder then?' asked Sir Patrick.

'No, we don't actually think that was the intention,' Jimmy said, 'although it could easily have led to that if it had gone wrong. No, we think it was actually meant to scare her such that she had a miscarriage. This case was all about the baby you see.'

'Yes, Jimmy's right,' Maggie said. 'We need to go back twenty-five years when Jolene was married to James Parrish. In some ways they were the golden couple, he the brilliant young surgeon, she the super-smart corporate lawyer on a fast-track to the top of her profession, and with a beautiful little baby on the way to complete the perfect happy family. But then they found out the child she was carrying would be born with Down's Syndrome. I expect they were as devastated as anyone in that situation would be, but at some point they decided that bringing up a disabled child was not part of their life plan. So they hatched their terrible scheme to rid themselves of the problem.'

'Enter Dr Helen Smith,' Jimmy said. 'We know now that Parrish is a serial womaniser...'

'Aye, he's a right chancer,' Frank said.

'...exactly,' Jimmy said, 'and even as she was carrying his child, he was already being unfaithful to Jolene. Dr Smith had been at medical school with Parrish and it seemed she had always carried a candle for him, and then at some point during his marriage they had began an affair. We assume it was just a casual thing for him, but she apparently fell head over heels in love with him.'

'Bastard,' Katherine McNally said.

Maggie nodded. 'And so he decided to exploit that love to execute their evil plan. We assume he told Helen that he loved her too and was going to leave Jolene, but the baby was a complication they didn't need in their lives.'

'It makes me feel quite ill to think about it,' Katherine said quietly, 'because they murdered their baby, didn't they?'

'Yes, they did,' Frank said, his tone sombre. 'Right now we don't know how because he's still denying everything and all she will say is he made her do it. But we think the wee boy was probably suffocated. And I know I know, it doesn't bear thinking about. Truly horrible.'

Maggie could hear his voice cracking as he said it, watching as he raised a hand to wipe away an emerging tear. More than anything she wished she could put her arms around him and hold him close and then they could both have a good cry and make it all better. One day perhaps. *One day.*

'So the baby was born at their home,' Jimmy continued. 'Nothing unusual about that of course, plenty of people choose to do that now just as they did back then. And then when the awful deed was done, Dr Helen Smith signed the Certificate of Still-Birth and that was it. The wee baby was taken away for cremation and as far as the Parrishes were concerned, it was all over and done with.'

'Except of course it wasn't, not for Dr Smith,' Maggie said. 'Because we assume shortly afterwards that Parrish dumped her and devastated by what she had done, her life went into a downward spiral. A spiral that only ended when she stepped in front of that Edinburgh express.'

'Good god,' Sir Patrick said.

She nodded. 'Leaving behind an eleven-year old sister who had worshipped the ground she walked on.'

'Emily Smith,' Katherine said.

Maggie gave Jimmy a concerned look, worried how he was going to cope with having the tragic story played out in front of him again. But he seemed ok, on the surface at least.

'Yes it was Emily,' she said softly, 'and she was as much a victim as anyone in this whole sorry tale. Her parents never recovered from the loss of their beloved eldest daughter and of course poor Emily suffered too. She carried the pain for twenty years or more, and somewhere along the line she decided that only revenge could fix the overpowering hurt she felt inside.'

'Justice,' Jimmy said quietly. 'Emily only wanted justice.'

Maggie gave a sad smile. In her time as a barrister, she had heard the line time and time again from her clients. *We only want justice.* No they didn't, they wanted revenge. It was basic human nature.

'I don't think Emily started off with any real plan or idea of what she was going to do,' she continued, 'but at some stage she must have decided it would be easier to get close to Jolene than to James. She was qualified in human resources and it would be relatively easy to get a job in the same firm as Jolene, which is exactly what she did. She reasoned too that as each year passed Jolene would be becoming more certain that her terrible crime was never going to be discovered, and the fact that a woman called Smith had joined Fortnum Price wouldn't have raised an eyebrow, given how common the name is.'

'That's right,' Jimmy said. 'So Emily just bided her time, watching and waiting until the right opportunity presented itself.'

Maggie nodded. 'When Jolene moved to Addisons, Emily moved too, waiting in the wings, hovering like a kestrel over its prey. And then when Jolene became pregnant she saw her chance. She knew what had happened to Harry Newton and Lucy Wu when they worked at Fortnums and that gave her the idea. She realised with Addisons recruiting like crazy on the Hampton Defence deal, she could bring them both in, putting them neatly in the frame for all the harassment stuff that was going on.'

'Aye, exactly,' Jimmy said. 'And Harry Newton was an especially good patsy because it turned out he had had a brief fling with Jolene, which Emily knew about, and he was bitter that she hadn't stood up for him when he was sacked for gross misconduct. So he had motive in spades.'

'That's right,' Maggie said, 'and as human resources manager, Emily was able to get their usercode and passwords, and she used that to plant these web searches that incriminated the two of them. We found out that any dodgy stuff found by the firm's Web-Guard security software was reported to HR *first* before going to the line manager. That's why Jolene knew nothing about it. Emily held it back from her until the time came to use it against the pair.'

'Aye, but Emily's masterstroke was bringing in Kylie Winterburn as Jolene's PA,' Jimmy said. 'Jolene Cavendish was a bloody difficult woman and her PAs didn't last long. There was always a vacancy and Winterburn neatly filled it. And with *her* criminal track-record, it wasn't hard for Emily to persuade her to become her accomplice, for an appropriate fee of course.'

'But this Emily made a *bomb*, didn't she?' Sir Patrick said, his tone mildly sceptical. 'How did she manage that?'

'Sorry to disappoint you Sir Patrick,' Jimmy said, 'but it's not that hard actually. A wee search on the dark web will reveal all. A litre of petrol in a plastic bottle, a bag of ammonium nitrate fertiliser and ten-quid electronic gizmo to detonate it. As I said, not hard.'

'Dark web, what's that?' he asked, addressing the question to his pretty researcher.

'Internet for bad guys is the easiest way to describe it,' Jimmy said before she could respond. 'Bad guys like Kylie Winterburn for example. She would have known how to access it, given her previous associations.'

'Ah yes,' he said, nodding. 'Jolly good. So Maggie, I assume you are going to tell us how you figured out that Emily Smith was behind all of this?'

She smiled. 'I suppose it began to crystallise when I learned about what happened to Newton and Wu when they worked at Fortnums. He was sacked for being a football hooligan and she for falsifying her qualifications. These are very serious offences and there was no way that a pair with that kind of blot on their CVs should have been working at Addisons. So that made me suspicious that Emily might be involved, since she was solely responsible for their recruitment. And then of course when Jimmy figured out that Kylie Winterburn had to be involved too because she was the gatekeeper to Jolene's office, and we found out from Frank about her criminal record, then I was ninety percent certain that Emily was responsible. That made me look at that old photograph again, and that's when it struck me. Because the blonde in the picture was the absolute spit and image of Emily Smith.'

'Aye, that was really good work,' Frank said admiringly. 'Of course in parallel we were looking to find out who this blonde woman was, and after some excellent work from PC

Macdonald here, we established her name was Doctor Helen Smith and that she had been the doctor that had signed the Certificate of Still Birth for the Parrish baby. And that was it, everything popping neatly into place.'

And he was right, Maggie reflected, it was all so neat and tidy and if it had been only some kind of intellectual puzzle, it would have been deeply satisfying too. But behind it there was the most awful human tragedy. The death of an innocent child, murdered in cold blood by evil and scheming parents, the horrible suicide of the beautiful young doctor, and the ruined life of the sweet and lovely Emily Smith. Yes, there would be justice, but there was nothing to be satisfied about.

But now Sir Patrick was on his feet again, evidently preparing to make another speech.

'Well I think it goes without saying that this has been the most fantastic piece of work all round,' he said. 'A great credit to every single one of you.' He turned to look at Commissioner Compton. 'I can take it Amanda that there'll be no more of this nonsense about closing down Department 12B? In fact I agree with the Home Secretary when he says we need to look into the decision-making process that led to such a stupid idea in the first place. But that will need to wait for another day.' And for another Commissioner too, Maggie suspected.

'So it just remains for me to ask you to raise your glasses. To Maggie Bainbridge Associates, to Department 12B and to teamwork.'

'To teamwork!' everyone shouted.

'Eh, just before we finish, would it be ok if I made a wee speech too?'

Frank was on his feet, looking awkward and holding a scruffy-looking scrap of paper in his hand.

'So like Sir Patrick, I just want to say how amazing everybody has been. Lexy, Eleanor, Ronnie, Katherine and of course Maggie and Jimmy. But that's not what my wee speech is about. Because you see, the fact is over the last two years I have been the most monumental arse.'

There was laughter all around the room, Jimmy augmenting it with a *hear hear*.

Frank gave an awkward grin. 'Aye, thanks. So as I said, I've been an arse. I've let something that happened years and years ago stop me from appreciating something wonderful that was happening right now in front of my eyes.'

'He was like jilted,' Eleanor piped up, 'by a girl called Mhari Black. She didn't turn up at the wedding and then she married someone else six months later. Me and Zak looked it up.'

'Aye, all right Eleanor,' he said, looking flustered, 'We don't really need to hear about all of that right now.'

Maggie laughed. She didn't know Eleanor Campbell well, but she knew her well enough to know she wasn't going to be stopped as easily as that. And this was a story that she herself was desperate to hear.

'You told me you hoped she'd had a shit life,' Eleanor continued, prompting another gale of laughter around the room.

'...Aye, *all right* Eleanor.'

'Well, so the man she married was like a builder or something. He became a millionaire and they live in a huge place on the edge of Loch Lomond...'

'...Aye, *all right* Eleanor,' Frank said again.

'... and they've got four children and a holiday home in Mallorca...'

'Leave off Eleanor,' Jimmy said, in a kindly but firm tone. 'It's not fair to kick a man when he's down. So come on Frankie-boy, we want to hear the rest of your speech.'

Frank glanced down at his note then gave a nervous sigh.

'Aye, well I suppose I'd better get right onto it. Maggie Bainbridge, the fact is I'm absolutely nuts about you and so I hope you will do me the honour of...'

Jimmy leapt up, beaming a broad smile. 'Hang on bruv, if you're going to do this you need to do it properly. Come on, no messing about. Down on one knee.'

Around the table, everyone began to clap, slowly at first then rising in both tempo and volume. Shouts of *go Frank* and *bravo* echoed across the room and several diners got to their feet to offer encouragement.

Frank raised a hand in acknowledgement, waiting for the hubbub to die down before continuing.

'...so I hope you will do me the honour of joining me for a romantic wee dinner in the very near future. And I'm paying.'

Maggie shot him a sharp look across the table. In her heart, she knew there could of course only be one answer to the question.

But after everything he had put her through, she was going to bloody well make him wait to hear it.

A THANK YOU FROM AUTHOR ROB WYLLIE

Dear Reader,

A huge thank you for reading Past Sins and I do hope you enjoyed it! For indie authors like myself, reviews are our lifeblood so it would be great if you could take the trouble to post a review on Amazon.

If you did enjoy this book, I'm sure you would also like the other books in the series:

- A Matter of Disclosure
- The Leonardo Murders
- The Aphrodite Suicides
- The Ardmore Inheritance

All available on Amazon. Search for 'Maggie Bainbridge.'

For special offers on my books, why not join the free Maggie Bainbridge Fan Club? Details at www.robwyllie.com

Thank you for your support!

Regards

Rob

Printed in Great Britain
by Amazon